She pressed harder into him and he groaned softly. "It will feel better in a minute," she promised.

"No pain, no gain?"

"Something like that."

He closed his eyes and sighed. "That feels great," he said. "You might not do this for a living, but you're good at it."

She shifted and he tensed. "Don't move," she said as she slipped out from behind him, leaving him to recline against the cushions. "Let me work it from the front."

She dug in again and her hands trembled. She braced her hand beside his head, intending to use her elbow to get at the muscle in his joint, but she lost her focus. Instead of continuing with the massage, she leaned all the way down, bracing her hand on the other side of his head. Fleetingly, she thought this was such a bad idea for so many reasons. But the impulse came over her and she couldn't help herself. He seemed so alone, so isolated; she wanted to comfort him in a more intimate way. She brushed her lips across his.

Dear Reader,

Special Ops Rendezvous brings together U.S. army ranger Sam Winston and P.I. Olivia Owens and is the third book in The Adair Legacy continuity. Olivia's psychologist brother had asked her to look out for Sam, one of his patients. He was worried Sam was in trouble. Then her brother is murdered and Olivia tries to get close to Sam to not only protect him, but get to the bottom of her brother's death. Thrown together, a chemistry that is volatile, Olivia and Sam fight their attraction as hard as they fight each other. Sam likes to give orders, but finds that tough-as-nails Olivia has a mind of her own. She discovers Sam is a loner and a sexy, alpha male. Her brother was right. Sam is being followed and is mixed up in a deadly conspiracy, and it seems that Sam is the linchpin. This wounded hero, who's experiencing blackouts and memory loss and is tortured by nightmares, has the answers locked up in his mind. Desperately they search for answers in a deadly game that could cost Sam and Olivia everything.

I was thrilled to be asked to write this compelling and sexy U.S. army ranger for the continuity. Don't miss the heart-pounding conclusion to The Adair Legacy, *Secret Service Rescue* by Elle James!

Best,

Karen

Chapter 1

"Dr. Owens?" Sergeant Sam Winston called out into the empty outer office of Dr. John Owens, a well-respected Raleigh, North Carolina, psychologist in private practice. To keep Sam's visits as private as possible, Dr. Owens had agreed to meet Sam before his receptionist arrived at 9:00 a.m. Sam looked at his watch. Normally Dr. Owens was waiting for him the minute he walked into his office at seven o'clock sharp.

As a Ranger in the Seventh Ranger Regiment of the United States Army Special Forces, Sam was used to rising early and getting very little sleep. He'd already been up for two hours doing some PT stress relief. Even six months later, his shoulders and hip still provided a challenge to getting back into fighting shape after he'd been captured and tortured for three months.

Also, the recent assassination attempt on his mother's life and the fact the would-be assassin was one of his buddies from his unit, captured and tortured at the same time as Sam, not only pushed him to seek out a therapist, but had shaken his very foundation. How could Mike have gone from a decorated Ranger to an assassin? That image didn't fit with the man Sam had known. Dedicated and tough-as-nails Mike. A hard, hollow ball of pain and regret mixed with a healthy dose of anger constricted his chest.

That incident made Sam question everything but gave him no answers. He was blacking out, losing time and having horrific nightmares that he couldn't understand or even sometimes remember. He would just wake up standing in his room screaming at the top of his lungs.

If Mike could somehow be coerced to kill his mother, Sam had to wonder how he had been compromised. Mike was one of the toughest men Sam had known.

Thank God his mother was tough, too. She was a formidable woman, formerly a very popular vice president of the United States and, later, an ambassador to France. The thought of losing her unhinged him. He would have been devastated, and although his mother was a cagey politician, she was still his mother. The fact that she was mulling over running for president wasn't something Sam exactly hoped for. Along with the prestige and honor, there were a lot of complications and sacrifice. He would be proud of her, but shining the limelight on him and his work with the U.S. Army wasn't exactly something he wanted.

Mike's betrayal and implications that Sam himself might be compromised prompted him to leave his family estate and rent a modest house in north Raleigh. In the back of his mind, he didn't want to be in too close proximity to his family. He didn't want to think too hard about his motivation. A terrible sense of looming disaster hung over him.

He stopped dead only steps from the door to Dr. Owens's office. An icy feeling of dread came over him when he saw the half-open door.

"Dr. Owens?" he called again, just in case he hadn't heard him the first time, but deep down, Sam knew he wouldn't get an answer. After being in Special Forces for a decade, Sam had a sixth sense about violence. He could almost smell it in the air.

He pushed the door open, braced for the worst. Dr. Owens's office was trashed. Papers and files were strewn everywhere and amid the chaos was Dr. Owens lying near a smashed computer monitor, his eyes open and a pool of blood beneath his head.

Sam barely noticed the unmistakable stench of death permeating the room. He had experienced death so many times in the past, often at his own hands and delivered in close proximity, it was now second nature to him.

Even as these thoughts were rushing through his head, he hurried over to Dr. Owens, knowing that he was dead, knowing there was nothing he could do.

His blood ran cold as he knelt down and felt for a pulse. There was a neat round hole in Dr. Owens's forehead. A head shot meant it was done by a professional.

Which meant what?

Tattered images came to him and his breathing doubled. He rose, backing up, gasping, starting to sweat. The dream he'd had last night! He'd killed somebody.

His back hit the wall and he looked down at his hands, trying to sort out what was real and what was fabricated by his tortured and damaged mind. When would this shit be over! When would he be himself again!

One thing was for sure. Dr. Owens couldn't help him anymore.

He looked down at his hands again as if he could find the answers. But there never were any answers.

He could easily have pulled off a head shot. But why would he have killed Dr. Owens? He reeled at the thought that his own mind somehow wasn't his own. But commit unspeakable acts against a civilian who was trying to help him? That just didn't make sense, and yet the dream burned in his memory. Had he killed someone or was he supposed to kill someone? The jumble was just too chaotic to make sense out of.

He could even be remembering a long-forgotten mission for all he knew. For a man with a very regimented life, who had been in the military since he was twenty-three and understood control, having these kinds of doubts only seemed to make him angry. Which didn't help at all.

In Special Forces, there was no margin for error and second-guessing.

But the torture… A fist of anxiety tightened in the pit of his stomach. Those bastards had tried to break him, the relentless beatings, the withdrawal of food and water, the cold, the discomfort and the pain. He endured it all for three long, torturous months.

He wasn't normally a paranoid kind of guy, but that didn't mean Dr. Owens's death had anything to do with Sam. But after Mike's inconceivable behavior, Sam couldn't discount that somehow the government might be involved. He'd admitted as much to his brothers. Hence the need for secrecy. Sam hadn't even told his superiors he was seeing a psychologist. Presumably, no one besides his brothers knew anything about it. So most likely Dr. Owens's death didn't have a damn thing to do with him.

Or it had everything to do with him.

He pulled his cell phone out of his jeans pocket and dialed his brother, a forensic specialist with the Raleigh Police Department.

"Thad Winston."

"Thad, I want to report a murder."

Sam had to admit the cop they sent, Detective Evans, was pretty sharp, asked really good questions, but again, Sam didn't really have any answers. He hadn't seen anything, didn't know anything. When the cop heard his last name, he recognized it, glancing over at Thad, who was present but had recused himself from working the crime scene because of Sam's involvement.

The Adair/Winston family money had come from tobacco and shipping. All his life, growing up in Raleigh, he'd had respect just by virtue of his wealthy political family. It was one of the main reasons he wanted to get out, do something where he could really earn respect. He wasn't cut out to sit behind a desk like his older brother, Trey, the CEO of Adair Industries, who, with his easygoing attitude and a politician's smooth way, charmed just about everyone, nor like his younger brother, Thad, who had wanted nothing to do with the all the privileged trappings of the Adair legacy.

"Sam, you're free to go. If Detective Evans has any more questions, he'll let you know," Thad said.

"I'd like to know when you catch whoever did this to Dr. Owens. He really helped me a lot."

"Of course, I'll keep you posted. I'm really sorry about this. I know you liked him and he was really helping you. Are you sure you don't want to move back home or bunk with me?"

Sam gave his brother an affectionate punch in the shoulder. "Stop being a mother hen. I'm a Ranger. I can take care of myself."

"No one said you couldn't, Sam, but with this shit going down with Mom, I'm just on edge. And when I think about Mike it makes me crazy all over again."

"I don't blame you for killing Mike, if that's what's bothering you."

"No. I wish I could have avoided it, but he gave me no choice. He was going to kill Lucy…and I had…"

Sam touched his brother's shoulder. "You did the right thing, Thad. No matter how much it hurts." Sam was pretty sure this was going to hurt for quite some time.

Thad nodded. "I have a feeling this isn't over." He looked at Dr. Owens's body. "Mom's assassination attempt was thwarted, but that doesn't mean they won't try again."

"At this point, I don't trust anyone."

"Not even the Secret Service? They're guarding her night and day."

"I told you and Trey. I feel the government is involved somehow, and the Secret Service is a government agency. I worry about her, too. But I like Agent Dan Henderson. Not only did he save her life, but he's intelligent and dedicated. I have a good feeling about him."

Thad nodded. "Yeah, I like him, too. He took a bullet for Mom. I will always be grateful for that."

"Yeah, a guy involved in shady stuff doesn't do his duty and stop a bullet."

"I've got to get going. But if you need anything, call me, brother."

Sam nodded and walked out to the curb with Thad. As he drove away, he was still unsettled about Dr. Owens's death and its possible connection to him, his family and his mother's assassination attempt.

Sam looked at his watch. He still had time to make it to his therapeutic massage appointment. Another suggestion Dr. Owens had given him. First, to help with his rehabilitation and second, to reduce stress.

He arrived with about ten minutes to spare and checked in at the front desk. The receptionist smiled flirtatiously at him, but he didn't respond. She was interested, but his life was such a complete mess right now. He had no intention of trying to carry on any type of relationship. He wasn't fit for a relationship, even a temporary one, or for duty. Right now he was in limbo until he figured it all out. As soon as he got his head on straight from the damage done by the insurgents, he was shipping out again.

Although it was something he'd thought about often. Maybe he should retire and find something else to do with his time. Serving his country had been a privilege and an honor, but after Mike's unpredictable and violent behavior, Sam wasn't sure that returning to active duty was a good idea.

He walked to the locker room, stripped down and

stored all his clothes in the locker. Shrugging into the robe, he dropped his wallet into the pocket and tightened the belt. He made his way to the room and went inside. Slipping off the robe, he slid under the sheet facedown.

He'd only lain there for a moment when the therapist entered. "Hello, Helga," he said. "I'm going to need some work on my shoulder today. It's been giving me some problems."

"I'm not Helga, but I'll be happy to take care of that for you." Her voice was beautiful, soft and melodious. Perfect for a massage therapist.

He turned his head. The delicious sight of the woman in front of him almost made him want to lick his lips. She had sun-kissed skin, wavy caramel shoulder-length hair, the front pinned up and away from her striking face with high, slashing cheekbones, and a plump bow of a mouth. She was lovely, delicate, feminine, her skin as flawless as fresh cream. She wore no makeup, no jewelry, nothing to enhance or draw the eye. But she drew attention, his very interested attention.

He left her eyes for last because that's where all the information about a human being was. Right now he was savoring the anticipation of the moment their eyes met.

Hers were dark brown, fringed with thick lashes. They were direct, assessing and…communicated her attraction. He knew most women liked muscles, and he was ripped. As soon as he got out of Walter Reed in D.C. and was cleared, he'd resumed his fitness routine. Being honed both in body and mind was what made a Special Forces commando a lethal son of a bitch. Besides the effects of his injuries, his body was back to normal now, but not yet his mind. He was still working on that.... Regret washed through him as he thought about Dr. Owens's death.

So he'd seen that shell-shocked look before. It wasn't the first time the sight of him half-naked, or completely naked, had put that expression on a woman's face. It happened all the time.

He'd had zero interest in the pretty receptionist, but this woman was a different matter. She certainly wasn't the middle-aged, somewhat dour Helga with the strong hands that he was used to. No, this woman was hard to look away from and hard to dismiss.

But unfortunately he had the same problem that he'd had with the receptionist. Getting involved with anyone at this point in his life would be a mistake.

But he suddenly wanted to make a lot of mistakes.

"Helga's out sick. My name's Olivia Marshall."

Trying not to show any reaction to the change in his therapist or the affect she had on him, he smiled and nodded. She was dressed in a white cotton T-shirt with the logo of the spa just above her full breasts and a pair of black, stretchy pants that were modest but did nothing to hide her curves.

"Why don't you tell me what you need taken care of, Captain Winston?"

When she pulled the sheet from his back, she gasped, but she tried to stifle it.

He turned to look at her again. "I should have warned you about that."

Her gaze was riveted to his back. She was affected by the sight of what the insurgents had done to him, but there was more than just shock in her eyes. Was

there…heat, too? "I should have been more professional. I'm sorry."

"There's no need to apologize. My back is a mess.
I was tortured for three months before I was rescued.
As you can see, they weren't easy on me. My shoulders give me the most problem. They hung me from
the ceiling every day."

Sam met those dark brown eyes and watched her
struggle with her compassion and her shock. And
something loosened up in him at her look, something
that brought with it intense heat. Suddenly he wanted
to get close to this woman on more than just a physical level.

"Okay, your shoulders. Anything else?"

"My left hip and quad. I got shot there."

She nodded. This woman should have come with
a warning label, Sam thought. She was much too potent, and he was, lethal son of a bitch or not, feeling
just a tad vulnerable.

It had never happened before. Not even when those
bastards were pounding on him.

Yet the brown eyes of a beautiful massage therapist
seemed to do it without effort.

She dimmed the lights in the room and put on soft,
chiming music that was really relaxing.

As the anticipation of her touch built up in him,
he sighed softly when her hands started on his upper
shoulders. Her touch was sure, gentle, soothing. He
tried not to read into it, but her hands just didn't feel
impersonal. He wasn't sure if that was just his perception.

He didn't really care. He liked it too much.

He heard her shift her position, felt her move closer, working the big muscles down the length of his back.

The bitch about getting injured was it sapped his energy. He had gotten up early and had worked out hard. The shock and dismay at Dr. Owens's death had taken a toll, too. He fell asleep.

He drifted, but then flashes of images disturbed the silky, comforting darkness. He blinked and he could see vivid evergreens around him as the sharp scent of pine smoke from the fire drifted across their camp. Flashes of the images lit his brain, powerful and tantalizing. Trey, his big brother, was there and Thad, too. All of them teenagers. He frowned. Was this Yellowstone? Were they camping with their father? How was that possible? Anger against his mother swamped him when he realized she wasn't there. Why couldn't she be here, too? He looked at his brother Trey, and his heart lurched.

Darkness swirled around him and his face was blank. There were no eyes, mouth or nose. It was just flesh. Then the scene changed and darkness surrounded Sam. The smell of his own filth and blood disturbed his sleep, and he shifted. He was huddled on the floor, trying to breathe around his agony. He couldn't find the will to lift his head. But the face of one of his tormenters thrust into his. His eyes widened and his mind reeled. It was Trey.

Foreign voices spun around him. Strong hands pulled at him and he made a sound of anguish, breathing hard and trying to prepare himself for more pain on top of what his aching body had already endured.

Pain exploded in his hip and he jerked away. With a cry of agony he reached for the hand that had touched him. He came fully awake and pushed himself up on the table. In the dim room, Olivia's startled eyes met his. The memory of that place, his helplessness and the excruciating pain throbbed through him.

And she saw it immediately.

"You fell asleep and must have had a nightmare. It's okay," she whispered, her voice so soft and soothing.

Her wrist beneath his hand was delicate, her skin soft and warm. He took a breath and closed his eyes as he let her go. Damn nightmares.

He lay back down, trying to control his breathing. "I'm sorry. I hope I didn't scare you."

"I don't scare that easily. You just surprised me. But I totally understand. I'm sure what you endured was something I can't even comprehend. No harm done."

He really liked the way this woman was so frank.

"Are you comfortable moving on? I just have your lower body left to do, but if you'd prefer ending the session, we can."

"No, it's fine as long as you're okay."

"I'm fine."

She touched his lower back and he sighed. The small room seemed to get smaller as she bent over him, removing the sheet from one leg and tucking it securely under his opposite thigh.

She was close to him.

Very close.

Practically on top of him, and he was enjoying it a little too much—the whole thing, with her hands on him, and her voice close, and her fingers kneading and smoothing over his muscles, sliding over his skin. With every moment of contact, the heat in the small room rose another degree.

From then on it was pure torture trying to keep his body under control and in check. But as she moved around him to his other hip and then his hamstrings, her every touch sent a hot thrill straight to his groin.

And the sensual feel of her not-quite-impersonal hands caused a reaction.

He tried to minimize it. Tried to think of something to curtail his response, but it was no use.

He got an erection.

"I'm ready for you to turn over."

He wanted to attribute the reaction of his body to not being with a woman for a long time, or to the fact that he'd just woken up from sleeping, but he knew better.

"Olivia, I have to let you know that I have an erection."

When he looked at her, she didn't bat an eye, but she looked a bit guilty. "That's totally normal."

He'd bet a lot of men got erections around her.

He really, really liked this woman's direct and no-nonsense attitude.

"My job as a massage therapist is to help you integrate into your body. I'm here to help you heal not only from physical pain and injury, but also from emotional traumas that can be held in the body. Your body is the way it is and I don't pass judgment on the normal and healthy reaction of a man. While an erection may be an uncomfortable topic for some, I have a different attitude about it."

He laughed for the first time in a long while. "Well, if that's the case, go ahead and finish."

"Are you comfortable with it? I don't want you to feel at all uneasy."

He rolled over, sat up and stuffed the sheet down between his legs, trapping his dick between his abdomen and the tightened sheet, then lay back down.

She smiled and nodded. "Good. I like a client who is in tune with his body and accepts it. I might also mention, in case it happens, that you might even discharge semen, as well. Also, totally normal."

Oh, jeez, she would have to bring that up. He had no idea why this woman was having such an effect on him. There was something about her that really turned him on. So, he wasn't sure if he wouldn't ejaculate, either. "Good to know," he said, amused at her complete trust in him. "Just so you know, I would never be inappropriate with you, Olivia."

"I trust that you would never do that, Captain Winston."

"It's Sam," he said. "If you're comfortable with my erection, you should be comfortable with my first name."

She smiled at him, and although he saw her struggle with her impartiality, her interest was wholly there.

When she put her hands on him again, there was some distance this time. He wondered if she felt a little responsible for making him hard, since he was still pretty sure her touch had not been as professional as she was with other clients. He also had to wonder if she was feeling soft toward him because he had been so wounded.

Regardless, she did a wonderful job. His shoulders felt great and she'd done wonders on his hip. Now she was kneading his quad.

After about ten minutes she finished and stepped

back. He was drifting, enjoying the rhythm of her hands and the feel of her palms against his skin.

"Make sure you drink plenty of water when you get home."

"I know the drill."

"I'm sure you do, but we always remind our clients."

"Thank you, Olivia. This has really helped."

"My pleasure, Sam."

She smiled at him and left the room. He got off the table, shrugged into his robe, went back to the locker room and showered. Getting dressed, he navigated his way out of the spa just as Olivia was pulling the outside door open. He hurried to hold it for her. She glanced back and then smiled.

They walked to the parking lot.

"Sam, would you be interested in having a coffee with me?"

He looked down at her, those candid eyes never wavering. He felt himself leaning closer, breathing in her scent. Which was dangerous given his current state of mind. But he seemed helpless to curb the impulse. Olivia Marshall wore her confidence like a well-worn sweater. He was so tempted with all that soft skin and a slightly lush bottom lip that just begged a man to taste it. Bite it. Just a little.

He got a hold of himself. "I'm sorry, Olivia. I can't. I've got an appointment."

"Are you sure you couldn't spare just half an hour?" she said, disappointment clear in her eyes. There was something else there, too—something that was there and then gone.

He hated to be paranoid, but something made the hair on the back of his neck stand up. Something in her voice that made him think…what? That she had targeted him? That was paranoid. She was a massage therapist, for Pete's sake.

"I'm going to visit my mother."

"Of course you would be. How is she doing?"

"She's up and around along with Dan Henderson, her Secret Service agent."

"That was so terrible. It must still be a difficult time for you."

He nodded.

"Maybe some other time, then, for that coffee?"

"Maybe," he said noncommittally.

As Olivia walked away, everything seemed to pile in on him all at once. Mike's betrayal, his mother's shooting, Dr. Owens's death, the blackouts, the nightmares and feeling as if he couldn't trust himself.

It was such an alien feeling and he wouldn't have minded a nice woman to take his mind off it all. But it wouldn't be fair to subject her to all his crap. Letting her go was a smart move.

So why didn't it feel right?

He shifted his shoulders. Had he killed Dr. Owens?

Had it been a dream?

Or had it been reality?

As soon as Dan Henderson heard that Trey Winston was on the estate, he stepped inside Kate Winston's sumptuous all-white master bedroom suite and spoke quietly to her while she was handling some correspondence from her desk. He let her know he was going to be right back and brought up another agent to stand guard outside her door.

Moving silently through the house and down the

wide mahogany staircase, he went looking for Trey. One of the agents said he had gone into the library. When he knocked on the library door, then walked in, he was brought up short. Trey and Debra were playing kissy face near the desk. "Henderson, aren't you supposed to be watching my mother?" Trey said, his eyes never leaving Debra.

Newlyweds, Dan thought. He had more important things on his mind than romance, but he smiled at Trey's wry tone. "Sorry, I didn't realize you were with your wife, sir."

"That's all right," Debra said. I was just leaving. "I'll go up and see Kate. You'll join me after Agent Henderson is finished?

"Yes, sweetheart."

Walking past him, she smiled, blowing Trey a kiss from the door, slipping out and leaving the door ajar.

"What is it? My mother…" Trey said, his blue eyes, so like his mother's, looking immediately worried.

Dan shook his head. "She's fine. Everything is quiet."

"But something is bothering you."

"Yes. Were you aware that Captain Winston moved off the estate?"

"I'm aware. We argued about it, but, Dan, Sam is a mess right now and he's understandably upset about Mike Harris. He wanted to be on his own. He's rented a house over near Six Forks Road. Under the circumstances, I can understand his pain. He and Mike were extremely close."

"Do you think it's a good idea for him to be at a different location rather than here at the estate where we can give him protection?"

"You're talking about Sam, right?" Trey laughed. "Dan, he's a U.S. Army Ranger. He can take care of himself. He wasn't targeted. My mother was."

"With all due respect, sir, he and Harris were captured and detained at the same Afghani camp, and now with Harris going off the grid, I…"

"You know I value your opinion. Hell, man, you saved my mother. I'm glad to finally see you up and about."

"Yeah, on a cushy security detail," he groused.

Trey smiled. "The estate *is* pretty cushy."

Dan laughed. "Yes, sir."

"What is it about Sam that is bothering you?"

"During my recovery, I had time to think about this. What could have happened at that place or to them…I mean, for such a dedicated soldier like Harris to turn against his own country and try to commit murder? As you said, sir, Harris was tough, both mentally and physically. He was in Special Forces. It just makes me twitch and spin conspiracy theories."

"Like what?"

"I wasn't here that night and I didn't witness Harris's meltdown, but another agent was and he was described as being disoriented. Thad even discovered the chief of police was involved and that this might go higher than we all think."

"I'm aware of that, but all we can do at this point is let the feds do their job, while it's business as usual for us."

"But, sir. If Harris and your brother were captured together and your brother even admitted that there might be government involvement…aren't you worried that Captain Winston—"

"What the hell are you saying? Are you accusing my brother of being involved in some crazy political organization?"

"Not exactly."

Trey stiffened and his mouth flattened out. "Well, you'd better explain it and explain it to me good. Sam has been through enough and I won't take anything said about him lightly."

"I understand, sir. I'm just concerned that he's out there alone with all that's come to light."

"I trust Sam with my life. He would never hurt anyone in this family, ever. Is that clear?"

"Yes, sir."

"Don't bring this up again."

Trey walked past him and out the library door. Dan stood there absorbing everything he'd said, but he was still not convinced that Captain Winston wasn't somehow compromised in this whole situation. His instincts were honed and he'd almost felt that sniper even before the first bullets started to fly.

He was getting a hinky feeling about Trey's brother.

His vow was to protect the former vice president of the United States. He didn't answer to Trey Winston, although the man had powerful connections and could cause quite a few problems with his superiors. But Dan was never one to give a damn about chain of command. He'd taken a bullet for Kate Winston and he wasn't about to let anything else happen to her.

Dan was going to keep his eye on Sam Winston whenever he was anywhere near his mother.

Chapter 2

Sam stepped into the foyer of his family's estate. He paused in the hall, not sure if his mother was upstairs or down in the sitting room.

"If you're looking for your mother, she's out near the pool enjoying a cup of tea."

Maddie Fitzgerald smiled at Sam, her plump face and eyes crinkling. She had been at the Adair Estate ever since Sam could remember. He adored her. She used to sneak him a chocolate chip cookie every day before dinner, saying that a strapping boy like him needed the calories and it wouldn't at all ruin his dinner.

"I was. Thanks, Maddie."

"How are you, Sam?"

Her sympathetic eyes roved over his face as she squeezed his forearm.

"I'm trying to just take one day at a time."

"Best way to handle it. I just took a batch of chocolate chip cookies out of the oven." She winked at him. "I'll be serving luncheon in about fifteen minutes, but I'm sure it won't spoil your lunch."

He laughed even though he was here to deliver very unhappy news. With all the death and betrayals they had all experienced in the past few months, the news about Dr. Owens would be taken hard.

"I'll come by the kitchen before I leave," he said.

Sam made his way through the house. When he got to the pool area and walked down the stairs, Agent Dan Henderson moved in front of him.

"Captain Winston? Is everything all right?"

"No, not really," he said to the dedicated agent. He was probably about six years younger than Sam, tall, fit, his dark blond hair combed off his face, his green eyes wary and alert. He filled out his suit jacket with a pair of broad shoulders that had sheltered his mother during the shooting. Sam was humbled by the younger man who, from reports he'd heard, had selflessly and courageously thrown himself in front of his mother. The bullet had almost killed him.

"Sam."

Sam turned around to find his brother Trey, dressed as usual in a dark gray summer-weight, impeccably cut suit with a red power tie, coming down the stairs. His wife, Debra, her belly slightly rounded with their child, was beside him.

Debra hugged him hard and didn't let go for a few minutes. Sam indulged her. She was a good match for his brother and he was happy for them. "Hello, Debra. How are you doing?"

"Fine. We're happy to see you, Sam. How about you?"

She clasped his upper arms after she let him go, her sweet, pretty face full of concern. She'd been working for his mother ever since she'd been in the White House. He forced a smile for her sake and said, "One day at a time."

She nodded and let him go. He shook Trey's hand and got a jolt to his mind as he remembered the dream when he'd fallen asleep on the delectable Olivia Marshall's massage table. He shifted his shoulders, letting go of his brother's hand early. Trey gave him a quizzical look, but his mother was there to interrupt Sam's gaze as she enveloped him in a hug.

"My boy. It's good to see you. Come sit down, all of you."

They moved toward the small table set up on the patio, the turquoise water of the pool looked inviting even in the early spring heat.

As they settled into their chairs, Sam's mother turned her attention to him. "Is this just a visit to see how your old mom's doing?"

"You'll never be old, Mom," Sam said. "I'm here to see how you're doing and to deliver some very upsetting news."

"Oh, no," Kate said, her blue eyes clouding. "What is it?"

"Dr. Owens was murdered this morning."

"Your psychologist? Oh, my God. I'm so sorry, Sam. I know that he was a very good doctor."

"He was."

Trey studied his face. "What is it, Sam?"

"I don't know. I can't help thinking that this may

have something to do with Mom's assassination attempt and Mike's..." Sam's throat constricted. "Mike's meltdown."

"This is all such a terrible business and I'm so sorry all of you got so involved in it. I know my political aspirations haven't been easy on you all."

"You did what you thought was good for Dad's seat and for the family. We all know that, Mom," Sam said.

As Maddie brought the lunch down, Sam stood up to help her with the tray. He saw Dan Henderson watching him with more than just a passing interest. He was watching him like a serious, vigilant Secret Service agent.

Late morning the next day, Sam entered his local coffee shop and stepped into line. He was behind about four people when he felt a tap on his shoulder. He turned around, and his gaze collided with Olivia Marshall's.

"Well, hello there," she said, beaming.

Even with that sudden prickling sensation back, he couldn't help smiling at her, feeling as if his day just got a bit brighter.

She looked good today, too. Her brown eyes sparkling, her multihued hair swinging free around her beautiful face. She was dressed in a butter-yellow shirt and a pair of snug, well-worn jeans. She looked delectable and smelled delicious.

"Olivia? You following me?"

She cocked her head and gave him a wry smile. "What if I was?"

He flashed a grin. "Ah, then I might have to think you were flirting with me." His frustration with himself and the whole freaking ordeal was finally what had driven him out of the house today.

She laughed. "Oh, Sam, if it's not clear, I must be terrible at it."

"No, you're fine at it." Damn, this woman intrigued the hell out of him. She was so at ease in her skin, which, he realized, most of the women of his acquaintance, regardless of their beauty, were not. And by not playing on it, she had somehow managed to seem all the more sensual and attractive. Which should make absolutely no sense, but the fact that he couldn't get her out of his mind was proof enough.

"How about we share a table?" she said.

He hesitated. The prickling sensation on the back of his neck refused to go away and, in fact, only grew stronger. Instincts this strong were rarely wrong. But they were usually rooted in something substantive. There had to be more here than he was seeing. And yet, at the same time, he'd never wanted more to be wrong.

All last night—while he'd been distracting himself with a Chicago White Sox game and found it increasingly difficult to keep his mind on any of the innings for longer than a few minutes—he could only think that had to be some babe to interrupt his baseball obsession.

He wanted—needed—to create more distance because he thought about Dr. Owens a lot last night. He'd checked both of his handguns and neither of them had been fired. That gave him a measure of relief. But if he hadn't killed Dr. Owens, maybe he'd been the reason he was murdered. He wasn't used to his thoughts being so clouded and paranoid, and he knew his judgment could be off. He simply had to find an edge and hold on to it.

Keeping his distance from this woman wasn't giving him the clarity he wanted. And all the thinking and distraction weren't going to help.

"Sure. I've got nothing but time to kill."

She gave him a smile, and there was absolutely nothing impersonal about it.

"What can I get you, sir?"

He realized that he'd been standing there staring at her. He forced his attention away from her face to the barista.

After placing and receiving their orders, he and Olivia walked over to a table by the window. People were walking by on the sidewalk.

"So, how did you end up at Rosebud Spa? Not exactly a place where a rough-and-tough Special Forces guy hangs out."

"Ha! No, not exactly. I got referred."

"By whom?"

He wasn't exactly sure he wanted to talk about his mental issues with this woman. She had seen him after he'd woken from that disturbing nightmare and she was so open and easy to talk to. "Dr. John Owens, he's a psychologist."

She made a small reaction, her eyes dimmed. "I heard he was murdered."

"Yes." His chest got tight and he had to look away. Damn his mental state. He felt he was acting like a little girl, but he had to admit a great fondness for Dr. Owens. "He was a good man."

"I'm sure."

"How did you end up working at the Rosebud?"

"I was looking for a job that would give me some pickup work. The owners were looking for a fill-in. It works out for me."

"You have only the one job?"

She looked away and he got that prickling again. Could just be his paranoia and he was reading something into nothing, given his fixation with trying to figure out what set off his instincts with this woman.

"I work another job. A boring office job. Nothing special."

He couldn't detect anything out of the ordinary in her statement. But in this situation he always followed his gut. "I can't imagine that. I've been in the field so long serving Uncle Sam I don't know what I would do if I wasn't enlisted."

"I can tell it's something that you've been thinking about. You looking to retire?" She took a sip of her coffee, keeping her gaze trained on him.

"I don't know. I'm tired, and to be honest, I have thought about getting out."

"Burned out? I've seen that before in my job."

"I bet." He finished his coffee and decided it was a good idea to nip this in the bud and get the hell away while the getting was good. He rose.

She rose, too, and stood directly in his path. "Look, what do you have planned today?"

Startled by her question, he didn't answer right away. "Like I said, I'm killing time." He regretted the words immediately. She was fixin' to ask him to spend more time with her. He was sure.

"I'm going to the flea market at the fairgrounds, then the Museum of Art. They have a really nice park nearby. You interested?"

Was he ever, and not in just spending the day with her! His initial reaction was to be pleased and flattered as a man would be when a woman he was interested in showed the same in return. Which was the wrong reaction entirely. His gut was telling him something was off. But it might have nothing to do with her. And yet…that was the first thing he'd felt. A good wake-up call that his gut was probably as paranoid as his head.

"Am I reading you wrong?" she asked.

He didn't move away. He told himself he just wanted to see her eyes up close, get a better idea of what he might be reading in her.

"If I am, I apologize. But I don't normally have to work this hard for a date."

Thoroughly charmed, he laughed. Up close like this, with the sunlight illuminating that captivating hair, he got caught up in her look. For someone so forthright and confident, the innocence she projected seemed incongruous. And yet he found her so sweet and compassionate, and it reminded him that no matter how tough the exterior, everyone was vulnerable in some way.

"My life is complicated, Olivia. More so than most people would want to deal with."

"Oh, well, it's just the flea market and the art museum and a walk in the park. Sounds like those are uncomplicated things. You look like you could use a simple day. There's a great café at the museum."

Sam's smile came slowly. "I bet you won all your debates in college."

Her smile spread to a grin that was unaffected as it was honest. "Well, as a matter of fact, I did."

An afternoon with a beautiful woman—simple, uncomplicated. He could really go for that.

And it was a great afternoon. Olivia was a great conversationalist, lively, with a wicked sense of humor.

So it was easy for him to understand how she ended up at his house on the couch watching baseball with him after he'd grilled some steaks they had picked up on the way there. He was really comfortable with her, and he couldn't make himself send her on her way.

It didn't help that she'd snuggled up to him in an open, warm way. He wasn't going to kiss her, but the urge to do so plagued him.

He was so glad he had that straight in his head. So little was straight in his head these days.

He leaned his head back, enjoying her warm body so close to his. With every breath she took, an irrepressible longing was building inside him, making his chest tight.

It would be good if he could take a full breath, but it seemed as if his lungs were at only half capacity. Maybe that was why he was lightheaded. There was only one truth here: he wanted her.

It had been so long since he'd wanted a woman. Well, he always wanted one. He just hadn't bothered lately to find one, something he used to do without putting out too much effort. Usually women were just there.

But if they'd been anywhere lately, he hadn't noticed, not since Afghanistan.

He'd noticed her, though. Noticed her in a way that was impossible to ignore, deep down in his gut, viscerally.

Man, the day had taken more out of him than he realized and before he knew it, he was back in that sunlit glen, back in Yellowstone with his father, the tents, the campfire, the anger, no, *hatred* at his mother. Only this time, no one was there. In the distance, he heard growling and it got closer and closer until a bear materialized out of the forest. He stood frozen as it watched him, its eyes feral and menacing. Then it was just his brother Trey standing there, that darkness all around him and his face blank again, just blank.

He started awake and found that the game had ended, but Olivia was gone. Had she left without saying goodbye?

Then he heard something from his office and he rose, that prickling starting up all over again. His training kicked in and he ghosted through the house to the room. The door was ajar and Olivia was in there on his computer, files strewn across his desk. Files she'd obviously been nosing through.

The look on her face was rapt, professional and determined. He felt all kinds of betrayed and a little relieved. His instincts weren't totally off and he wasn't paranoid for nothing.

When she turned off his computer and carefully put his files away, she rose and he made his move, grabbing her from behind.

"What are you doing here?"

"I'm a private investigator," she said, not at all intimidated.

"Who the hell are you working for?" he growled.

"Dr. John Owens.... I'm his sister."

Chapter 3

The fact that he had his forearm snug around her throat and her waist, his warm, hard chest against her back made her lose focus for just a second. She'd thought last night about all that warm skin that she'd had her hands on. She'd even found it extremely difficult to get to sleep not only because her dear brother had been murdered, but because memories of touching Sam had plagued her. He was a very attractive man, his chiseled features memorable. He had a set of blue eyes that were intense, focused with a lethal edge, and a full bottom lip that was distracting all on its own but, when matched with his perfect bow of an upper lip, made a deadly combination. Very gorgeous, very kissable. The memory of the shape, size and feel of his body was burned into her mind. She wasn't at all worried that he was going to hurt her. She didn't know how, but she just knew.

"If you could let go of me, we can discuss this. I mean you no harm, Sam." Damn, he was tall, six two to her five ten. The arm around her waist was immovable. He was holding her so tight against him, she could feel the beat of his heart against her back. Her backside pressed up against his muscular hips.

He released her and she turned to face him. Sam just stared at her and she couldn't blame him. He looked so confused, his blue eyes full with a sense of betrayal. She did feel very guilty about that. But she wanted to understand who this man was and why her brother had been so insistent that she follow him and, if the need arose, protect him. That made her pause because Sam Winston looked as though he could quite easily take care of himself. He screamed *warrior* in a potent way that made her only want to get closer to his dangerous edge.

In the short period of time that she'd known him, she was beginning to understand why her brother cared about Sam so much. Her brother was the kind of man who worried about all his patients, but he considered Sam special because of what had happened to their father. Now she understood why her brother was so keen on helping Sam.

"You're Dr. Owens's sister? Let me see proof."

His eyes were hard and filled with a distrust that Olivia totally understood. "I'd have to get my purse in the living room."

He nodded sharply and followed her out there. Picking up her handbag, she reached inside and snagged her wallet. Dragging out her license and P.I. ID, she handed both to him.

He studied them. "They look legit, but in my line of

work, I can never take anything at face value. People disguise themselves and fabricate identities as easily as breathing."

He handed the IDs back to her. "I don't understand why you're here."

"I know you don't. But, in light of my brother's death, you can't blame me for being cautious about you."

He ran his big hand over his dark brown hair buzzed close to his scalp, his blue eyes wary and stormy. "Dr. Owens never mentioned a sister," he said.

"That's because my brother didn't talk about his personal life with his clients. The only proof I can offer you is the truth. John Owens was my brother. He left me everything as I am his only family, including the keys to his practice. I control all his files, notes, tapes, everything."

He let out a heavy breath. "I guess for the time being, I'll have to take your word for it." He shifted, his eyes still wary, but now there was sympathy there and what looked like…guilt. "I'm so sorry about your brother. I know what it's like to lose people close to you. I just lost a buddy of my own. We'd been through a lot together and he was like a brother to me."

She nodded. "Mike Harris. I always do my home-work on a case, and I read all about you and your family in the paper. I'm sorry about your loss, too, Sam."

He closed his eyes for a moment, the pain and the loss clearly on his face as he nodded. The distress in his voice and his eyes wasn't an act. She was very good at reading people. A sudden ache constricted her throat at the fresh memory of just speaking with John two days ago. His warm voice and the way he'd always given her a quick hug whenever they parted. Tears welled up in her eyes as the emotions rushed over her in a terrible sense of loss.

Sam's expression relaxed, his blue eyes going soft with his compassion as he reached out and squeezed her shoulder.

"Before Mike shot my mother, I would have sworn with total confidence that he wasn't capable of doing something that horrible. He was not just my friend," he said with conviction. "We were comrades and we'd been through more than normal men ever go through. I thought our bond was unbreakable. I can't count the times he'd saved my ass and the times I'd saved his. So it was natural to invite him into my life."

Her reaction to Sam was so visceral. On every level. Yesterday before she'd met him, she had thought he was a head case that could be a bit out of control, maybe even broken. But then she'd talked to him, seen the terrible scars on his back, the remnants of his agony. When he'd woken from that nightmare, the fear stark on his face, everything in her galvanized into a hard ball of need to help him any way she could.

"He took advantage of that for the sole purpose of murdering my mother." Sam's voice broke and she reached out and touched his shoulder. He sidestepped her hand and paced away. "After Mike shot her, I questioned everything I knew."

He paused and she could see how he was struggling with Mike's betrayal. Even more surprising was her need to comfort him, but he wasn't allowing that. She was so happy that Mike Harris had failed. Olivia was a big supporter of Sam's mother. She thought Kate Winston was a wonderful vice president. Of course, she had voted for her and would vote for her whatever office she was running for. She was one of those no-holds-barred politicians and she told it like it was. But Olivia wasn't going to gush all of that to Sam. She could only secretly hope there would be an opportunity to meet her.

He set his hands on his hips and faced her squarely. She appreciated his honesty. She didn't think Sam had anything to hide, really. John was tight-lipped about Sam's circumstances. Her brother was always aware of his patient's confidentiality, so Olivia was really in the dark here about Sam. She would have to rely on her own interviewing skills to decipher what was going on with this guy.

"I assume you suspect I had something to do with your brother's death and that's the reason for this subterfuge."

He wasn't one to pull punches, but she guessed that was true because he was a Ranger and those kinds of guys hit things head-on. There was something unsettled in his eyes, something apprehensive, with just a touch of fear there, too.

"No, going undercover was John's idea, Sam. He wanted you to be safe, but he didn't want to break or damage your trust with him. So he asked me to be totally discreet. I got a job at the spa to stay close. But I will admit that after my brother's murder, the thought had crossed my mind. My brother asked me to follow you for a reason. Now I wonder if it got him killed."

"You don't think I killed him?"

"He was concerned about you, Sam. He thought you needed protection. Why would I think such a thing?"

"Because I wasn't sure. Olivia, I have memory loss

and sometimes I black out and do things I don't remember."

"You didn't kill my brother. I don't believe that."

"Thank you for that." He glanced away, then back. "Dr. Owens hired you to protect me?" That made him smile wryly. "Damn, Dr. Owens," he said, shaking his head. "He thought I needed protection…yet he was the one who suffered for trying to help me."

"So you think his murder has something to do with you?"

"I don't know, Olivia. I truly don't, but it *feels* like he was…*assassinated*."

That jolted her with a sudden fear of who was behind this, but it wasn't going to get her to back off. There was more here with Sam, but they were just getting started and she would get Sam to open up to her later when he trusted her more. Because now that she was here, she had no intention of leaving until she got to the bottom of her brother's death and the threat to Sam. Sam was very much alive, and Olivia believed he was in danger…. She *knew* he was in danger. Walking away from this wasn't an option. She owed that much to John.

But even with that determination, her stomach knotted. She tried to get detached from her brother's murder and think like a private investigator, but she couldn't quite get to that level of objectivity. She said, "What do you mean? The police won't tell me anything."

He looked at her as though he didn't want to go on.

"Tell me, Sam. I can take it. I need to know."

He crossed back to her and stood close, his voice a low rasp, his teeth clenched. "He was shot in the head. A kill shot that, to me, says professional."

Her stomach jumped and tumbled. That information was certainly cause for alarm and made it clear why Sam was worried. "Even if that's the case, I intend to find out who killed my brother."

He set his jaw and looked past her into the darkened kitchen. "Olivia, you don't have a clue what you're up against. I don't know who could be involved here, but ever since Mike and I were captured and imprisoned, I haven't trusted my government. Hell, I can't even trust my own memories. What I have of them."

"Why don't you trust them?"

"I'm only telling you to convince you of the folly of pursuing this." The reluctance in his voice indicated to her that he was clinging to his training and the "need to know" edict that he lived by. What he was telling her must be classified information. "Very few people knew where we were on that mission. It had to have been compromised. I can hardly remember the details, but what I do remember feels like a damn ambush. I don't trust the army and I don't trust the CIA, even though they rescued me. I don't even know if I'm going back, if I can even get my memories back and feel fully functional again."

Olivia watched his face, saw the way his jaw hardened against the uncertainty of his life, saw the anger in his eyes and the vulnerability that lay beneath it, and her heart ached for him. He was close to her, leaning slightly toward her to make his point. She wanted to cup his jaw, give him some comfort. The memory of her hands on him came back at her with a sizzling jolt, the feel of his hot, slick muscles beneath her palms. She had totally tried to remain cool, but with each stroke of her hands over his skin, she'd lost that impartiality in the heat of him.

It was clear that he was attracted to her, and that gave her a thrill. His blue eyes dipped to her mouth and she shivered at the thought of him leaning in, pressing that mouth against hers, the tactile memory of his body only fueling the sudden need. They stared at each other.

She held his gaze for what felt like an eternity. Then he broke it and stepped back out of her reach, battling with the temptation that only made her heart pound that much harder at the sheer promise of giving in to it.

"I'm sorry for what you went through. I'm sure it was horrible, intense and extremely terrifying," she said with compassion. "But the fact remains that my brother was murdered and I'm sticking like glue to the man who may be the key to discovering who killed him. I can't back down. John wouldn't want me to." Her voice was a bit unsteady as the emotion and enormity of what she was saying sank in. "I've lost my brother and I can't...*won't* abandon my promise to him to protect and help you, Sam."

"There are some dangerous people out there, and you might be out of your league, he said, clearly exasperated as he ran both hands over his short hair.

The movement only tightened his powerful biceps and drew attention to his face. With his closely cropped hair, his maleness and his striking looks were pronounced, which made his impact on her even more of a gut punch to her senses. She could only marvel at how calm her voice was. "I'm aware of that." That calmness seemed to set him off. His eyes went a hot blue and he was in her face again. He clasped her upper arm roughly and shook her slightly.

"Dammit, Olivia. I won't be able to sleep at night knowing you could now be in danger because of me. I can't bear another innocent death on my hands. If you are going to continue with this investigation against my advice, then you are sticking close to me, rather than blunder into something that will get you killed."

"Sam, I'm a private investigator, not some innocent woman off the street. I understand the danger and the consequences."

His eyes narrowed and he shook his head. "You have no idea what you're getting into. I can use just about any weapon to kill—silently with a knife, with a gun from a distance, and even my bare hands.... The people we could be up against have all those abilities and one thing I don't have."

"What's that?"

"A complete and utter disregard for human life."

She met his tough gaze with her chin up and her eyes hard. She took in the wild gleam of pain in his expression, the muscles and tendons that stood out in his neck, the heavy rise and fall of his chest as he breathed. She suspected most women in her shoes would back off, turn around right now and bolt, trying to get as far away from Sam Winston as was possible. But Olivia wasn't one of those women. In fact, Sam intrigued her, a devastating combination of warrior and hero.

"I'll be careful."

He smiled then, but it wasn't in amusement. "That's right. Here with me."

"I don't think that's—"

"It's nonnegotiable, Olivia."

"Don't get high-handed with me, Sam. I make my own decisions."

He let go of her arm and stepped closer, and she tensed. She tried not to show it, but the man unnerved her. The stabilized world she lived in had suddenly become filled with this irresistible and wholly captivating man who had a very destabilizing effect. She wasn't sure what to do about that. She wasn't a shrinking violet, and Sam would have to get used to that. She faced things head-on, too.

His eyes went hard and flinty, and she had to resist the urge to shiver. He had intimidating down to a science. Gone were the soft eyes and the soft tone. In their place was blue granite and a flat, steely voice that brooked no argument—something she would expect of a man who lived by his wits and honed strength, one who was used to giving out orders. "You're moving in here with me until this is over. I won't take no for an answer. We've just become roommates."

"Giving me ultimatums only makes me want to be contrary," she returned flatly.

He did smile then and it relieved the tension in his face. "Why doesn't that surprise me? I'm not too happy about it, either, Olivia."

"Are you using reverse psychology on me?"

He laughed. "Would that work?" He sobered. His gaze locked on hers, so intent, so focused. So trustworthy and steady. "Okay, then do it for me so I can sleep at night knowing that if you need me, I can be there in a flash." He said it quietly, but somehow the softer tone wasn't the least bit comforting. In fact, it only served to unnerve her further.

She had to take a breath because he made her lungs

feel compressed. "Now you're preying on my emotions, but I'm inclined to let you win this one. Safety in numbers and all that. We'll make a good team."

"I'm not exactly a team player. But you're not the only one who owes something to your brother."

She told herself she was agreeing to stay with him for safety reasons. But that might have been the biggest lie she'd ever told herself. Even though this man stirred her blood, she wasn't a pushover. But it was clear he was dangerous in so many ways—to her equilibrium and maybe to her very life. She was going to have to be vigilant about both. A cocky loner wasn't exactly her type. They didn't usually play nice with others.

"This Lone Ranger act doesn't work well within a team."

"Would that be Team Owens?"

She tilted her head. Okay, he was quick on the uptake.

"I'll show you to my guest room. The bathroom has an extra toothbrush in it and I can find you something to sleep in."

She nodded, her heart fluttering just thinking about being under the same roof as Sam. He headed toward the back of the house and she grabbed her purse and followed him. He opened the door to a modest room with a bathroom.

"I'll be right back."

He disappeared through the doorway across the hall, and Olivia set her purse on the bed. She would have to go to her apartment and pick up some things tomorrow. She also still had arrangements to handle with her brother's funeral, which was the day after tomorrow.

For a moment, the loss of her brother overwhelmed her and she closed her eyes against the sudden stab of pain, her arm banded around her waist.

"Olivia?"

She started. She hadn't heard him come up to her.

"Are you all right?"

She nodded. "I was just thinking about John. Were you planning on coming to his funeral?"

"Yes, I was."

"It's the day after tomorrow."

"I know." He looked sad and guilty all over again.

She couldn't even tell him it wasn't his fault, because she didn't really know if it was. All she knew was that her brother was dead after hiring her to watch one of his patients. That patient was in some kind of trouble that Olivia couldn't even fathom. After the attempt on his mother's life and the involvement of one of his army buddies in the shooting, it was clear it was on a much deadlier and wider scale than she'd ever dealt with.

She couldn't imagine what Sam was going through. He looked stressed, but that wasn't a stretch. He was seeing her brother for therapy. Whether that had to do with his military service, the turmoil in his private life right now, or something else, Olivia couldn't guess. She was determined to get answers regarding John's death.

But she wasn't going to back off and let her brother or Sam down.

"Let's get some sleep," she said. "We'll tackle it in the morning when we're fresher."

"Sounds like a good plan." He held out a camouflage T-shirt that was large enough that it would come to her about midthigh.

She accepted it and their hands brushed. His were as warm as she remembered his skin had been. There she was again, thinking about him totally naked. When he'd gotten that hard-on, she couldn't help wondering if it was because she'd been touching him...okay, not in a therapeutic way. She probably was the one who caused it. She couldn't seem to feel sorry about that. She liked the fact that she turned this man on.

But it would be smart to keep her distance now that she didn't have to pretend to date him. They could do away with that altogether. Well, she could pretend, couldn't she?

"Good night, Olivia."

"Night, Sam."

He left and closed the door behind him. She set the shirt on the bed and went into the bathroom, finding the spare toothbrush and toothpaste. She washed her face and brushed her teeth, still pondering Sam's mental state.

Once that was done, she stripped down to nothing but her undies and pulled the shirt over her head. The soft cotton settled against her body, and her skin flushed as she thought of this fabric having at one time been against Sam's hard chest, broad shoulders and thickly muscled back.

She slipped beneath the covers and wondered how she was going to even get to sleep. So much had happened in just two short days.

She'd have to watch herself and try to find her professionalism somewhere in all that melting she did around Sam.

Any way she sliced it, Sam Winston was trouble.

Chapter 4

Sam started awake, standing in the middle of his room again. His chest was heaving as if he'd been running. His skin was slick with a cold sweat, his shoulder throbbing. He felt sick with fear, the taste of it like bile in his mouth. He was shaking as if he were freezing, but it was warm in the room. Waves and waves of pain, that's all he could remember. Unending. When he reached for some remnant of the nightmare, there was nothing there.

There should have been.

Plenty.

These bits and pieces of what had happened to him were almost more torturous than actually remembering. Maybe.

The blank place where his memory should be was a wall of darkness.

A black freaking hole.

He walked on shaky legs back to his bed and sat down. Sam eased in a steadying breath, reaching down deep inside himself for calm.

He hovered on the edge of panic and he didn't know why.

He wanted to call Dr. Owens. He had even risen to go look for his cell when he stopped and...felt that panic inch a bit closer.

"Damn!" he said into the quiet room. Maybe it was because his defenses were down or it was because he needed Dr. Owens, but tears pressed on the backs of his eyes. He wanted to rip out the heart of the person who had stolen Dr. Owens's life. If he ever found out who that was...and if it was because of him...that was something he would regret for the rest of his life.

The panic intensified and Sam thought he was going to jump out of his skin. Then deep brown eyes flashed in his memory. Then that caramel hair and that soft, kissable mouth. He took a deep breath and the panic receded a little bit more. Olivia's curves. How she had felt against him, her shapely butt pressed against his groin, the warmth of her skin beneath his forearm. He took another breath and more of the panic retreated.

He went into the bathroom. He caught a glimpse of himself in the mirror. His pupils were dilated and he wasn't sure if this was from the fear, the memory of Olivia or his nightmare.

He turned on the shower and stripped off his shorts, soaked with sweat. The warm water felt amazing. As amazing as Olivia's hands running over him, giving him relief from the pain. His skin was sensitive as he soaped up and rinsed himself off, the memory of his reaction to what he couldn't remember being replaced by thoughts of Olivia, thoughts about her wet and soapy against him, her delectable mouth on his, his hands all over her.

He got hard and lost in the fantasy, desperate to push his failure to find peace, to understand what had happened to him, and to make a damn difference away from him. Unable to help himself, he cupped his raging erection and leaned one hand against the wall as he imagined himself deep inside Olivia. He bit his bottom lip as the pleasure built, wondering, imagining how she would move, how she would feel, slick and warm. He came hard, grunting with the spiraling pleasure. Damn, that woman turned him on and she'd been what he needed to push back the darkness.

Outside the shower, he toweled himself off, still vibrating from his powerful orgasm. He went to his dresser and pulled out another pair of army-green cotton shorts with Army Strong stitched into the hem.

He walked out into the hall and then into the kitchen. He pulled a cold bottle of water out of the fridge and unscrewed the cap and downed the whole thing in a few gulps, then grabbed another one.

"Sam?"

He started and spilled water down his chest, grimacing and gasping as the cold liquid hit his hot skin.

She blinked in the light from the kitchen, her expression apologetic. "Oh, I'm sorry."

"Olivia?" Her hair was tousled around her face with a half-lidded sleepy look that said she'd just rolled out of bed. The thought of her all warm and soft against him arrowed right into his groin. She looked luscious in his oversize shirt. It fit her like a dress. He liked that she wasn't at all self-conscious around him.

That heated fantasy came back to him and he reached for a towel, dragging his eyes away from her.

"Are you all right?"

"I'm sorry I woke you. Just a nightmare." He wiped off his chest, displacing his dog tags as Olivia's eyes followed his movement. Was she looking at him or what he was doing? His blood surged.

"I thought I heard running water."

"I took a shower."

Her eyes traveled over him and he got his answer. She was looking at him. Definitely. In the past, he wouldn't have hesitated in making time with a woman. But this was Dr. Owens's sister and…well… He rubbed the back of his neck. Hadn't he just jacked off thinking about her? He was an idiot and, on top of it, he was so messed up. All he could allow himself to do was think about it. But his mind went there anyway. He knew that reality would be much better than his fantasy.

"Did it help?"

He hid his smile. "Yes, it did."

He rolled his shoulder to try to alleviate the dull throbbing there.

She came into the kitchen when she saw the expression of pain on his face. "Is your shoulder bothering you?"

If he said yes, she would probably offer to help, and he couldn't quite hold on to his resolve. His family was great as usual, but with all the turmoil in his professional and personal life, it was nice to think about a beautiful woman giving him some measure of comfort. The fact that it was Dr. Owens's sister was ironic.

"Yes, it's 24/7, honey."

She gave him a wry look at the flippant endearment. "Come into the living room and I'll work it for a bit."

Without giving him any time to answer, she took his wrist and pulled him into the living room. He'd met some forceful women in his life, and his mother was at the top of the list, but he'd had yet to meet one he'd let drag him around by the nose or his dick.

But he was beginning to reassess that whole thing since not only was Olivia steal-his-breath beautiful, but her assertiveness was a turn-on.

She sat down and with her hands on his hips, turned him so his back was to her. "Sit."

He chuckled as he complied. "Yes, ma'am."

She slipped one of those silky bare arms under his armpit and around his shoulder joint to hold him steady as she began to knead the muscles connecting to his shoulder.

He breathed a sigh of relief and relaxed.

"You can lean back if you want, Sam. I'm not a delicate flower."

She pulled him toward her and he sank into her, her chin just over the shoulder she was working, her breath warm against his skin. The wisp of her exhale sent a shiver of pleasure along his nerve endings. He was glad he took the edge off in the shower, because this was pure sensual torment.

"Wow, you're still a bit tight. Have you thought about seeing a chiropractor?"

Reclining against her now, listening to her voice, which managed to be both soothing and no-nonsense, and breathing in her enticing scent, he could barely register what she was saying.

"Sam?"

"Huh."

"Chiropractor?"

"Um, no. I hadn't," he said, sighing again as the pain lessened with the pressure of her warm, insistent hand. "How do you know all about this therapeutic massage?"

"I was actually a massage therapist. In fact, I've had a number of jobs that have now come in quite handy as a P.I. A jack-of-all-trades makes it easy to fit into any kind of job you might need to carry out your client's wish. I did once have certification but faked it this time to get the job. They might have discovered it eventually, but it was only a temporary situation. Or so I thought."

He dropped his head back against her shoulder and looked up at her, into eyes that easily held his own when challenged.... Yeah, he was finding his rationale a little harder to hang on to.

His body was finding it even more difficult. He had to chalk that up to being a man, one who didn't hesitate to take what he wanted most of the time. Her hair smelled good and he breathed deeply of her scent, the strands tickling his cheeks.

"You need to do it."

Those words immediately evoked the image of him on top of her *doing it*. "Huh?" he said, feeling drugged and sluggish with the intoxication of her.

She laughed softly, "The chiropractor? Are you getting sleepy?"

No, he was getting turned on even more. This close he could see that her eyes were a deep brown, like melted chocolate. "Yes, ma'am."

"Was that a yes to the chiropractor or yes to being sleepy?"

"You are very pushy."

"Ha! Isn't that like the pot calling the kettle black, Sam?"

"Yes, ma'am."

She narrowed her eyes and gave him a hard look. "Don't patronize me."

He chuckled and her face softened, her eyes roving over him. Ah, damn, he didn't need her looking at him as if she was thinking any of those same things in return or getting turned on by him. Temptation, in this case, was not a good thing. He had enough to handle just trying to keep his head on straight—make that both his heads.

He couldn't afford to be noticing things, or noticing her noticing things, either.

But her gaze stayed on his face and then dipped boldly down to his mouth.

Olivia had never been one of those coy women. She had always dealt with men just the same as she'd dealt with women. They needed to be handled differently, of course. Men were action-oriented, relied on logic and concise communication. Say exactly what you meant around a man and he would get your meaning every time. Even Olivia found that read-between-the-lines crap some women liked to peddle annoying.

So her reaction to Sam was intense. Much more intense than it had been with any man she'd dated. His looks aside, he was intelligent, compassionate, tough, obviously courageous and had a good sense of humor.

She liked so many things about him, which was

good and bad. Like where she was right now, taking his weight against her, touching all that tanned, gorgeous muscle.

She pressed harder into him and he groaned softly, and that had a very volatile effect on her, sizzling her nerve endings. "It will feel better in a minute," she promised.

"No pain, no gain?"

"Something like that."

He closed his eyes and sighed, his dark, impossibly thick eyelashes like half-moons on his cheeks. "That feels great," he said. "You might not do this for a living, but you're good at it." The stubble shadowing his jaw accentuated his mouth. She really, really needed to stop looking at that mouth. But the stubble gave him a rugged edge, emphasizing all the more those beautiful lips of his.

She shifted and he tensed. "Don't move," she said as she slipped out from behind him, leaving him to recline against the cushions. "Let me work it from the front."

She dug in again and her hands trembled. She braced her hand beside his head, intending to use her elbow to get at the muscle in his joint, but she lost her focus and her damn mind in the beauty of Sam. Instead of continuing with the massage, she leaned all the way down, bracing her hand on the other side of his head. Fleetingly, she thought this was such a bad idea for so many reasons. But the impulse came over her and she couldn't seem to help herself. He seemed so alone, so isolated, she wanted to comfort him in a more intimate way. She brushed her lips across his.

His eyes flashed open and he looked up at her with those stark blue eyes. She held his gaze for what felt like forever. She could feel the power of his personality in that gaze even while she could read nothing of his thoughts. She started to draw back, but he cupped the back of her neck and pulled her mouth against his with a soft groan. His movement gave his dog tags a sexy, musical jingle.

The touch of his mouth made her want so much more, that bottom lip, so sensual, so full she couldn't help using the tip of her tongue to savor the taste and feel of him. His open mouth was so inviting as he groaned again at the slide of her tongue. His chest heaved against hers, the thin T-shirt no barrier against the heat of his broad chest. Her breasts ached, her nipples tightening and hardening. Both of them panting, she took his mouth again. His fingers caressed the back of her neck when she opened her mouth, and the kiss just got hotter.

Warm, moist lips met hers, still open and so inviting, offering. He slipped his tongue inside, tracing slowly around the inner edge of her lips, then slipped deeper, probing, exploring. Olivia tried to catch her breath, but he kept stealing it every time his mouth moved over hers.

The heat flowed down over her, followed by Sam's hands. He ran his hands down her back, sending shivers, setting off new ones, sliding lower. Desire swelled inside her, pushing aside sanity, blazing a trail for more instinctive responses. She arched against him, losing herself in the kiss and in the moment.

She slid her hand over his dark brown cropped hair, soft and smooth against his scalp. She molded her palms over the curve of his head and slanted her mouth across his as needs took over with a burning edge.

His hands slid over her buttocks, kneading, stroking. He caught the hem of her T-shirt and dragged it up, his knuckles skimming over the taut muscles of her back, skating along the side of her rib cage. The skin just below her breasts and on her stomach made hard, searing contact with his, and it was her turn to groan.

He was so silky soft and sizzling hot against her. He jerked the T-shirt more and her tight nipples made contact. His whisper of pleasure vibrated against her lips. She felt as if she were tumbling through space, dizzy, hanging on tight to her only anchor. Then suddenly she was on her back looking up into the blazing, passionate eyes of Sam. He dipped his head, focusing on her breasts and she arched in reaction to his gaze.

Then he was at her breast, his tongue grazing against her nipple, his lips tugging gently. The sensation was incredible, setting off a flutter of something wild inside her.

A car alarm close by went off and they both jolted at the sound. Sam lay against her for a moment, tense and alert. Then he sighed when the alarm abruptly cut off.

He looked down at her and swore vehemently as he pushed off her and sat back.

For a moment she let the regret wash through her as his eyes caressed her still. Reluctantly she pulled down her T-shirt and sat up.

He rubbed his hand over his face. "Olivia…"

"I know. There are so many reasons why this would be a bad idea."

He nodded. "But I want to say the hell with all those reasons."

"But you're worried. About me."

She was trying not to fool herself. She knew he was

a stranger, but that kiss…she'd melted into him, disappeared inside him and had been more with him than she'd ever been with anyone in her life. Right or wrong, the feelings were there and they were real.

She just wanted to bury her face in the curve of his neck and start all over again. She didn't get embarrassed about her feelings like other women, and she sure as hell didn't get them hurt often. She was methodical about who she chose to date.

Sam…was an American hero, a military man. Normally that would suit her. Gone a good bit of the time was okay in her book, but when she thought about Sam going anywhere, she didn't like that idea.

He stood and moved away from her as if he didn't trust himself. "I'm so messed up, Olivia. So messed up. I don't even know if I'll ever be right again. Normal. If I am, it's back to Special Forces for me. Uncle Sam is all I really know."

"In the short time that I've known you, you've never sounded so unsure about anything."

He rubbed his hand over that short sexy hair, and Olivia just wanted to get her hands on him again.

"I don't really know you, but it must be a trait that runs in your family, because I'm close to spilling my guts and I'm not used to that. I barely talk to my family. In Special Forces showing any weakness is unacceptable. But I can't go back to my unit until I figure out what happened to me."

"Sam," she said, rising and going over to him. "If you need someone to talk to, you can talk to me. I won't ever betray your trust. It has to be ironclad if we're going to weather all this."

He backed away from her and ran his hand over

his head again. That was fear she saw in his eyes, and she suspected that he'd had plenty of that in the six months he'd been back in Raleigh. She figured he was tired, too. The kind of tired you didn't get from one difficult day. Those nightmares must be awful if the look on his face when he had woken on the table was any indication.

"Talk to me."

She shut up then, deciding to let him find his own way into the conversation they both knew they had to have.

He leaned against the wall and closed his eyes, his breathing shallow. She was a bit worried he might hyperventilate, but she held her tongue and let him work through it in his head. Men like Sam powered through fear, and the courage it must have taken for him to seek out her brother humbled Olivia.

He brought his head down and opened his eyes, then settled back a bit more. He released a shaky breath, his eyes dark and tormented. He tried to speak, but his voice gave out on him. His face contorted in an agony of emotion. Finally he said, "Do I feel freaked out because your brother is dead?" in a hushed voice. "Yes. I have a tremendous amount of guilt about it. And that's bad enough, but he can't help me anymore. And, Olivia, I need that help. I've got to unlock what's inside my head. That's where the answers are, but it's just blank. Like a black wall."

As she watched him, an enormous need unfolded in her. A need to comfort him, to assure him, a need to simply wrap her arms around him to let him know he wasn't alone. But she sensed he wasn't open to that right now, the muscles along his bristled jaw tensing. "Then we should find someone else to help you."

He shook his head, his eyes stark. "I can't...." Folding his arms across his chest, he didn't move for the longest time; then he let his breath go in a heavy sigh and rubbed his eyes, swallowing hard. Finally he spoke, his voice gruff. "I can't trust that what I might have said to your brother somehow got him dead. I can't see another psychologist and put anyone else in danger. I don't even think you should be involved."

She shifted and looked directly at him even as he gave her an exasperated look. "We've already discussed that and I'm not changing my mind about that, Sam. Especially now."

Letting his breath go in a ragged sigh, he pushed off the wall and said, "Why? Because you feel sorry for me? Olivia, I can take care of myself.

"I don't doubt that, Sam." He just stared at her with the look of annoyance on his face. "I don't. I understand that this is risky and dangerous, but I'm not leaving you. I think you're under surveillance."

"Why didn't you tell me this last night?"

"Because you'd had enough last night and I can't be sure. It's a gut feeling, but I haven't been able to pinpoint who might be watching you. I took a lot of footage when I was following you. I just haven't had a chance to look at it all. Whoever they are, they're pros, slippery and elusive, very good at what they do."

"I must be really off my game if you were following me and another set of people." He sounded so weary. "I've had this prickly sensation ever since I got home. Where is this footage?"

"In my camera at my apartment. We can pick it up tomorrow when I get my things."

He nodded. "That's at least something."

"We should get some sleep, Sam. We have a lot going on in the next few days."

He nodded and they headed toward the back of the house. As she drew closer to him, she noted the compressed lines around his mouth and the tension in his body. She hated the thought that while she would sleep well, there was no guarantee that Sam would. Was that what was causing him this tension or was it her and what had happened between them in the living room? She touched his arm and he hesitated. "We'll figure it out, Sam. We'll work at it until we do. Try to rest if you can. We can take…everything slow."

He turned to look at her, and a genuine smile released some of the strain on his face. "Babe, if we ever decide that we want to move forward with what happened on the couch, it won't be slow. Believe me, it was the best part about this whole screwed-up situation we're in."

Unable to drag her eyes away, she stared at him, her heart fluttering, an unexpected longing clogging her chest.

The men of her past faded away. Right now there was no one but Sam. He had that certain aura about him, the stamp of unadulterated masculinity, of sexual intensity, that somehow magnified his physical strength. But it wasn't his looks or his rugged body that made him stand out in the crowd. It was his quiet assurance in spite of his fears and doubts. He was a man very secure in his own masculinity, whose strength of character had shaped and molded his life. There were no half measures in him. He handled everything all the way.

"I can see why John was so keen on you and so adamant that you deserved the attention. And as for what happened on the couch…let me say you know what you're doing very well in that respect."

He leaned down and whispered softly, "You'd better get inside your room, babe, before I forget why I stopped kissing you in the first place."

"You like giving out those orders, don't you, Captain?"

"Hup to it and march, Olivia."

"The more I get to know you, the more I like the man you are."

They shared a grin before she did as she was told, not because she wanted to, but because at this moment it was prudent. Would it always be so? No, she didn't think so. The attraction between them was volatile and she wasn't sure whether, when it exploded, they could keep it in check.

After closing the door, she leaned against it. Sam Winston wasn't just some client now; he was more.

She just wasn't sure what that was exactly.

Chapter 5

After one more nightmare that wasn't as bad as the one he had on the massage table and one erotic dream about Olivia, Sam rolled out of bed at 6:00 a.m. and went for a run. He needed the time to get his head together before facing Olivia.

The nightmares, the memory loss, the blackouts, the death of a therapist who'd been making progress with him and the fact that he was being followed not only by Olivia but by others put Sam in a very bad place. His sixth sense had been screaming, and it was good to know his instincts weren't as off as they appeared to be, but he must have been terribly preoccupied not to notice the tails.

Of course, Mike had taken up a lot of thought process and emotion. This was still a very sore place for him to go. Mike had gotten Sam to open up about some things. He now had to wonder if Mike had been feeding this to someone else or if he had been in the same boat as Sam. Totally blindsided by his descent to madness…or had it been madness?

Frustrated, Sam pushed himself harder than in his previous workouts. By the time he got back to the house, the humid spring air had drenched him in sweat.

Before going back to his room, he decided to look over his truck quickly, checking for tracking devices. Then he went inside and got the coffeemaker going.

He heard the shower on in Olivia's room. Keeping his mind completely neutral so that he wouldn't think about Olivia's body, now that he knew what she looked like beneath her clothes, he went straight to his own room and took a quick shower, dried off and was back out before she'd finished.

In the kitchen, he poured himself a cup of coffee and took a sip.

"Good morning. That smells very good."

He turned to find Olivia, in the clothes she'd been wearing yesterday, standing at the entrance to the kitchen. Her hair was damp, just starting to become wavy, her eyes bright enough that he guessed she'd gotten some sleep. She looked good—really good.

"Would you like a cup?"

"Do you have creamer here?"

He shook his head. "No, just milk. I drink mine black."

She smiled at him and he was suddenly liking having a woman in the house first thing in the morning. "A necessity in the military?"

He shrugged. "Sometimes we're lucky to get coffee at all."

She nodded and stopped by the fridge to pull out the milk while he reached into the cabinet to get her a travel mug. When he turned to hand it to her, she was right there. Too close. Her brown eyes taking in his face as she reached for the cup.

Their hands met and the air heated. What was it with this woman? This happened every time he got close to her. Hell, who was he kidding? It happened every time he even thought of her.

"Thanks," she said, and poured out a cup and added a splash of milk. Taking a good swig, she sighed. "Sam, I was thinking. Maybe it would be a good idea to take a look at your file from my brother's therapy sessions. Maybe there is something in there that might help you to remember or give you something to think about."

She stood next to him as she drank her coffee, and the scent of her drifted to him, clean and sweet. "Didn't the police take everything for the investigation? Plus, it's still a crime scene, right?" He wasn't sure he wanted Olivia to see how messed up he really was. But she was here to help him. Not one to seek help, which was considered another sign of weakness, he had to put aside his military way of thinking and accept her help. It was hard to admit it, but he needed her.

"No, they released it already. And they can't have my brother's files. Those are confidential, and as the sole inheritor of all his possessions, I told them they would need a warrant. They can't go digging into patient files looking for a motive. They need probable cause."

"What about his computer?"

"They didn't really have a reason to take it, but even if they had, my brother didn't keep paper files.

He had a therapy management database he used, so we'll have access to it anywhere. They wanted access to his emails, but, again, that's a tricky thing. Some are private and confidential and some aren't. I told them if they get a suspect, I'd revisit the email question. My brother would be horrified if his confidentiality was broken. I promised him that if anything ever happened to him, I would ensure that never happened."

"Well, that's to our advantage. We had a lot of taped sessions, as well."

"I know where he keeps those, too. We can bring them back here to listen to them."

He tensed. Some of the stuff on those tapes was deeply personal. He wasn't sure he wanted her to hear them. Some of the stuff was when he was under hypnosis, and still more was when he was remembering bits and pieces of his captivity, and it wasn't at all pretty. He set down the coffee mug, the easygoing atmosphere suddenly growing tense. "I don't think you should go. Just give me the key and I'll take care of it."

Her brown eyes darkened and she got a mutinous look on her face. Damn, he loved the way this woman took no guff from him, even though this once he wished she would just comply.

"What? Even after all that we discussed yesterday, you are still trying to protect me? I'm going, Sam. You may not believe it, but I'm in my element. I found myself when I became a P.I., so you can argue all you want, but I'm going!"

"I usually give the orders," he said flatly, all the irritation he'd felt while he was running earlier coming back at him in a rush.

"Well, I'm not one of your soldiers, and guess what? I don't have to follow them."

"Olivia. The key."

She made a noise that clearly stated she found him completely insufferable. He could be, so there was no point attempting to change her mind. But before the day was over, she'd also find out he was doggedly determined about keeping her safe. Her brother had died in that office, shot down like an animal. *Eliminated.* The blood was probably still on the floor. He could be in and out in a jiff without her having to see that so soon after her brother's death. He wanted her clear of it.

"This is a team effort, Sam. I'm keeping the key, and unless you want to try to wrestle it from me, this is going to remain a team effort."

He ran his hand over his hair and threw his head back to gain control over his temper. "You're exasperating."

"I'll take that as a compliment."

"Just give me the key and stop arguing with me."

"No! What is your problem?" she snapped.

"I don't like that you have to go to the place where your brother was murdered." His voice was quiet.

Understanding came over her face slowly, and her eyes immediately softened. "Oh," she said, sounding a little surprised by his kindness, but then so was Sam.

He didn't usually get in touch with his *sensitive* side, but with Olivia it just seemed to come out naturally. He wasn't sure that was a good thing.

His mind spun back to that moment last night right before they said good-night when she'd made the comment about liking the man he was. From someone else it might have come across as flirty and provocative, but she'd said it rather straightforwardly, more as a measure of respect.

After that kiss and her obvious growing regard for him, it was no surprise why his entire body had begun to tighten when she teased him and then disappeared into her room.

And yet he couldn't get his mind to let it alone. That moment he'd looked into her eyes and seen that she was as affected by their forced togetherness as he was. He wasn't sure he'd be so chivalrous and self-controlled the next time. If there was a next time. He stared into those tender brown eyes as she looked up at him. He damn well knew he wanted there to be a next time.

"I know that it won't be easy. But I have to remain detached. For now. There will be a time to mourn my brother. But I explained to you why I need to do this. Put your protectiveness aside."

"Olivia—"

"No, Sam. I appreciate it very, very much. But my intuition is telling me to stick close to you. That you are somehow the target here."

"I'd be the first to say never ignore your gut. It might not always be dead accurate, but that feeling is usually grounded in something." Sort of like his instinct that Olivia was someone special. He'd gotten all hung up on his own stuff, and all that crap had dulled his instincts. Now? Now he was just all hung-up. "Something is going on and I am at the epicenter. There's no doubt in my mind. It's why I left my family's estate and rented this house."

Her eyes went even softer. "Oh, Sam. You really are something."

He shifted under her scrutiny. He was so used to

being a shadow warrior. He was silent and deadly behind the scenes. No one really knew what he did or what kind of sacrifices he had to make, except for the men who served with him. Men like Mike. "You ready to go or did you want to get something to eat?" he grumbled.

She tilted her head and gave him a wry smile. "Don't be such a sore loser. Let's just stop by the coffee shop for some bagels. Something tells me you don't have much here."

"See, those instincts are working for you."

She laughed and nudged his shoulder with hers. "Sounds like we'll need a trip to the grocery store at the very least for half-and-half."

"Yes, whatever you need. I do want you to be comfortable here. How is the bed?"

"Very comfortable, thank you, but I think I'll get my own pillow."

Okay, it was time to get his mind off beds and pillows. He grabbed up his car keys and headed to the garage door. Holding it open for her, she stepped through and they got into his truck.

Pulling out of the garage and driveway, he was hyperalert for anyone who might be watching them. But if it was the government, they had so many toys to easily keep track of him. Trying to find them was like looking for a needle in a haystack.

When he checked his truck over after his run he'd found no tracker. Didn't mean it wasn't there, just not in a package that was obvious to him.

"When you have a chance, Olivia, could you go over my truck and your car to make sure there are no tracking devices? I looked this morning, but I didn't see anything conspicuous."

She looked pleased that he was actually giving her something constructive to do. "I already did that before you caught me in your office. No trackers."

After stopping for a bite to eat, they headed over to Dr. Owens's office. It didn't matter what Olivia said, she was feeling something. He could tell by the way she took a deep breath before she fit the key in the lock and opened the door.

She pushed it open and took another breath before she stepped inside. The outer office looked the same as it had when he was there three days ago. As they approached the office door, the only evidence that a crime had been committed was a piece of the yellow crime scene tape that was stuck to the frame of the door. He wished he could somehow lessen the impact of seeing her brother's life destroyed.

But no matter how much he wanted to, he couldn't change that reality. He'd learned to live with that after seeing countless injustices in his almost ten years with the army. But in this case, he had a direct personal connection to the other victim here. Olivia.

After so recently enduring the assassination attempt on his mother's life, he wasn't so sure that he could have had anywhere close to the amount of courage that she had in facing her brother's death and, taking it one step further, following through with what he would have wanted had he lived.

The thought of losing either Trey or Thad, let alone his mother, was too painful even to contemplate. His respect for Olivia went up a notch. Her bravery humbled him.

"Olivia, are you sure…?"

"I'm sure," she said, giving him a look of gratitude and pushing the door all the way open. The impact of the office settled in her eyes as she scanned the room. She abruptly stopped and swallowed hard when she saw the bloodstain on the floor. "Oh, John," she whispered, clearly fighting her emotions. Taking a deep breath, she moved farther into the room and walked to one of the locked cabinets. After perusing the files, she pulled out a case.

"These are yours. We'll take them back to the house."

Sam looked closer at the lock and saw the very faint scratches on the wood. They could have been caused from everyday wear and tear, but his sixth sense was telling him that wasn't the situation.

He took the case out of her hands and opened it. Inside were five minicassettes. He pulled the last one out of the plastic. On the label, in neat handwriting, was the date from the previous week. The last session before Dr. Owens had been murdered.

He walked to the desk where the microcassette recorder was sitting on the edge of the desk. The back of his neck prickled. Most of the stuff had been knocked off the desk. He popped the tape in and pushed Play.

Nothing happened, no introduction to his session, no discussion about what was going to happen, nothing. He checked the volume. Up to full. He popped in the next and still nothing. He turned to look at Olivia.

"The tapes have been erased."

"I guess that's our confirmation."

He put his finger to his lips. He shook his head and opened the recorder and took out the tape.

She nodded her understanding.

His eyes traveled over the office, but he figured if there had been listening devices here, they had long been removed. Whoever planted them couldn't afford to have law enforcement find them. But he wasn't going to take any chances.

He set the tape into its plastic sleeve and returned the case back to the file, which Olivia locked up. There was no use in taking it if it had been erased.

They left the office without touching anything else. He could only hope that Olivia could find something in the notes on the therapy database, but after finding that the tapes had been tampered with, he was worried about the data online. They needed some idea why his therapy was so important, what Dr. Owens had discovered and how it impacted his life.

He was even more uncomfortable now that Olivia was involved, but he'd lost that argument. First, he really needed her. She was a connection to his retrieving information about his therapy, if it hadn't been compromised, and second, she was becoming important to him just by virtue of her character. It wasn't only that he wanted to get close to her, intimately close, but it was the way she interacted with him.

Once inside the truck, he started it and Olivia gave him directions to her apartment.

As he put the truck in gear, Olivia said, "My brother was killed because of what he discovered about you through therapy. We just don't know what that is. We're flying blind."

"We are because I can't remember a damn thing." He turned to her, feeling even more paranoid than usual. "The implications of your brother's death and my connection raise other red flags. If Dr. Owens was murdered because of something I had locked up in my mind, I had to guess that my captivity six months ago had to be in direct correlation. That was the topic we were working through. What happened to me during my imprisonment has to be related. Which only makes me think immediately about Mike."

"You're thinking, did he go off the deep end because of what happened to him?"

"I'm going to tell you what I remember, and I'm breaking federal law here, but I need your help. This is all classified information, Olivia. I was specifically told not to reveal anything."

"By whom?"

"The CIA."

"Holy shit. You weren't kidding about this being out of my comfort zone."

"No, I was dead serious."

"This smacks of the CIA and exactly what they would do, but aren't they forbidden to run missions on American soil?"

"Of course they are, but do you think that deep black ops cares about whether the soil is red, white and blue?"

"Why would our government be running a black ops on you, Sam? What are they hoping to gain from it?"

"I don't know."

She reached out and settled her hand on his forearm. It wasn't something she consciously did, because she never even looked down, but her touch made it difficult to keep his mind on what she was saying. "Maybe we're just jumping to conclusions here. We really have no proof of anything and nothing to go on unless we can unlock your mind."

He bit his lip to keep his focus. His gut was churning with the implications of Dr. Owens's death and the blank tapes. "I keep coming back to Mike. He was a tough son of a bitch, mentally tough, Olivia. We're trained specifically in resisting torture. We're chosen because of our mental and physical attributes. That's why this attempt on my mother's life and his subsequent meltdown is so disturbing. What got to him? Was my mother a target or in his delusion did he perceive her as one?"

"Are you saying what I think you're saying?"

"Did they get to Mike and mess with his mind so that he would kill my mother?"

"Oh, God, Sam. What does that mean for you?"

"I wish I freaking knew. Maybe they got important information about my family from me. I just don't know. If this is about my family, I should really warn them."

"At this point, we really need to just get to my apartment, get my things and grab my camera. I'm anxious to get there now. Once we get some answers, that will help."

"If we get any answers. Without a professional, Olivia, how do we get to what's inside my head?"

"That is a good question. Do you know anyone you're willing to trust?"

"It's not a matter of trusting them. It's a matter of putting them in danger. Anyone I talk to is a potential target."

"Oh, you're right. This is very frustrating."

"I don't like any of this. It's a mess with you right in the line of danger."

Her hand tightened on his arm. Then she moved closer to him for protection as if she was trying to get away from the danger she must have realized she was in. His heart clenched at the thought of her considering him a safe haven. "Sam, I'm part of this now whether you like it or not. If the CIA or some clandestine black ops part of the army killed my brother, they must already know that I'm involved. I wouldn't be safe anyway. I say I'm much safer close to you."

No, she wasn't. She wasn't safe at all in either respect. What happened between them last night was smoldering right now. It wasn't a habit of his to take a woman to the edge like that and then walk away. And it took considerable control now not to nudge her in that direction again. But then, he hadn't expected resisting her would be easy. It was downright torturous.

He clenched his hands around the steering wheel the pressure of her next to him wore down his self-control. She stroked his skin, her palm warm. But it wasn't at all soothing.

He resisted the urge to touch her, knowing it was the right thing to do, but he couldn't quite draw his arm away. Tangling themselves up any further than they had already done was begging for trouble. They had more than enough trouble as it was. He needed to stay focused on the situation and not think about getting her naked. He swore under his breath. The little tugs he was experiencing inside his chest whenever he looked at her were downright terrifying. He'd been in her presence for only a couple of days. No way should she be having this effect on him. But there was no denying she was affecting the hell out of him. And it was more than sexual need fanning those flames.

"Things may seem calm now, but there are forces at work in the shadows."

"I'm beginning to buy in to your paranoia."

"Oh, confirmation. Isn't that just peachy? Do you know what we call that in special ops?"

"No, what?"

"A double cluster."

She laughed and finally drew her hand away and sat back.

Olivia lived in an apartment off Millbrook Road, tucked in the back with trees bordering the complex, making it seem almost as though they were off the beaten track, yet still in the busy city of Raleigh.

As soon as she opened the door to her apartment, she cried out and ran to her computer, leaving Sam to close the door and follow. Accessing her hard drive, she saw that all the files on Sam had been deleted. "Dammit," she said as Sam looked over her shoulder.

"What?"

"They got rid of everything, but I have a drive that stores all my files on a server instead of my computer." She clicked frantically. "Dammit, they got to that, too." She opened up an email and wrote a quick note to the company who had provided the drive about recovery. Then she shut off and packed up her laptop into the carry bag to take with her.

She looked over to a bookcase behind her desk and swore. "Sam, they took my camera. All my surveillance footage was on it. Wait, no. I did load my last session to the cloud. Hopefully they can recover something from it."

"We'll have to see. I'm sorry about this…your apartment."

"It's a mess all right. After all this is over, you're helping me clean it up."

"Yes, ma'am."

In spite of everything that had happened this morning, Olivia's eyes sparkled at him with amusement. She disappeared into the bedroom and he noticed some pictures on the wall. They were mostly of her and her brother hugging each other, mugging for the camera. He took one off the wall and held it in his hand. Would he ever get over the deep-seated guilt? The two of them looked so happy. Their love for each other prominent.

A lump formed in Sam's throat as he thought about his own family.

"Sam?"

He turned with the photo in his hand. Her face softened when she saw what he was holding. She set her bag down and took it out of his hands.

"That was last Thanksgiving. We had just battled for the last crescent roll, and one of my friends took this."

"Who won?"

She turned to look at him, her eyes tearing up. He knew that look. He'd seen it on faces plenty of times when his unit came back without one of its members. The loss just hit her like when he'd turn, expecting that buddy to be there, and find he'd forgotten that vivid soul was lost to him.

On the verge of tears, she said, her voice breaking, "My brother let me win and then I…gave him half."

She dropped her chin and her shoulders shook, her mouth twisting. He gently took the picture and set it aside so no tears would drop on its surface. When he turned back to her, she looked up at him and his heart rolled over so hard pain settled in his chest. He grabbed her upper arm and dragged her against him. For one brief instant she remained motionless. She slipped her arms around his neck, a soft sob wrenching loose from her when he gathered her up in a tight embrace. She buried her face into the hollow of his neck, sending his hand over her soft hair.

He'd never been in this position before. Comforting wasn't really one of his roles, and he'd never had a long-term relationship to ever get in deep enough to share this kind of emotion. His reaction to her was doubly strong, and it was surprising because of the short time he'd known her.

He murmured soothing words to her, not even sure what he was saying. But all he knew right now was that this raw pain she was feeling lived inside him, too. His relationship with Dr. Owens's was as close as a hardcore Special Forces commando could get to someone outside the unit that was as much family as Trey, Thad and his mother were.

Tight-knit didn't even begin to cover it.

So while he held her, wishing there was some action he could perform, then suddenly realizing he was being active by comforting her in his own awkward way, he again wanted to rip out the heart of the person who had pulled that trigger.

Solely because he'd hurt this beautiful woman cradled against him.

Chapter 6

Fighting against another swell of tears, Olivia yielded to the pressure of his arms. It felt so good to let go of that hard ball of pain that had been building ever since she'd heard that her brother had been killed. It wasn't until she'd stepped into his office and spied the blood on the floor that reality got terribly stark.

Sam had been right. It had been hell to go to the place where her brother had lost his life. But she guessed that Sam knew all about death. It was something that he lived with every day, saw every day.

She had no idea how he dealt with that. She wasn't sure she had that kind of courage.

Mourning her brother was going to take some time, and being overwhelmed by her emotions at a time like this was probably indulging herself, but Sam held her and she took advantage of his comfort once the initial tears and pain had passed.

Finally she loosened her arms and he released her.

"You have everything you need?"

She nodded.

He bent down to look into her eyes. "You okay?"

She met his eyes and smiled at his concern. "Yes, Sam. Thank you."

He looked uncomfortable for a minute, then nodded once.

She leaned forward and kissed him on the cheek.

He looked surprised for a moment. "What was that for?"

"You know what that's for, Sam."

"Aw, crap, don't get all mushy on me now. I need that warrior spirit."

She stared into those blue, steady, reassuring eyes of his. Their chemistry was always there even when they weren't acknowledging it.

"To hell with that." She copied his gruff tone. "Thank you," she said more softly, and kissed his cheek again, but this time he turned his head. She found that she was kissing his mouth instead. She'd been craving the taste of him since their first mind-blowing kiss. It would have been easy for her to think that she'd overreacted. A kiss was simply a kiss. No way one kiss could be so consuming, so intoxicating…so addicting.

But even a P.I. who knew what the hell she was doing most of the time could be wrong.

His lips were so soft, and the way he caught his breath in the back of his throat, that little guttural moan, made her instantly melt. It was all she could do not to plaster him back against the wall and devour him whole. He wove his fingers into her hair, tilted her head and took the kiss deeper. There were times when he drove her crazy with his orders, but in this case, she loved his command of her, the way he took what he wanted, yet fully gave to her, as well.

She really had expected him to come to his senses sooner and push her away. She clutched at his shoulders for balance because her mind just spun out of control. When his lips parted beneath hers, she drew him in almost greedily. God help her, she wanted him.

He broke the kiss and she was suddenly disappointed that his rationality had prevailed, but he lifted his head only a fraction, so she could still feel the warmth of his breath, his skin. He looked just as dazed as she was.

"Olivia, why aren't you…angry? Why don't you blame me for your brother's death? It's my fault."

She brought her hand up, wondering how long it would take before he really let go of that guilt. "Sam, it's not your fault. All you did was ask for help, and all my brother did was provide what you needed. The person who pulled the trigger on the gun is the one responsible for his death. I could never blame you. My brother wouldn't, either. So let that go, but I'm probably wasting my breath, because you probably won't."

He sighed. "I'm a stubborn son of a bitch."

"That's for sure," she groused.

But something shifted in her. It might not happen soon, but she knew it was going to happen. Before Sam left to go back to his unit, she was going to have him. All of him. Even if she had to seduce him into bed with whatever womanly wiles she had.

If she didn't take him the way she wanted to, she would regret it for the rest of her life. Even if he broke her heart. Which she was pretty sure might happen... was happening already.

He ran his thumb along her lower lip, watching her reaction as she gasped at the contact.

His chest heaved and his eyes went molten blue. "I used to think my control was ironclad, but you keep pushing past my barriers, Liv."

He gave her a nickname and she liked that very much. "Liv, huh? Can I call you Sammy?"

He chuckled. "Not if you want me to answer."

"Oh, come on, Sammy."

"Okay," he said with a smile, "only in private and never within hearing distance of my brothers or anyone in my unit."

"Deal." She homed in on his sexy mouth, and the air heated up between them.

"We really should get moving," he said, but he didn't move. Didn't let her go.

"We really should," she agreed, also remaining immobile.

This time he lowered his mouth to hers. "You're addictive..." he said as he kissed her gently, almost sweetly, and she felt her heart catch a little as he held her head, keeping her mouth on his, wanting as much as she did. He sighed when their lips finally parted.

"This...it's the *damnedest* thing."

"Yeah," she agreed, her hand reaching up and curving around his head, the feel of his soft hair filling a need inside her. "The damnedest thing."

He grabbed her bag before she could reach for it. "You know I can carry that."

"I know, but I've got it."

They stepped out of the apartment and Olivia followed Sam down the stairs toward the exit. As soon as they walked outside, someone grabbed Sam around the throat and hauled him backward. The man was big and wearing a mask.

Sam dropped her bag and broke the man's hold, but before Olivia could even think about helping him, another man materialized from behind one of the bushes and grabbed her around the waist and started dragging her away from Sam.

He punched the guy in the face and lunged after her, but the man recovered and had him in a choke hold again. It was clear whoever Sam was up against had the same kind of training as he did, because they seemed evenly matched. Olivia struggled against the other man's hold, but she couldn't break his iron grip.

She lost sight of Sam as the man half carried her, half dragged her around the side of the building.

"Sam!" she screamed.

When she saw that he was hauling her toward a van parked on the side of the road, fear exploded in the pit of her stomach and determination fired off in her blood. Olivia doubled her efforts.

But it was no use, he was just too strong. When they were almost to the van, someone, also masked, threw the doors open. Using her leg, she jammed it between his and he tripped and fell, letting go of her for just a minute. They wrestled on the ground and she ripped off his mask in the struggle, getting a good look at his face. With a shock, she recognized him from her surveillance before he pulled the mask back on. He had to have been one of the men following Sam.

He cursed and punched her in the face and knocked her back onto the grass. Then he reared over her, but she recovered enough to slam her fist into his groin. He blocked most of her swing, but her blow still landed.

He swore and doubled over, still reaching for her. It was all she needed. Bracing both hands on the ground, she kicked out and caught him in the jaw. Scrambling away, she was almost to her feet when Sam came barreling around the corner of her building, his gun in his hand. He started firing the moment he saw them.

The man chasing her stopped dead and backpedaled toward the van, his partner returned fire. Something hot and excruciating hit her arm, and she cried out, her legs buckling at the sudden shock of the pain. She dropped like a stone.

The man who attacked her jumped into the van and it squealed away from the curb.

"Olivia!" Sam shouted as he ran to her. The agony traveled up her arm, radiating out with a burning, stinging sensation that brought tears to her eyes. When she clutched her arm with a reflexive action, her hand came away slick with blood.

When Sam saw the blood, he looked into her eyes. What she saw there she was sure Sam rarely showed. Fear. Stark fear for her safety. He ripped off his T-shirt and pressed it against her arm.

"Hold that there tight," he ordered. He scooped her up and sprinted for his truck as sirens sounded in the distance.

"Sam, the police."

"No police. I'm getting you to someone who can help you." He set her in the truck and ran to get her bag.

Sam banged on the door of a modest residential house, cradling Olivia in his arms, angry and feeling as protective as hell.

"Sam," Lucy said with a calm concern as she opened the door. "What happened?"

"I need your help, Lucy. She was shot."

Lucy bit her lip.

"I know I'm asking a lot, but I just need you to trust me."

"Come in." Once the two of them entered, she closed the door.

"Hello, I'm Lucy Sinclair," she said to Olivia. "I'm engaged to Sam's brother Thad." She turned to Sam. "Do you want me to call him?"

"No. It's complicated, Lucy. I need you to just patch her up. Can you do that?"

"I'm Olivia Owens." She rubbed her uninjured hand over Sam's forearm. "Sam. I'm all right."

He still kicked himself for what had happened. He should have been more vigilant, more aware instead of getting lost in that damn kiss.

"Follow me," Lucy said, leading him into the living room. "You can set her down on the couch. I'll be right back."

Sam put Olivia down. By this time the cotton of his T-shirt where it was pressed against her arm was soaked with her blood.

He closed his eyes, swaying, the world shifting around him. Blood. There'd been plenty of it the night he and his unit were ambushed. Two men had gone down, one with blood gushing out of a neck wound, the other man shot in the head.

Sam braced himself on the arm of the couch as the memory of the ambush rolled over him like a freight train. They had been caught by surprise as if the men who had been lying in ambush out of the desert were specifically waiting for them.

He saw Mike go down as three men overwhelmed him and one shoved a needle into his neck. Even as Sam brought his gun up in reaction, three men were on him, the foreign voices yelling at him.

They had drugged him and Mike. It had only been a four-man mission. His C.O. had told them that was all that was needed.

"Sam!" Lucy shouted in his ear, and he started out of the flashback. Sweat rolling off him, his fists were clenched tight.

"Are you all right?" she said.

"Yes, I'm all right. I know this is asking a lot because I'm sure you have to report gunshot wounds."

"No, it's okay. You're family."

Olivia was looking at him with concern, but when Lucy pulled away the T-shirt, Olivia hissed with the pain.

"I know this hurts, but we've got to clean it and I have to make sure there's nothing left inside the wound."

He knelt down next to her and took her hand. "Look at me, Olivia," he said softly. "You were amazing. Fighting that guy off like a tough warrior." He was royally pissed still, but he found a calm place inside him for Olivia.

She met his gaze, hers going tender. The chemistry between them was almost too potent to handle.

Olivia closed her eyes against the pain as Lucy worked inside the wound. "No, don't focus on the pain. Focus on me."

"You're as distracting as the pain, Sam."

"But in a much better way," he said with a cocky grin.

She chuckled and then gasped. He squeezed her hand and drew her attention again. "I haven't told you, but you have the most beautiful hair. So many shades of brown. I always think of it as caramel, you know, just like the sauce."

Her eyes widened and instantly dropped to his mouth.

Lucy glanced at him and smiled softly and he gave her a mind-your-own-business look.

She rolled her eyes at him.

Olivia dropped her gaze down his neck to his chest. He was still shirtless with Olivia's blood on his chest.

He flexed and her eyes jerked back to his face. He smiled wickedly for her benefit, but the anger smoldered inside him like a burning ember deep in his gut.

"Sam, what is that heart-shaped tattoo you have over your heart?" she said, her voice uneven with her pain, and he clenched his teeth, then tried to relax for her benefit.

"It's the periodic table's chemical symbol for iron, Fe."

"Ironheart?"

He nodded. "Hooyah," he said.

"Okay, there was some cloth in there from your shirt, but I think I got everything," Lucy said. "I'm going to rinse it out with hydrogen peroxide and it's going to sting a bit. Are you ready?"

Olivia tightened her hand around his and he kept his gaze steady on hers. Out of the corner of his eye, he saw Lucy tuck a towel under her arm and pour.

Olivia made a small gasp, but she kept her eyes on his. Their communication was silent, powerful and absorbing. His breathing slowed and she followed in sync and her face smoothed as if the pain receded and all that remained was their connection.

"That wasn't so bad," Lucy said, patting Olivia's arm dry, then picked up a tube of antibiotic ointment and dabbed it on. "I want you to watch her for the first twenty-four hours. If she gets feverish, she's got an infection."

"Do you think that will happen?"

"No. I think I got it cleaned out really well. But change the dressing before she goes to bed and again in the morning. The bullet grazed her, so she's got some major swelling, but that should recede. Ice will help when you get her home."

"Thank you, Lucy," Olivia said.

"Sam, can I talk to you for a second? We'll be right back."

Olivia closed her eyes and nodded, resting her head against the couch.

Lucy led the way out to the kitchen.

"Sam, what do you think this is about?"

"I don't know."

"Sam…"

"I don't know, Lucy! Believe me, if I knew who shot Olivia…"

"Okay, I believe you, but I'm really concerned here. Why can't you go to the police? You were the ones who got attacked."

"I can't trust them, Lucy. That's all I can say."

"Surely, Thad—"

"No, I trust Thad."

"Is she any relation to Dr. Owens?"

"Yes. She's his sister."

She reached out. "I know that we don't know each other that well and you're dealing with so much, but Thad and I are here for you."

"Thank you, Lucy. That means a lot."

"Does this have anything to do with Mike?"

"I'm not sure." Sam lowered his voice. "I think what happened to Mike wasn't an accident, but I have no proof."

"All right, Sam, just be careful. I'm sure I can find you a shirt to put on before you leave."

"Thanks, Lucy." He squeezed her arm, turned and walked back into the living room while Lucy disappeared upstairs.

Sam stood there, the anger he'd kept in check threatening to boil over. It scored his gut, mixing in with the unadulterated terror that had run through him like a virus.

Lucy came back down and handed him one of Thad's T-shirts.

"Bathroom," he gritted out.

She pointed to the right. "I'm headed off to work, so just pull the door closed when you're done. It was nice to meet you, Olivia."

"You, too, Lucy. I'm just sorry it was under these circumstances."

Sam went inside the bathroom and washed off the blood. His got angry all over again and that fear for her safety that was still heavy in his gut only made his anger intensify. He'd banked it for the sake of comfort when she was being stitched up, but now he couldn't contain it. After pulling on the T-shirt, he strode toward the couch. Olivia was sitting up, and when her eyes met his and she saw the blaze of anger he couldn't hide, she looked immediately mutinous.

"Don't start, Sam."

"Don't start? I warned you something like this was going to happen! I told you it was dangerous to be around me! Now you've been hurt. It's not bad enough that I got your brother killed… Dammit!"

"Stop it. This isn't your fault! How many times do I have to tell you that?"

"I take responsibility for my actions!" He was beyond pissed. More so because she could have taken a fatal bullet instead of the minor wound on her arm. His gut clenched at the idea that there was even a scratch on her beautiful skin.

"Of all the pigheaded, stubborn jackasses…!" Her eyes were furious, and he had a feeling most of her reaction was adrenaline. She knew the score.

"Name-call all you want, but you know I'm right!" He scoffed. She got in his face then, and his breath caught. She was lucky the bullet had missed anything vital. He shuddered thinking what could have happened if the guy who dragged her away from him had gotten her into that van.

"I'm sure you think you're always right!" She shoved at his chest with her good hand, but he wasn't budging. He liked it right here close to her where he could feel her intensity, take in all her wrath and sputtering and anger. That suited him just fine—it meant she was alive. The brown lights in her eyes, the heat of her skin, the warmth of that mouth looked so inviting. Her caramel hair slid down around her flushed face. Suddenly he was totally, utterly distracted.

He wanted to feel her up against him again.

"I am always right!"

She shoved him again, but it had no effect. Her brown eyes flashed, and he knew it was really messed up that he couldn't get enough of feeling her fire. He loved the way she stood up to him.

"Jackass!" she yelled. "You are pushing all my buttons!"

"I'm pushing your buttons! Honey, you have no idea how many of my buttons you're pushing right now." He crowded her back until she was against the wall.

"What buttons? Because everything is your fault. Are you going to take the whole world on your shoulders as if I'm not in control of my own actions? I make my own decisions and I'm the one responsible for them!"

"Dammit!" He ran his hands through his hair. *"Unbelievable!* Are you under the impression the guys that tried to kidnap you are run-of-the-mill guys who cheat on their wives?"

She narrowed her eyes. "Don't denigrate my work, Sam!"

He just stared at her, speechless. He closed his eyes, trying to breathe around her beauty and his attraction to her. Everything in him was primed to protect her with his bare hands if need be. Didn't she get it? She looked so warm and alive. Her mouth so soft. The curve of her jaw so tantalizing. Her cheeks, the silky fall of her hair against her throat were he wanted his mouth. He planted his hands on his hips to buy time to get a grip, but his chest just grew tighter. She was so female, she had to bring out every primal instinct in any man who looked at her. Including him. Especially him. He wasn't civilized. He was Uncle Sam's honed weapon and he had cut his teeth in firefights she couldn't even imagine seeing let alone live through. Rough, coarse and brusque. He didn't know how to handle this direct woman.

She was down-to-earth, courageous and made his blood rush in his veins, and he was having a hard time resisting her, for Chrissake. He realized he should. Hell, he didn't even know her, and whether she thought so or not, it wasn't prudent for her to get to know him—he was a moving target. He was contrary, gave out orders and expected them to be followed. That's the way he marched. Even on a good day he was difficult. Here she was embroiled in this cluster of his all because he happened to choose her brother as his therapist.

They didn't have a damn thing in common.

Except the instense burning attraction they had for each other. "No, offense, Olivia, but your work is a walk in the park where these guys are concerned. They must have wanted us alive or they would have tried to take us both down."

Her eyes filled with tears and he swore vehemently under his breath. Great, now he had scared her and made her cry. He was a jackass!

"I know all this!" she shouted, obviously insulted. "It doesn't change anything! Not a damn thing. I have no intention of leaving you alone."

"That's exactly the problem!" he bellowed back. They stood there for a few minutes, both breathing hard.

"Too bad!"

"Dammit, Olivia! Can't you see that I don't want

anything to happen to you? That I want you safe? That's all I want right now. You safe."

"I will be safe. With you!"

"No, you won't!"

She twined her hands in his shirt. "If you think yelling at me and barking orders is going to change my mind, it isn't!"

He made her back up and realized she had her hand in a death grip on his shirt. "You are the toughest, most direct pain in the ass!" He'd stepped into the kill zone where he could smell her scent, feel her heat, and his worry for her safety, his attraction to her, just swamped him. His resolve broke at nothing more than her soft exclamation and her small fist twisting tighter.

He swore softly, and he couldn't ever remember doing that before when he'd wanted a woman this much. Without warning he dropped his mouth on hers, his kiss hard, a bit out of control. She tasted hot and comforting and so sweet. Something indescribable and irresistible overtook him. Whether it was a part of his nature or his reaction to the taste of Olivia, he didn't know. He couldn't find his balance, and that sent him even more off the deep end. He had to have her. He pressed into her, and her response tightened everything in his body.

A low sob broke against his mouth, and he shoved his hands into her hair. The strands were soft against his fingertips, against his hands and wrists, jacking up his breathing and the fierceness of his mouth sliding over her lips.

The scent of her, like the grass and flowers, a force of nature, was like oxygen, giving him energy and life.

Now that he'd breathed her deeply into him, he wasn't sure he could do without it.

He gently cradled her head so that he could *take* her mouth in a sizzling, hungry and ravaging way. Locking her arms around him, she yielded, melting against him, her hands curving over his scalp, loving the heat of her hands there, trailing fire over the nape of his neck. Her touch drove him wild.

Widening his stance, Sam dragged her up against his groin, which was so hard he ached. He forgot where he was. Forgot who he was and just sank into the sensation of her.

He was so damn crazy, he told himself. Why did this woman affect him so much? Their chemistry whispered along his skin, tingling in his nerve endings. The sensation made him hot-blooded, explosive.

He gave himself up to the can't-help-himself feeling. He was in deep kimchi. Just like that, she disarmed him before he could even draw down on her.

Chapter 7

The kiss was as good as the first one. Better. She welcomed this primal side of Sam, inhaling his hot, male scent, the way he could so easily lose control with her.

How could a man's mouth be this soft and pliant? She ran her hand down his throat to his collarbone, reversing her fingers to caress the satin skin on his chest beneath the neckline of the T-shirt. He might feel like velvet, but he was definitely hard in all the right places.

She opened her mouth for him, inviting him to take her. He tightened his hold on her face and stroked his thumbs along her jaw. When his tongue touched hers, she groaned and he sucked on her bottom lip, igniting a fire that coursed through her bloodstream.

She was well aware why Sam was so jacked up—adrenaline, fear and his need to protect her, which had made him act like such an asshole. She understood.

And even as she fought with him, her heart was melting and melding with those needs in him.

It wasn't that she wasn't scared. She was. Out-of-her-mind scared. But she couldn't, wouldn't back down in the face of that fear. Sam needed someone. Whether he wanted to admit it or not, she was going to be that someone. Without her, he would be alone in this. She was well aware that he would not involve his family. He was already an uptight, angry, frustrated man right now. What would he do without someone to help him get through this? At the very least, she could protect his back. She had no intention of being caught off guard like that again.

He took a deep, uneven breath and broke the kiss, resting his jaw and head against the hollow between her shoulder and neck.

He growled as he stepped away from her. "You drive me crazy."

He gave her a long, heated look. It made her a little sick to think about how much blood had soaked into his T-shirt. Lucy had told her to take it easy, so no wonder she was feeling a bit light-headed. Or it could have been Sam's kiss. She wasn't sure.

"Are you ready to go?"

She nodded.

Back in the truck, he still didn't say anything. It was as if he'd been drained after the argument and then that mind-blowing kiss. Olivia didn't want to set him off again, erring on the side of caution, so she kept her mouth shut.

Once he pulled into the garage, he zipped around the truck to help her out. She didn't protest too loudly; her arm was hurting a bit.

When he saw the grimace on her face, he said, "I have pain reliever."

"That sounds good. Thank you."

He reached in and snagged her laptop. She lost her balance, feeling a bit woozy, and he caught her against him. Setting the laptop on the hood of the truck, he slipped his arms under her legs and picked her up.

"We didn't get a chance to get to the market, and I barely have anything here for you to eat. Need to get something into you."

"Do you have eggs?"

He brightened. "I do. I'll scramble us some as soon as I get you situated on the couch."

"While you're doing that, bring me the laptop. I need to check my brother's database, but after seeing that they wiped my drives, I don't hold out hope that the database will be untouched. Also, I'll see if there are any messages from the company about my deleted drive."

He set her down on the couch and dashed back out to the garage for her laptop, then went into the kitchen.

Olivia booted up her computer and accessed her email. Sure enough, there was a message from them. They were able to recover only a few files from the past two days, which worked fine because those were the surveillance photos she'd taken of Sam the day before her brother had been murdered.

With a sinking heart, she accessed her brother's therapist database. When she looked for Sam's file, it wasn't there. It had totally been erased. Damn those bastards!

Sam came back into the room with two plates of eggs and some toast. He set one plate down on the coffee table beside her laptop and settled on the couch next to her so he could see the screen. "Any luck?"

"Yes, I was just about to bring up the photos, but no on the database. They erased your electronic file. I'm sorry, Sam."

He looked so disappointed, but nodded his head. Sam then leaned forward to look at the photos shook his head. "I can't believe I didn't notice you."

"You were preoccupied and just got out of a session with my brother. I'm sure you had a lot on your mind. At least, that's what I thought when I saw you and took these pictures."

She scrolled through them, and then she saw him. "There, that's the man who tried to drag me into the van."

"You saw his face?"

"Yes, his mask got pulled off when I tried to get away."

"Dammit. I'm sure that's going to make them nervous."

"Is there any way we can find out who this guy is?"

"I could talk to my brother, Thad. He works for the Raleigh Police Department. He'd be discreet."

"I thought you didn't want to involve the police. We'll have to be very careful who we confide in."

"My brother is trustworthy, but he might be difficult. Since he's a cop, he thinks he can save the world and he won't like it to find out we're both in danger and not do anything about it."

"Sounds like that runs in the family," she muttered under her breath.

He didn't look at all apologetic. "Eat, and if you want, we can argue some more later."

She sighed. "I don't want to argue with you, Sam."

"You could have fooled me."

"You were the one… Oh, never mind."

She picked up the plate and dug into the eggs. Sam had already finished eating and he took his plate back to the kitchen, disappeared down the hall and brought back aspirin and water.

"Thanks," she said, taking them out of his hand.

"I don't like it, Olivia. I know that you're not going to back down and I can't take the risk…*we* can't take the risk that they'll try to snatch you again."

"We should put our energy into trying to figure this out, rather than fighting each other."

"And we've come full circle. I don't know how to unlock what's in my head. I don't know what caused me to lose my memory. But at Lucy's house I had a memory return to me when Mike and I were taken. It was an ambush. They were waiting for us and they drugged Mike and I and killed the other two S.F. guys. We were targeted and there were only a few people who knew about that mission. The four of us, some tactical guys and my commanding officer with probably a couple CIA guys also in the know."

She bit her lip. "So we don't know if we can even trust your commanding officer?"

"No. We don't."

"Do you remember anything about your captivity?"

"Not much, but my injuries say it was completely brutal. I don't know if I even gave up anything to them at this point. All I remember is bits and pieces—a lot of beatings and continuous pain, thirst, hunger, cold. Sensations really."

She swallowed hard. It was one thing to have the

vague notion of what had happened to Sam, but it was another to hear the details of what he had suffered.

His words whirled around and around in Olivia's mind, every picture uglier than the one before it, every possibility too terrible to be absorbed. But Sam had survived. This amazing man had been through excruciating hell and had survived. She seized on that notion with a rush of relief and resolve. She wouldn't fall apart. They would solve the mystery.

She tried to keep her reaction under wraps, but something in her face must have been revealed to Sam, who was probably very good at observation and reading people, because he leaned forward slightly.

"This is going to be tough, not just for me, Olivia, but for you. Your brother was a trained professional, and it even horrified him. What happened to me is part of going to war. I know it's difficult for you not to personalize it, because any compassionate person is going to feel something about what I went through. But we need to analyze what I can remember to get the answers we need, regardless of how it makes us feel. Okay, so you don't have to hide your reaction from me. It is awful. I know. I have lost it in my sessions before when I remembered something especially terrible. So I can't say that won't happen, either."

She took a deep breath and covered his hand, the tension his words created lodged in her chest. "All right, but I might feel the need to hug you."

He chuckled. "Okay, well, I won't have a problem with that." His gaze roved over her face, and her stomach got that fluttery feeling all over again.

"Another thing. I have nightmares. Really bad ones. Some I remember, some I don't. I've often woken up in the middle of the night just standing and yelling at the top of my lungs and I don't know why. So I'm sorry if that happens, but at least you'll be forewarned."

Fingers of tension curled around her stomach and squeezed.

It didn't help that Sam knew the consequences, that what he did was part of his job. He belonged to the army 24/7, an elite soldier.

"What can you tell me about your treatment?"

"Dr. Owens used something called recovered memory treatment. Some hypnosis. I don't know what he got out of those sessions because he didn't want me influenced by anything I said. He asked me tons of questions about my childhood, my mother, father and brothers."

Olivia watched his face, glued to his expression, saw the way his jaw hardened against some unpleasant memory, saw the frustration in his blue eyes and the vulnerability that lay beneath it, and her heart ached for him.

"I don't really know what those were all about and what my family and my experiences growing up have to do with what happened to me. But he looked like he was onto something. But again, he didn't want to reveal anything until he was ready, because he worried it might skew my answers."

"Oh, Sam. I'm scared for you."

He sat there looking handsome and sad, his eyes locked on her as if he were gazing at her for the very first time, memorizing her every feature.

"I know who I am, Liv. I hold on to that with both hands," he whispered, that low, deep voice touching her.

"That's something good, Sam. Something they didn't take away from you."

"They tried to break me down. That's the fundamental concept of torture," he said unevenly. "Take a person down to the basics. Deprive him of food, water, the necessities, and that's when it's easy to lose it. Lose your humanity." He rubbed at his forehead and took a deep breath.

The depth of Sam's psychological damage was most definitely out of her expertise. She was just glad that she'd stuck with him this far. It was so unfortunate that those bastards had erased Sam's tapes. She and Sam could at least have figured something out from those. It was clear John had known what he was doing, and she missed her brother's presence more than ever. She also felt helpless in this situation. How could she help Sam?

"I think we could find some answers if we could get our hands on one of the guys who tried to kidnap you."

"How do we do that?"

"We go on the offensive. I got the license plate number off that van. I thought we could go over to the Raleigh Police Department and talk to my brother."

"It's a blessing you can trust him, and Lucy is very nice. When are they getting married?"

"In December, a Christmas wedding. My confirmed-bachelor brother is tying the knot. Trey, my older brother, got married to his fiancée, Debra, only recently. There was a second attempt on my mother's life at the reception. That's where Mike was killed."

"We'll have to be careful, even with your brother."

"My brother will be discreet. He heads up the CSI unit, so he can run an inquiry for us without too much fuss."

"Okay, then what?"

"We'll figure that out once we find out who that van belongs to."

"We?"

"Don't press your luck, Olivia."

She smiled at him. "I won't if you won't."

This time he smiled. Even with the intensity of what Sam was facing, he still had a sense of humor. "You good to go, or do you need a nap?"

"Only if I get some milk and cookies and my blankie first."

Now he laughed. "I'll take that as a yes."

"You could have hit Winston! If he'd been *killed,* then where would we be?" These guys only knew him as "the Suit." His identity was secret and had to remain so. None of these guys would give him up. They were much too loyal to their organization. Lenny Jeffers faced him, along with the driver of the van, Sasha Burroughs and Hemp—Jimmy Hempstill—who was the one who shot at Owens and Winston. Jeffers was supposed to grab the woman. They were all dangerous, all highly trained and they couldn't kidnap one slip of a woman! He was livid, his face almost purple from that emotion. In a sudden movement, he backhanded Lenny across the face. The operative took it as though he knew he deserved it.

They all shifted nervously. They understood the rules and the consequences of failure. This was how guys got dead.

"That bitch is a damn wildcat! I underestimated her," Jeffers said.

The Suit paced and the tension in the room ratcheted up another notch. "It was our error to underestimate Owens and his private investigator sister! Where are they now?"

"He took her to a residential house where his cop brother and a Lucy Sinclair live," Jeffers said.

"She's a nurse. Took care of Kate Winston after Harris botched it. Looks like our Sam is a bit paranoid of the cops. Could be an aftereffect of the drugs we pumped into him. He has no idea how high this goes, which is also perfect. That damn doctor could have ruined everything! At least you did that part right, Jeffers. We don't need Winston enlightened at all about what happened to him or the good doctor's diagnosis."

"We can breach Winston's residence and grab her."

"No! If Winston is in the dark, that suits us fine. But we don't want the pressure of added tension pushing him over the edge. I want you three to lie low for now. Follow them and keep tabs on them. If you get another opportunity, bring me the woman, but don't engage Winston again unless you have a clear path to the girl!" The Suit got right into Jeffers's face. "He's a dangerous son of a bitch and he's unpredictable right now. There's no telling what he will do. I want that girl alive. I have questions! I can't question a dead woman!" He shoved Jeffers, the tension in him winding up to off-the-chart intense. Everything was riding on Winston.

The Suit knew Winston's profile. Hell, there was a rumor in D.C. that he would be the next Medal of Honor recipient. But after what he'd been programmed to do, his illustrious career—and probably his life—was over.

The Suit knew everything that was possible to know

about Captain Samuel Winston. He was a freaking American hero, literally. They also didn't make them tougher than Sam. From what the Suit had read about the Ranger, it hadn't been an easy task to break him down and get him primed for what they needed from him. Harris had been a walk in the park compared to Winston. But men like Sam had a way of surprising even the most confident enemy. Getting the drop on him out in the desert had been a delicate and monumental task. And he had almost slipped the noose.

The bottom line with Army Ranger Winston was he was a lethal, volatile and crazy warrior. He wouldn't hesitate to protect Olivia Owens, especially if he became attached to her. The Suit didn't want that. Isolating Sam from others by virtue of taking over his mind was the goal. And women—they were also an unknown equation in the mix. Olivia could undo everything that they'd done to Winston. That would be unacceptable.

She would need to be questioned. Then she would need to disappear. *Poof.* Drop off the face of the earth. It was all about survival…his and the family he dearly loved.

But for now, they had to bide their time.

"We wiped everything and took her camera. That'll keep them in the dark until Winston can be used."

He'd have to contain the situation so that they were on schedule with their timeline. Their leader didn't have to know anything about this screwup. The Suit was a key player in this action, so he was relatively safe and so was his family. For now. The leader wouldn't be forgiving. "You wouldn't have had to do that if you'd been aware she was shadowing Winston in the first place!"

"She's good, sir."

"You all need to up your game and be better. Or there won't be any game at all!"

"Yes, sir," they all said in unison.

Thad was at his desk in that maze of cubicles when Sam and Olivia got to the Raleigh Police Department. "Hey, Sam. How are you doing?" He cut a quick glance to Olivia, then back to him.

"I'm muddling along," Sam said. He had been tight-lipped with his brothers and his mother. They were worried, but he really didn't have anything to say. What happened to him wasn't something either Trey or his mother would understand, but Thad? Maybe. He'd seen plenty in his job. Yet Sam was reluctant to confide even in Thad. He'd gone it alone for a long time serving his country. Now he questioned whether going back was even something he should entertain. Being a soldier was all he really knew. Even though he was burned out, it was still a comfortable fit. "This is Olivia Owens." He slipped his hand around the small of her back and brought her forward in introduction.

Thad's sharp hazel eyes flashed with the name. "Owens? You related to Dr. Owens?"

Sadness dragging at the corners of her mouth as she said, "I'm his sister."

Remorse washed over Thad's face, compassion in his voice. Sam hadn't seen Thad in action before. They had lived very separate lives. But after seeing the confidence Thad had shown during and after Mike's shooting, he'd gotten a healthier measure of respect for his little brother. "I'm sorry about your brother's death, Olivia. We'll do everything we can to find his killer. I'm not personally working the case because of my connection to Sam, but I'm keeping an eye on it." Then he turned to Sam. "Okay, what's going on?"

"I need your help."

Thad sat up straighter. Sam was well aware that everyone was on edge in his family since his mother had almost been gunned down. Thad carried guilt from his inability to see it before it had happened. But how could they have suspected that Sam's friend, his teammate would be the one responsible? The fact that Thad had been the one to pull the trigger on Mike to save Lucy must have been very difficult.

"You in trouble?"

Sam met his brother's gaze directly. The memory of that dream from Yellowstone made the back of his neck prickle. He'd have to find time to ask Thad about it. For some reason that Sam couldn't pinpoint, he knew it was extremely important. "I think so, but I don't have any answers for you, Thad, and at this point, Olivia and I are kind of running blind."

"Maybe you should take the time to explain it to me." He indicated the chair next to his desk. Getting up, he snagged one from an empty cubicle. Sam sidestepped so Olivia could sit down; then he occupied the chair Thad brought over.

Sam leaned forward and kept it short and sweet. By the time he was finished, Thad looked unsettled.

"Lucy patched her up?"

"Yes, I'm sorry to drag her into this. But I couldn't have the police involved. Do you understand? I—" he glanced at Olivia and she slipped her hand over his forearm "—we can't really trust anyone, except you."

Thad sighed. "I don't like it." He looked between the two of them.

"I don't know, but they tried to kidnap Olivia and they only attacked me to slow me down so I couldn't intervene."

"What do you know?"

"Just what I told you. I think Dr. Owens may have made a breakthrough in my therapy, and I'm afraid he was murdered for it."

"You think someone… Like who? The CIA?"

Sam shrugged. "I don't know. Professionals."

"Damn. After what I went through with Mom's assassination attempt, I know how cagey those bastards can be."

"The answers are locked up in my head. I feel that anyone around me is in danger." He looked at Olivia, and her lips tightened.

"Sam, I'm not leaving you."

Thad looked from him to Olivia, his eyes speculative.

At Sam's hard stare, Olivia huffed. "Where's the restroom?"

After Thad directed her and she was out of earshot, he gave his brother an atta-boy shove.

"What?"

"She's a beautiful woman."

"She is. What's your point?" Sam wasn't so far gone that he didn't recognize that, but Olivia was more than the sum of her parts. If he was being honest, he was thankful for her support. Letting her into this whole mess seemed to make slogging through it all that much better. Didn't mean he wouldn't get her out of it in a heartbeat. But she wasn't going to listen to him. And he'd prefer her close to him rather than out there investigating her brother's murder and then end up disappearing herself. That wasn't going to happen. He wasn't losing another innocent life to whatever it was that was going on with him.

"Just making an observation."

"Sure you are."

Thad shrugged. "Hey, I was in the same boat you are in only a little while ago. Now I'm totally in love with Lucy and can't live without her. I was sure I'd never settle down, but now that's all I want to do. With her. Don't let that pass you by, Sam. You've served your country long enough. We want you home and back living in Raleigh. Time passes way too fast, and it looks to me like Olivia has a thing for you, too. Don't squander that, man. Open up to it."

Olivia did have a thing for him, and he was resisting… Okay, he was mostly resisting. "Yeah, Lucy did a number on you." He'd rather be back in Afghanistan than give in to the wants and needs trapped inside him. If he gave himself fully to Olivia, that would give her power over him, and he wasn't interested in giving up control. Didn't mean he didn't want to be with her. His thoughts strayed to how incredible it would feel to slip inside her, pump uncontrollably against all that softness. He got hard just thinking about it.

Thad chuckled. "Just think about it."

Sam was thinking about it. Way too much.

"Now back to this mess. We both know that Mom's assassination attempt goes up higher than we can imagine. But the chief killed himself before we could get the information we needed. And all that stuff I found in Mike's apartment feels to me like a setup. Sure, the sniper rifle was there and we both know that Mike pulled the trigger. We also know that something had to have happened to Mike to coerce him to do that. But with the red tape the feds are wrapping around his death, it's hard to get any straight answers."

"I know. It's all very suspicious and that political organization, whoever it is, must have strong juice to put up all these roadblocks and corrupt civil servants."

"Agreed. What's the license number of the van that was used this morning to snatch Olivia?"

Sam handed him the slip of paper that he'd written the number on. "There's something else. Could you run this guy through facial recognition? He's one of the guys that tried to kidnap her."

Thad nodded. "I'll run it, but if he's CIA, he's not going to show up. Those guys are ghosts."

"That's still information. If he's not in the database that tells us something."

Thad nodded. "I'll help any way I can, so don't be shy about asking for help."

"I won't. Keeping Olivia safe is at the top of my list."

"Yeah, I bet it is," Thad said with a nod.

Chapter 8

They took the time to stop at the market on the way from the police station, and Olivia could tell that Sam was on edge, hypervigilant.

He looked as though he was in his element.

And she was sure that anything he did, any damn thing, looked sexy on him.

Protector. Yep, he was rocking that.

Scary. Yep, that, too. She'd had him in her face, so she had experienced that firsthand.

Dangerous.

Oh, God, yes. On many, *many* levels.

To the unknown bad guys—a given.

To her equilibrium—she didn't think she'd been on solid ground since she'd met him.

To her heart—most assuredly.

She was feeling the effects of adrenaline, too, and to think that Sam lived, worked and breathed this kind of lifestyle *every day*. She loved being a P.I., but a lot of the work was tedious.

"You're thinking really hard over there." Her arm was throbbing, and along with all the food they'd gotten, she'd thrown in extra strength pain killer. The regular wasn't cutting it. Now they were packed to the gills with bags and headed back to Sam's house. The eggs she'd had before going to the police department hadn't been enough, but it was almost dinnertime anyway.

"I'm more frustrated that the van was stolen and that gives us zero leads on those guys. My gut tells me we are still being followed." He glanced in the rearview mirror for the tenth time.

"I'm not betting against your gut."

"Short of getting our hands on one of those guys and getting information out of him, we're kinda dead in the water."

"Then maybe we should try to do that."

"How?"

"By setting a trap."

He frowned.

As he pulled into the garage, he turned to her and without even saying anything, he felt her forehead.

"What are you doing?"

"Seeing if you're feverish."

"I'm not." Although his hand was as hot as a brand, and the way he touched her jacked up her heart into a fluttering beat.

"We can do it, Sam."

"You go lie down on the couch and I'll get all this stuff inside and get it put away. Are you hungry?"

"Don't dismiss me."

"I'm not, Olivia. You're on my mind now 24/7."

He swore softly, the curse tumbling off his tongue; then he bit his lower lip.

She heated from the inside out as if she did have a fever. The tension between them always seemed to just be *there*. So easy for it to flare. All it took was a curse and the way he took that full bottom lip into his mouth just as she'd been fantasizing about doing for the past hour.

He sighed, dropped his head and rubbed at his temple.

"I can feel you all primed for an argument, Olivia. And I'm tired. Bone-tired. Can we just…get the food in the house and eat?"

She relented because now tenderness welled up in her. She understood he must be tired. She was hurting and she was primed for a fight. Maybe it was all that unfulfilled sexual tension that was tormenting her, making her take offense at every word that came out of Sam's sexy, full-bottom-lipped mouth.

"I'm sorry, Sam. I usually am an easygoing person."

"Well, I'm used to giving orders." He looked at her. "So get going."

The laugh was unexpected as it cut the tension, and both of them heaved a sigh of relief. She got out of the truck and did as he asked, mostly because her arm did hurt and she really couldn't help him carry stuff, and second, because she needed a break. She stretched out on the couch and turned on the TV.

Before she knew it, Sam was gently shaking her awake. "Dinner's ready." The sun had gone down and the heavenly smell of chicken drew her off the couch into the kitchen. They settled at the table and dug in.

Now that she had some food in her, she felt ten times better. Sam picked up and started to take care of the dishes. The sight of him being all domestic was so cute. Obviously he was used to fending for himself, being a bachelor and in the military. Her curiosity about him had run rampant since her brother asked her to follow him. She guessed that was a good thing being a P.I., but now that she'd met him, she was even more curious.

"How long have you been in the service?"

He twisted from the sink to look at her. "Almost ten years. I enlisted when I was twenty-three."

"So you've been out on many missions."

"Yes."

"In the Middle East?"

"Mostly, but I've been all over the world. Can't say more than that because—"

"It's classified."

He smiled and turned back to the sink and started to load the dishwasher. "Right."

"Did you go to college?"

"Yes, majored in political science, but I'm no politician. I left that up to my mother and Trey. I went through two years of law school and hated it. Although I did love trying cases in moot court." He started the dishwasher. "You want to play gin?"

"Sure," she said.

He grabbed a deck of cards out of one of the kitchen drawers and sat down at the table. "We play a lot of cards when deployed. Passes the time."

"What other kinds of schooling did you get in the military?"

He dealt out the cards. "I went to officer training school at Fort Benning in Georgia. My other military training and education includes the Infantry Maneuver Captains Career Course, Ranger Course, Infantry Officer Basic, Infantry Mountain Leader Advanced Marksmanship Course and Airborne School."

"You jumped out of planes?"

"Hooyah." He made his first discard and it was Olivia's turn.

"I always wanted to try that."

"Jumping out of a plane? Piece of cake. The first step is the hardest."

She laughed when he grinned at her.

"Maybe someday…" He trailed off.

"What?"

He shook his head. "I was about to say maybe one day we could do that, but we both know that's probably not going to happen."

"Because you're going back."

"Yes, it's always been the plan."

"But is it still the plan?"

He shrugged. Then picked up her discarded card and set down one of his own. "Are you under the impression that I spill my guts to anyone who asks me questions?"

"Don't you?"

"No. I barely talk at all to anybody. Why is it so easy with you?"

Out of anything he'd said to her in the past, including that statement about how beautiful her hair was, this made her blush.

"Maybe because I'm pushy?"

"Ha! You're pushy, but that's not why."

"Maybe it's because you argue with me so much, talking is a relief?"

He chuckled. "No, that's not it, either, but, for the record, you can hold your own, honey. I like that about you, even though it drives me crazy."

She studied her cards, then chose one. Sam picked from the deck and after a second discarded one she could use. She picked it up, set down her cards and said, "Gin."

He counted up his cards and recorded their score on a pad of paper. "Did you go to college?"

"Several times. Wasn't for me. After the second time, I thought John was going to lose it, especially when I told him I was going to backpack across Europe."

"I bet."

"I've had good life lessons, got my certification in massage therapy, did other odd jobs like I told you, then settled down to be a P.I."

"Sometimes it takes time to find your niche."

"In my case it did. John was never really happy with my final choice, but he was always proud of me."

"Business is good?"

"It is and recently I've had more work than I can take on. I was thinking of hiring someone to work with me."

He dealt out the cards and they played a few more hands.

After the final hand, Sam went into his bathroom and got some first-aid supplies. "Let me change the bandage before we go to bed."

They went into the living room and Sam sidled up close to her to get at the bandage on her upper arm. His fingers were gentle and sure as he carefully unwrapped it and discarded the bloody bandage on the coffee table. He examined the wound. "Looks good. Lucy did a fine job."

"I guess you've done this a few times on the field of battle."

"More than I care to name. Most not this minor."

"Ouch," she said, wincing when he dabbed on more antibiotic ointment. "It doesn't feel minor from where I'm sitting."

"Sorry." He then put on a gauze pad and wrapped more gauze around it, securing it with medical tape.

"It really hurts to get shot," she said, "a burning and stinging pain."

"It's the temperature from the bullet. It comes out superheated from the chamber from friction. When it hits, it's literally burning lead."

"Have you ever been shot?" she asked softly.

"Shot at plenty, shot a couple of times." He dragged up his T-shirt and showed her the long scar on his waist. "Got between the body armor. Hurt like hell, same for my quad."

She had to take a couple of deep breaths, one for the scar and one for his tight, washboard abs.

"You ready?"

Her eyes popped up to his.

"For bed."

Not really, unless it was to snuggle up to him for both comfort and relief of some of that sexual tension.

They rose together and Sam headed off down the hall. Now that it was time to go to sleep, she felt apprehensive and a frisson of fear crawled up her spine. What if someone tried something in the middle of the night?

Sam realized about halfway down the hall that

she wasn't following. He turned to look back at her. "Olivia?"

"I'm coming."

When she came up to him, he put his hand on her arm. "Are you all right?"

"Yes," she lied. She didn't want him to think she was a baby or a coward, but she was definitely feeling apprehensive. Okay, more than that. She was scared.

"If you need anything…"

"I know."

"Good night."

She settled into the bed, her nerves on edge all of a sudden. Every noise made her start and she thought about the man who had dragged her away from Sam. Thought about his determination. What would have happened if he'd gotten her into that van? She shuddered with the thought. She didn't think she'd be breathing right now.

She closed her eyes tight and tried to relax until she finally started to drift. Then darkness gripped her by the throat and she couldn't breathe. The man in the mask appeared, the image of his face alternating between his masked and unmasked face until his eyes were deep black sockets of nothing. Those empty sockets sucked the very life from her.

She woke with a start and sat bolt upright in bed feeling pain shoot up her arm. She gasped softly.

She threw back the covers and rushed to Sam's room. Her steps slowed as she got to the bed. He was facedown, the sheet tangled around his hips so that it left his back and legs bare.

She looked at the long line of his body, from his bare

feet and strong ankles to the shape of his legs, his hips beneath the green shorts he wore and his broad back.

His back was a mass of scars, but the skin beneath her hands when she had given him his massage was soft and smooth. She followed the line of a vertical slash across his shoulder blade and down the taut muscle over his ribs.

Her gaze traveled back up again to his barely there hair that was so soft against her palm. Then her eyes fell to the nightstand and the wicked-looking pistol that was within easy reach of his hand. She wasn't sure if he'd put it there in response to what had happened to them today or if he always slept with it beside his bed.

She wanted to break down and cry to think of the pain and the agony and the fear he must have endured, and she wanted to curl up with him. Have him hold her against that hard, strong chest.

"Sam?" she said. She was unable to go back to her room, unable to face any more nightmares.

He sprang awake as if he were spring-loaded. He went from deep, even sleep to wide-awake and ready for action.

"Olivia. What's wrong?"

She tilted her chin to look up at him, the blue of his eyes like midnight in the semidark room. "I lied. I'm not okay." She bit her lip, the fear suddenly alive in her.

He was off the bed in a heartbeat. He came forward, silent on bare feet, setting his hands on her shoulders and looking into her face.

"I'm scared," she whispered. Without a sound, he pulled her into his arms, against his chest, careful of her injured arm. One hand delved into her hair and pressed her head beneath his chin. "It's okay. Every-one gets scared." His voice was hushed.

"Can I stay with you?"

He stood for a long moment with his eyes closed and his jaw set.

"Of course." He moved back onto the bed and set-tled against the pillows. "Olivia, so you want to—"

She shot forward and onto the soft mattress, slid-ing her body over his until she was against all that hard, hot muscle. It felt as though she'd wanted to be here forever.

He exhaled a long, heated breath, soft against her cheek. "I guess that's a yes."

Her skin caught fire just from that one soft puff of his breath. She knew what he was feeling because she was right there with him.

She moved her leg and it brushed against his. The warmth of him seeped into her, calmed her nerves.

"Oh, God, Sam, you feel so good. So safe."

His fingers tightened in her hair, her scalp prickling under the grip that tilted her face up to his. His kiss fierce; she could taste the resistance in it, but the hot need welled up the instant he touched her. He drew one hand down through her hair, pausing at the small of her back, spreading his palm until his fingertips curved around her waist. He held her that way, the peaks of her breasts pressed into his bare chest through silk and lace, their shape swollen and spread against him. It made no difference that she had asked to be here, that they were trying to resist this—it all whirled away and left only awareness, his body a bruising pressure against hers, his hand locked in her hair and the taste of him consuming her.

Olivia spread her hands across his bare skin. His chest was taut, hard and smooth, the broad muscled expanse beneath her fingers hot against her exploring palm. The heat and desperate longing to cherish and hold him spread to her body—she burned where she touched him; she burned all through, a hot ache that coursed from the fierce possession of her mouth down to her breasts and belly and legs—a pleasure that bloomed between her thighs and made her move and press and mold to him as if she could make him part of her.

"Olivia," he mumbled, a harsh breath against her lips. "We should stop. God…stop."

But he held her still; he didn't stop. He kissed her throat, pushing back her hair, coiling it around his fist. She opened her mouth and allowed her tongue to taste the bare skin at the curve of his shoulder.

She felt him groan. His powerful muscles moved, salty skin sliding past her tongue as he pushed her back on the bed. He hung above her on braced arms, cursing softly even as he grasped her shoulders and bent to kiss the base of her throat and nuzzle while his body pinned hers against the mattress.

She felt his hands at her waist, pulling the silky nightgown upward, tugging the fabric with rough and frantic moves. Soft air caressed her bared thighs and then her hips. He spread his palm across her flat stomach and made a sound of excitement, a rough note deep in his chest. His forearm drove her shoulder back against the cotton sheets as he bowed to reach her breast.

He kissed it through the silk, his tongue finding the tip and drawing it against his teeth until she arched and whimpered with the searing swell of pleasure. Her reaction touched off something primal in him, something that he'd never felt with any other woman he'd ever been with.

Growling, Sam lost himself in her body, tasting the delicious heat, sliding his hand into the crevice between her legs. He wanted her passionate, he wanted her arching her sweet body upward, begging for what he burned to give. He caressed her groin at the apex of her thigh and slipped two fingers into her slick opening, his tongue and lips closing on the peak of her breast.

She was moist and hot, insanely inviting. He drowned in her, in the tightness of her, in the way she closed her legs convulsively on his hand. His fingers slid, pushing, exploring deeper and deeper until she began to gasp and tremble beneath him.

He tugged at her nipple while his fingers went deeper to the spot he knew was there inside her, the spot that would ignite a fire so hot it would singe him. His thumb found her core, and he pressed there, rubbing with a slow and steady rhythm. Heat flashed through him, the fierce desire to thrust and sink into her, to spread her and take her delicious softness in absolute possession.

He started to withdraw, to reach for his shorts and free the aching pressure there, but her body followed the move. Her hips curved upward. She tossed her head, pushing into his hand while her fingers raked his back. Deep into the desperation for him, she clutched at him, holding his head to her breast. She arched with a strangled moan—that long, lovely strain of female ecstasy—and then her body was shuddering against him in a way that made him want to explode in response.

But he didn't. From somewhere amid her collapse into panting oblivion, he found a vestige of reality. He folded down next to her, dragging her against him, his chest heaving.

"Sam, please," she pleaded softly. "Please."

"I'm just not good for anyone right now. I shouldn't be…" He barely got out those words. This time Olivia went on the offensive. She slipped her hands beneath the waistband of his shorts and felt her fingers curl around his aching dick.

He thrust helplessly upward, his hips leaving the bed. He groaned. A sound he'd never heard before, intense and tight, and suddenly he felt the way he did right before a mission. Focused, intent. She let him go, slipping off her underwear, and then grasped the waist of his shorts.

He grabbed her wrists, even as she continued to jerk against him. "Olivia. Let go."

She tussled with him and he felt as if he had a tiger by the tail and he simply loved it. This woman, this beautiful, contrary woman.

He was trying to do the right thing here, and she was fighting him every step of the way.

"No, Sam. I *want* you."

He let go of her wrists, going for the side drawer of his nightstand, reaching for the condoms when she took him in her mouth and he lost his damn mind.

He closed his eyes and froze. Everything in him taut and hard. So hard. His hips jackknifed off the bed at the sensual feel of her wet mouth sliding over him. Her tongue curled around him and he knew that the first damn time he had her, it wasn't going to be like this. He used everything he had to focus on getting the condoms out of the drawer while she continued to work him over, give his reason a run for its money.

Finally he got a hold of them and pulled out one, quickly tearing open the packet. Then he reached down and grabbed her under her armpits, lifted her with brute force and flipped her onto her back.

"Dammit, Sam."

"Condom," he said. "Put it on me. Now!"

She stilled and her breath released in a heated rush right against his chest and he thought he was going to come right then and there. *Focus and wait,* he told himself. It would be worth the wait to be deep inside her.

She pushed his shorts the rest of the way off, her hands caressing his hips. She knocked away the condom and ran her hands over his stiff hard-on. "We don't need that. I'm on the Pill."

He shuddered, his voice hoarse and desperate. "Oh, damn. Oh, dammit." He pressed a line of swift kisses down the side of her face to her lips. "Open for me," he growled.

Then he forced her to do it without waiting, made her accept his tongue, seeking deep in the kiss. His weight spread her legs. She whimpered under the aggressive power of his body. His dick pressed to her opening. The stiff swell of his body pushed hard, seeking entry.

He was rough. Capturing her hands, he pinned them above her head, thrusting strongly into her warm, soft body. She tilted her head back and drew a sharp breath, and he felt her surrender to his invasion, arching up against his hard heat as he took her and sank deep inside.

Soft gasps and moans broke against his mouth as he filled her, her body tightening and moving beneath his. He made similar sounds deep in his throat. Every inch of her belonged to him, joined with him.

She buried her face in his shoulder as he thrust again and again, taking full possession of her in power and mindless passion—something that was so elemental, so electric and primal between them.

His arms tightened on hers convulsively from the soft slide of her hair against his skin.

She clamped around him, his dick rigid, rising beyond pure sensation. It was so different, so vivid—this was real, and all that had gone before a dream.

He needed the wonder of this, of being inside her, of being so consumed by her. He needed one place where he could let down his guard, one safe place, and he'd found it with her.

She touched him, slid her hands all over him in places that he'd craved her touch. He shuddered; he groaned her name. The feel of her was so luxurious, his body trembling as he took her, thrusting with potency instead of control.

"Sam. Oh…God…*Sam*."

She climaxed, stiffened as her pleasure ignited his, and it was all he could take as waves and waves of humming pleasure washed over him. His body emptied inside her. His hips moved hard against hers in that explosive tremor.

As he began to relax, she held him in a quivering grip. Her skin still burned against his. For a long time, he just floated. Just taking deep breaths because breathing was enough. It seemed his chest could not hold sufficient air to allow his brain to think or his body to move. So he just indulged himself and lay in her arms.

Her soft caress against his back registered. *Olivia.* Even when it came to sex, she was arguing with him. Damned if he didn't find it a turn-on, sexy as hell.

He lifted himself on his elbows and looked down at her.

So beautiful. So utterly beautiful. He cupped her face. She looked up at him, a match for him. Opposite, disagreeable and downright maddening.

He swallowed. He was past speaking, simply past it. He rolled and pulled her against him, holding her, holding her safe from everything that could hurt her—worrying that he would be one of those people. But how to protect her from himself.

His world shifted and twisted, challenging the status quo. Olivia was very, very special. Something very raw and painful moved in his chest.

He suddenly felt lost.

Rangers never got lost. He could have been dropped in the middle of the desert with a map and a compass and he'd find out exactly where he was. Piece of cake.

But even with a compass and a map, he didn't think he could find his way.

He always knew where he was.

That is, until he'd met Olivia.

She made him feel lost, then found.

Reaching up, she slid her hand around the back of his neck and drew his mouth down to hers. She kissed him softly at first, then more deeply, letting her tongue move inside his mouth, letting the taste and feel of her fill him up.

And he kissed her back, her hands rubbing over his head, holding him. He gave himself over to it. Her soft lips crushed against his mouth, her breath on his skin, the taste of her in his mouth. They kissed forever, deliberately, erotically, until he was drugged with the sensation of her body moving against his, taking his bottom lip into her mouth and sucking on it like candy. She consumed him, kiss after kiss, until he got hard all over again.

He buried himself into her again. Could only think that he'd been found. Again. He could get his bearings all because Olivia showed him the way.

Chapter 9

She lay there, knowing it was morning, that the strong, warm body against her back was Sam. Even in sleep he held her, his arm a band of steel around her waist. And she thought about her behavior. Her *behavior*.

She had lost it. Okay, really…self-control, reason, discipline. Out the window. Really, she'd just met him and she wasn't the kind of woman who engaged in… what would she call that? Wantonness. He brought out her inner vixen. She'd never in her life been that aggressive with a man, that forceful.

Then she thought about how he had taken her. That was a new one, too. Rough sex. He hadn't really hurt her in any way, although her mouth was probably bruised. It sure felt thoroughly ravished this morning. There was something…primal about what she needed from Sam. Only Sam. That aggressive taking that slaked her hunger for him in such a basic, essential way that she didn't know anything about until she'd shared it with Sam.

She couldn't help thinking about the way he had literally picked her up and flipped her down. Almost like a wrestling move and all the erotic and exciting things he'd done after that…man…she wanted to have him all over again.

He stirred beside her and she felt him stiffen for just a moment as if he had momentarily forgotten she was there.

A breath rushed out of him, and without even missing a beat, he snuggled his face into the back of her neck, his arm tightening on her waist, his hand flattening out against her stomach.

She moved then, wanting to see him. She turned against him, her hot flesh sliding against his hot flesh. When she got to her back, he had raised himself on his elbow.

"Hey," he said, his sleepy eyes regarding her, his lashes so long.

"Hey, yourself," she said, reaching up and sliding her hand along his jaw. The rasp of his stubble felt good against the pads of her fingers and her palm.

As he stared at her, a big grin spread across his face and she smiled in response.

"That's quite a grin, Captain Winston." And it was. It transformed his face from handsome to devastating. And this was the first time he smiled like that. It reached all the way into those blue eyes.

"You put it there, babe." He dipped his head and buried his face into her neck.

"Is that so?"

He shook his head, breathing her in. "Are you always so contrary?"

"I don't usually have such…resistance with my partners."

He raised his face, the grin replaced with stark toughness. She liked the grin much better.

"I was trying to spare you my crazy, messed-up shit," he said.

"Sam, we're just having sex. It's not a commitment or anything. But the attraction is pretty powerful. I will admit that."

He nodded. "I know, but, Olivia, I am messed up— you know that."

"I understand. But if there is something that I can do to bring you the kind of comfort you offered to me last night even though you didn't want to get involved with me, I will in a heartbeat. You're a good man, Sam."

"I hope I didn't hurt you. It got…a bit…out of control."

Every breath he took, she felt his washboards rise against her.

Just thinking about it made her tingle and burn.

His head descended. He took a deep breath as he locked eyes with her all the way down, his hand tightening on her abdomen.

His mouth hovered above hers, her hands sliding up his arm, molding over his thick biceps. "You didn't hurt me at all."

He closed his eyes and groaned softly, gently brushing her mouth.

"I…liked it. A lot."

He growled low and took her mouth harder, and she realized that her lips were indeed tender, but that didn't stop her from returning the same kind of pressure, taking him deeper, and it still wasn't enough— not even close.

His hips pushed against her and she felt the evidence that she turned him on, too. Pushing at his shoulders, she rolled him to his back. Without giving him a chance to even protest, she moved down his body, taking what she'd wanted last night. This time he didn't push back. It was a good thing, because she was willing to fight.

Later they moved to the shower, where it was more heat and steam, more of his mouth, his clever, clever hands and his ready and willing body.

Once they were sated physically, it was time to change her bandage and he did that gently and efficiently as he had done last night. Breakfast was a shared chore and consumed in companionable conversation.

"Sam, you'll drive me to John's funeral, won't you?"

"Of course. We'll handle that together."

The service was so hard, especially with the speakers who spoke about her brother so fondly. She kept herself together until they got to the graveyard and they lowered her brother's casket into the ground. Then she turned into Sam's arms and cried for the loss of her only family. She would miss him terribly. There was a small reception downtown where she greeted and accepted the condolences of her friends and his. So many friends and clients.

Later, back at Sam's, she was holding herself together, thinking how much she wanted to get the person responsible for taking him from her. She sat at

Sam's dining table drinking a cup of green tea and looking out into the sunny backyard.

Sam came into the kitchen. He'd changed out of his dark suit, giving her a soft, compassionate look. He poured himself a cup of coffee and sat down next to her, squeezing her hand, and she smiled weakly.

"Yesterday in the truck you said something about going on the offensive. Could you elaborate on that?" he said, leaning back in the kitchen chair.

"Since they wiped my hard drive and my brother's, we have nothing to help us. There is no information to gather to give you the answers you need. So I propose that we bait and capture one of the men who attacked us."

"You are something else. We. As in you and me? If I remember correctly, you were the one in my arms last night afraid of the bogeyman and now you want to storm the castle."

She was still scared. She didn't say this wasn't something that made her nerves jangle, but she didn't see any other way. "Sam…"

He leaned forward. Damn, the man was so intimidating when he was arguing with her. He put the command in commando. She raised her chin and he narrowed his eyes, his jaw hard and still sporting that delicious stubble.

"What do you propose we use as bait?"

"Me." She wanted to do this for her brother. To hit back at whoever took his life.

He slammed back in his chair, his blue eyes giving her an incredulous look. "What the hell! No!" He went to stand and she grabbed his arm.

"I knew you were going to react this way. Just listen."

He stopped in midair and froze, giving her an angry and exasperated look. But then sat down in the chair.

"What else can we do? I think time is important here, and these people are on some kind of timetable. They're just corralling you. Hemming you in for something they want out of you."

He shifted and looked away as if her words were hitting him like physical blows. For a man of action like Sam, this had to be torture.

"I fully expected them to try something last night, and after I thought about it this morning, I realized they weren't going to. But I'd bet my next paycheck they're out there watching us right now."

This time Sam stood and paced away from her, his hands clenched into fists, his back muscles bunching.

She didn't know for sure, but U.S. Army Rangers didn't take to being forced into something they didn't want to do. U.S. Army Rangers didn't take well to being followed and attacked and watched.

Sam was on the edge and getting closer and closer to going off it. She was just a simple P.I. That was all. She didn't have a lot of experience dealing with men like Sam. Men who knew exactly what to do in just about every situation, could jump out of airplanes and land in hostile territory and do their damn mission and get out. Tough men who lived by their wits and their training.

She also wasn't used to handling a man who had so much trauma he was losing himself. Losing himself in dark nightmares and emptiness. Not sure what he was remembering was real or imagined, twisted by his own psyche.

A man who was tortured enough to break anyone, even tough, strong U.S. Army Rangers.

But there was one thing she did know. She was going to stand by him and fight for him. Now it wasn't just about what her brother had made her promise. It was about what she had to do. For Sam. He was isolating himself from his family, from the military where he had drawn his strength and from the government who exacted such a toll on him. It wasn't a question whether for her own safety she should run away from him, but it was about what she was risking to remain with him.

She was just as stubborn.

He might not be a team player, but she was forcing his hand and he could just accept it.

There wasn't any alternative, and her resolve was absolute.

She stood up and walked over to him and wrapped her arms around his waist, pressing her face against his back. "If there was an alternative, I would take it. I am scared, Sam, but I'm also scared for you. At the very least, we can get some answers. I'm willing to do whatever it takes."

He spun around his chest heaving. "What if I'm not willing to risk you, Olivia? What then?" He covered his eyes with his hand. "What about that?"

She cupped his face in both of her hands, cradling his roughened jaw. "Sam, I trust you with my life. You know what you're doing. You plan it out and I'll execute it."

Indecision warred on his face as he gazed down at her.

* * *

Standing here having her look at him as if he were some kind of superwarrior only made Sam feel more like shit.

He wanted to kiss her so badly, but if he kissed her, he was going to devour her again, take her and drown himself in her. He was such a selfish bastard. He should never have let the situation get so far out of hand. But she'd been scared; then she'd curved around him, and she was soft, smelled like heaven. And what she'd said about him being safe, hit him in the heart.

He was so screwed up, and yet sex with her had been...mind-blowing. He had no other words to describe what had exploded between them. It wasn't bad enough he was fragmented and floundering, or that he was carrying around regrets and a colossal case of guilt.

He'd fallen off the edge, and that unnerved him almost as much as what he'd done. It wasn't like him to lose control, to break one of his own rules. He'd been running around the globe breaking rules for Uncle Sam since he was twenty-three, but not his own, never his own.

Until now.

"We're trapped, Sam, and it's up to us to figure a way out of this because I don't know about you, but I don't like being confined and forced into doing something I don't want to do."

He dragged his hand back through his hair and just held her with his other arm around her waist, his fingers gripping tighter than he should. He knew it, but he couldn't help it. Jeez, this woman was going to be the death of him. She was right. He didn't like being manipulated if that was what was happening here. Sometimes his mental acuity was blurred, but Olivia helped him to focus.

The whole situation made him feel a little wild, a little wildly crazy. Crap! He let his gaze run over her gorgeous hair, the soft arch of her cheek, down the side of her neck, back to her shoulder, then lower, down the sleek curves of her body.

In a situation where combat was the preferred choice, sometimes the only choice, he would have no qualms about engaging the enemy, but Olivia wasn't part of his unit and she certainly wasn't a commando.

She was a P.I., and a good one, that much was clear. Her intelligence and the way she handled her job... It took a high level of skill to track a Ranger, even one off his game. She took a problem and hit it head-on, and he really liked that about her.

He liked too damn much about her.

He let out a breath and with an act of pure will kept himself from touching her, but just barely.

He needed to think, not start feeling her up again. What she had said to him at the table made frustration ball up in him until he wanted to hit something hard, break-his-knuckles hard.

"Don't you feel that? Am I spinning my wheels? Some guidance would be good here."

The only thing Sam felt was trapped.

He couldn't seem to get himself under control. When she faced off with him, he felt trapped. Trapped with her blood already on his hands. Trapped by the death of her brother. Trapped in his attraction to her. Trapped with his needs and his desires. And trapped, so trapped inside his head, he felt ready to explode with the frustration. There was no outlet for him to release any of his tension, any of his concern for her safety, except one.

And that had felt too damn good.

Honesty. He was always true to himself, no matter what it cost. Last night was no different in that respect, and he knew the problem wasn't that he could resist her. The problem was that he didn't want to and, try as he might, he couldn't see his way around that one inviolate fact.

He didn't want this sick pain in his gut that said he'd put her in danger. He didn't want the heartache of knowing he really couldn't have her, not forever, if only because he knew himself, and he knew he would move on.

Oh, yeah, kissing her now, making love to her now was so perfect, but it wouldn't last. Nothing ever lasted for him, except the army. Even the friendships there hadn't always lasted. Men died, left service—that was the reality of the path he'd chosen. Mike was a case in point. The longest-standing friendship he'd ever had.

And somewhere inside him he was tired of it. Burned out. The missions, the loneliness, being constantly on the move. He wanted something permanent, something that would last, but he was too pragmatic for that.

The mistake he'd made with her was letting this rise above the friendship level.

But, hell, a friend didn't murmur your name when you shoved into her, didn't slay you with a sigh when you took her breast in your mouth. A friend didn't groan and clutch at you when you touched her, and didn't call out your name when she came as if you were the only handhold away from oblivion.

He'd felt her tighten around him, and he'd come hard and deep, as if she'd reached down into the depth of his soul. Everything was pulsing, tingling, aching. He'd just had her twice this morning and his balls were still tight. He still wanted her.

Every instinct in him was focused on one thing. Protecting her. Protecting what was his.

Yet he couldn't do this without her, and without doing this he would remain trapped.

"Sam, say something. Anything."

He moved his hands and slipped them under her armpits, the scent of her mingling with sweet, just-showered woman. He lifted her off the floor and she gasped. He drew her to eye level and gave her the fiercest I-mean-business look.

"You will follow my orders to the letter. You will not argue with me at all. Every freaking thing I say, you will say 'yessir' and carry it out. When I say jump, you will, without hesitation, say 'How high, sir?' Are we clear, sweetheart?"

"Captain Lone Ranger...*sir.*" She leaned in closer, sliding her hand up the side of his neck and pretty much freezing him where he stood.

Damn, he loved the way this woman interacted with him.

"Yes, Team Owens," he growled.

"You are a pushy bastard."

"Sir," he said.

A smile curved her mouth, slowly, sweetly. "What?"

His gaze narrowed on those sinful brown eyes, the

ones with the devil dancing in them. What would it take to intimidate this woman?

"You are a pushy bastard. *Sir.*"

She bit her bottom lip. "I'm glad you agree, sir."

"Olivia."

"I will follow your orders to the letter. I will not argue with you at all. Every freaking thing you say, I will say, 'yessir' and carry it out. When you say jump, I will, without hesitation, say, 'How high, sir?' We're clear, sweetheart. Very clear."

"Are you mocking me?"

"No. Not at all. I'm the one planning to be the bait here, and I'm well aware what happens to stupid bait. I don't want to be stupid bait."

"I don't want you to be bait at all. But if you have to be bait, we will play this smart, and if this goes wrong—"

"Sam."

He thought of Mike. How Mike would have been his choice right here, right now to cover his back, except Mike had been going through his own personal hell. He would never know what had driven him, but Sam was a realist. He knew that things could go wrong with even the best-laid plans. Look at what had happened in the desert. Four lethal Special Forces U.S. Rangers had been taken down during an ambush. He knew about clusters.

Betrayed from within. Someone was going to pay for that.

For eight of the almost ten years he'd been in the army, Mike had been the bedrock of his life. They'd been to hell and back, firefight hell where the odds had been against their chances of survival. The hell of losing him twisted Sam's gut up into mourning, his loss so deep it physically hurt.

The black hell where a man was more dangerous to himself than anybody else on the planet. They'd pulled each other back from the razor's edge more than once, and once was all it took to cement a bond that went deeper than blood. If asked before Mike had tried to kill his mother, he would have said nothing would ever come between them, nothing could shake their friendship. They were solid.

But he'd been wrong.

His judgment had been shaken.

He was second-guessing himself every time he turned around.

What had been done to him was to blame. Unless he found out what it was, unless he took the offensive and stopped letting them cage him, he would never get his answers.

When Mike needed him the most, he wasn't there.

Now Sam needed Mike and he was gone, as gone as he could be.

Sam was a loner. It was true. Mike had known that, as well.

He wasn't naive enough to gloss over the truth.

So he knew about how this thing with Olivia could turn into a mess in the time it took to take a breath.

"If this goes wrong, I want you to run." He shook her slightly. "Run to my brother Thad. He will help you."

"And leave you? Sam, I don't—"

"I'm out, then. If you don't make this promise, I'm out." His voice was completely rock-solid, and he would deliver on that promise in a heartbeat.

"This is emotional blackmail."

"I don't give a damn, Olivia. If anything happens to you, it might as well be a bullet to my heart anyway."

Her face twisted and she wrapped her arms around his neck and he set her down and wrapped his arms around her.

"I promise."

He nodded against her neck. They stood like that for a few minutes. "Okay, my next question is, do you know how to use a handgun?"

She released him, but only enough to slide her hands over his chest. "Yes, I have a permit to carry concealed. But I've always tried to resolve everything the easy way."

"There's not going to be anything easy about this."

"The only problem is I left it back in my apartment. I don't normally carry it on surveillance jobs, especially when I'm pretending to be interested in a subject."

"Pretending?"

"Okay, not in your case."

"Really, I was just joking."

"I wasn't."

There it was again. That straightforward answer, none of that coy beating-around-the-bush crap he hated. Mostly because it felt like being manipulated. "So that massage therapy appointment was an opportunity for you to feel me up while you were undercover pretending to be interested in me."

She looked down, then back at him. With a wry smile she said, "Busted, and busted good. Yes, I can't say I didn't enjoy touching you, Sam. Does that bother you?"

He took a breath. No man in his right mind would give a shit if a woman like Olivia liked feeling him up. And he didn't need to remember what it had felt like either that day on the table or what had happened on his couch only two days later. "Right. Let's get away from that. Guns, back to guns."

She nodded, her breath leaving her in a rush, and he could only feel relieved he wasn't the only one who couldn't keep his mind on what they were doing.

It was only because it was new. She was exciting and challenging. That's all it was, he told himself.

"Okay, so you have handled a gun. You a good shot?"

She rolled her eyes at him. "You are always ready to discount me with your Ranger elitism. Four-inch groups with a .45 at twenty-five yards. So, yes, I am. I practice with it on weekends just in case I need it. If I decide to use it, that will be an irrevocable situation. You're either all in or not. There are no half measures with deadly force."

He just stared at her as if she were an alien creature. "Are you sure you weren't a commando in another life?"

She tilted her head. "Well, maybe, because I have a couple of other take-no-prisoner moves that I could use that include ball breaking. Kinda dirty street moves that a retired cop showed me when I was taking my certification."

He grabbed her around the back of her neck and squeezed gently. "You are a sassy soldier. Street moves, my ass."

She punched him in the ribs and danced away and he laughed. "What was that? A love tap?"

For a moment they just stood there staring at each other and then she laughed. "I'd rather not show you any ball-breaking moves. I kinda like them right there between your legs. Why don't you show me what you have?"

The grin disappeared off his face and he snapped his jaw shut. He felt completely blindsided that he had somehow underestimated not only the lengths she would go to support him, her abilities, but the way she twisted him up.

He needed to figure out a way to work her out of his system without taking her clothes off, because that was so damn easy—easy for him but hard on her heart. If he wanted to he could have her now. He was so smooth, and she was into him. Deeply. But the reality remained. He'd move on, and she'd be here in Raleigh while he continued his odyssey for Uncle Sam.

He wanted her. Something that clashed with his goals, principles.

She was killing him.

He didn't give in to that thought. He just walked out of the room and went to retrieve the handguns. If he wasn't careful, he would have that woman beneath him again. They had serious things to plan out, so there wasn't time for that.

Although he wished like hell he was in a tropical environment where he could keep her naked and explore her for at least a week—maybe two.

Hell, who was he kidding? A month's leave wouldn't be enough.

Chapter 10

She stood by him as he disassembled, oiled and cleaned not only his weapon but the one he was allowing her to use. Then assembled it with ease. As they got closer and closer to the time where they were going to execute Sam's plan, she saw a change come over him. He was now in commando mode.

Gone was the relaxed, teasing man and in its place was a steely-eyed, tough, determined warrior.

And, dammit if that didn't turn her on, too.

The only thing still remaining between them was that sizzling, just-beneath-the-skin buzz that would probably never go away.

Sam had laid out the plan in a cool, detached tone that said he meant business, and he expected her to mean business. He explained in a low voice that she should never, ever, ever underestimate these guys.

They were putting their lives on the line just as much as she, and they had superior experience with a no-fail attitude.

She'd already encountered them and she had, in fact, gotten away from the bastard. She had no intention of underestimating them. Sam would discover that, although she had a healthy sense of fear and caution, she also wouldn't hesitate to pull the trigger on the handgun that nestled in the small of her back in a holster clipped to her jeans.

She also had a no-fail attitude.

So, as she pulled up to the curb outside her apartment, she felt exposed and a little rattled without Sam's presence to bolster her. They had agreed that she would leave the house alone as if she was going for something in her apartment. Draw them to her to bait the trap.

The trouble with being bait was that predators were unpredictable.

She took a deep breath, maintaining her focus and awareness of everything around her while trying to act as if she weren't hyperalert. She knew from experience that people did become more vigilant after a violent episode but then tended to relax once time had passed.

She drove slowly along, trying to look vulnerable because most burly men didn't think a woman of her size and statue was a threat.

That could work to her advantage, unless the bastard she had booted in the jaw learned from his mistakes. Remembering what Sam said, she should automatically assume that he had learned and this takedown would be difficult at best.

She stepped out of her car and came around the hood feeling a tingling at the back of her neck. There was no doubt in her mind that she'd been followed, but she hadn't seen anything. These guys were like shadows.

It was imperative for their plan that she get inside her apartment, so she took her time and walked along the concrete pathway that led to the stairs. The shadows were thick here, the security lights only illuminating so much. She took the first flight, then the second without incident.

Sam had already left without the people watching him being aware. He was already in her apartment hiding…for her to bait the trap.

Her nerves strung tight, she approached her apartment and slipped the key in the lock. It turned easily and she entered.

And that was when the man came out of nowhere and pushed her inside, his hand going to her mouth, covering it with brutal force. Out of the corner of her eye, she saw the hypodermic syringe heading for her neck.

Holy crap, they weren't going to subdue her this time; they were going to incapacitate her.

If that needle embedded, she'd be out of the game completely and Sam would be on his own. She pivoted away from his hold, exactly as she'd been taught in her training and Sam had reinforced. Since he didn't have both hands on her, she was free to slide away from his grip. Then without hesitating, she snapped her leg back and delivered a vicious blow to his abdomen. He cried out and doubled over, the syringe falling from his hand to the carpet.

She backed away and the only warning that there was someone else there was the sound of a heel scuff.

She tried to turn to face the oncoming threat, but the guy wasn't fooling around. He hit her so forcefully in the head that she flew into the wall, cracking her shoulder and temple so hard that she saw stars.

He was on her in an instant with his own hypodermic. While darkness hovered on the edge of her vision, she wondered where Sam was.

Panic iced her insides, thinking they got to him and she was on her own.

With her head clearing and the man thinking she was down for the count, she went for the eye closest to her and pressed against it with enough pressure to make him rear back. He lost his focus just enough for her to bat away the hypodermic and slide out from under him. She scrambled away, reaching for the weapon at her back. This wasn't what she wanted to happen, because she'd wanted at least one of them alive, but there was no way they were getting whatever drug they had into her.

She swung the weapon up, but the man in the entryway was on her too quickly for her to fire. The gun went off and he knocked it out of her hand. The other, his face murderous in the dim light, stood.

That was when Sam came out of her hall closet and with three blows, the guy was down and unmoving. He hit her attacker like a freight train and knocked him to the floor. He got him into a hold like a wrestler and held his arm around the guy's throat.

Olivia caught her breath and expected Sam to let the guy go as soon as he was unconscious, but Sam didn't let go.

Alarmed, Olivia knelt down by him. "Sam! Let go! You're killing him."

But it was as if he couldn't hear her.

Oh, God. Was he having a flashback? This was bad.

In the distance, she heard sirens. Crap, someone had called the cops because of the gunshot. She slapped Sam as hard as she could and with a soft huff, he released a breath as if he was coming out of a daze.

"Olivia? Are you all right?"

"I'm fine. We've got to get out of here. The police are coming."

Sam moved quickly. He stood, picked the guy up in a fireman's carry and headed out of the apartment. Olivia ran to her bedroom, grabbed something that she would need and retrieved her gun. When she saw the hypodermics on the rug, she snatched them both up and followed Sam out. They left the second guy behind.

He secured the guy's hands and feet once he'd dumped him in the backseat of his truck. Olivia left her car out front and jumped into the passenger side of Sam's truck.

She looked over at Sam. He didn't look good. He was sweating, his shirt sticking to him, his features drawn and his eyes a bit wild.

"Sam, what happened?"

"I need to focus on driving right now."

"Okay." He was right. Now wasn't the time for questions. They needed to get to her brother's office, which was where they decided they would interrogate their prisoner.

Sam parked in the private parking lot in the back so they were obscured by the buildings. Once inside, Sam secured the man to one of her brother's chairs, zip-cuffing both his wrists and his ankles.

When he was finished, he grabbed her arm and went to the outer office and closed the door. He leaned back against it, his breathing more ragged than it should be.

"What happened?"

"Lost time. Freaking lost time. I don't know. It's unpredictable." He looked at her, his eyes stark blue, tortured. "I left you unprotected without backup. I'm so sorry, Olivia."

She went to him and wrapped her arms around him. She knew what this was doing to him, because he cared deeply about people, but she knew that he was more tortured because it was her.

She had told him she trusted him with her life, and she still did. "You came through, Sam. That's all that matters."

"We're lucky he's alive. I could have killed them both."

Sam was in pain. It was all over his face, in the way he was holding himself. There wasn't anything Olivia could do, because Sam was so good at beating himself up. God, he needed help. He needed it so bad and she was a really poor substitute for her brother.

She was starting to get really worried about him; he looked even worse. His skin had gone pale and his breathing was still shallow as though he couldn't catch his breath.

"I'm having a hard time…focusing right now. I'm losing it."

"What?" Panic clawed up her gut, making her feel even more edgy.

His arms loosened from around her. His chest heaving as he started to slide.

"Sam!"

But there was nothing she could do as he simply dropped down the door until he hit the floor.

"I'm sorry. Everything is such a mess in my head. Sometimes, with you, I think I have it all sorted out, but then it all goes to hell again. Like now. I'm just screwed up."

"I'm going to help you," she said as if she knew what she was doing, as if she could clear everything up through sheer force.

He shook his head, as if he didn't quite believe anything was going to help.

"I don't know, babe. I don't know what I gave them. It could have been everything. I could have answered every question they asked. I don't know what they did to me. What I'm capable of now. I don't trust myself. I warned you this could happen. I told you that you couldn't trust me. I can't even trust myself. I—I need…" His voice trailed off.

"Sam, tell me what to do."

He was looking at her so intently, his gaze so confused, as if he couldn't quite get her into focus, but whatever he was trying to say, it was damn important to him, important enough for her to give him another couple of seconds, even though they had some crazy, professional killer/operative sitting in her brother's office where that operative probably had killed him. Time was running out for them.

"What?" she whispered when he didn't continue.

A frustrated sigh left him, followed by a muttered curse.

"Zip-tie me. I can't… Just do it."

"What are you saying?"

"Do it, Olivia! I don't know what I'll do. Just do it to be safe."

Oh, God, he was having a massive episode set off by the stress of the situation they were in and he wasn't fully healed, not mentally and just barely physically.

She thought fleetingly of calling his brother Thad but discounted it. If she did, they wouldn't get any answers.

"No!"

"You promised you would do everything I said! Do it!" he said in a voice so cold Olivia felt the hair on the back of her neck stand up.

She didn't say a word for a full tension-filled minute. She had promised him, but the thought of binding Sam as if he were the enemy made everything rebel in her.

Then his eyes, his beautiful blue eyes glazed over and he started mumbling, "I'm not breaking. I'm not breaking!" his voice splintering, his breathing jagged. "You can't break me," he said low, then louder. "You're not breaking me!"

Tears filled her eyes as she searched around in his pocket and found the zip ties. He grabbed her wrist and looked at her as if he didn't know her. For one split second she was terrified. Sam was dangerous. Sam was lethal and right now he didn't know who she was. She could see it in his angry, frantic eyes.

Shaking, she pulled the gun out and pointed it at him. "Put your hands behind your back."

He stared at her, then at the gun and then he collapsed. Went out like a light and lay still.

Tears streamed down her face as she slipped the zip

cuffs around his wrists, then sobbed as she took his gun and backed away.

She had no illusions here. Sam was on his own, and she by association was, as well. Because she'd made the decision to stick by him. She didn't regret that. Not one bit. But what they had done was so illegal she didn't even want to think about the laws she'd broken tonight.

But they'd had no choice. They were desperate to get her. That was clear and the hypodermics said that they wanted her alive. Which meant to her that they wanted to question her. About Sam. About what she knew and about what he might have told. They probably wanted to know that more than anything right now.

She looked at his prone body, then at the closed door. From somewhere deep inside her she found the courage to stop the tears. They were making her lose focus.

She had to stay calm. Sam would come out of this. He had to.

She needed him.

His wrists ached, he was shivering with cold and he was so, so thirsty his lips were crusted and dry. Even his tongue barely moistened them. His shoulders throbbed. Agony screamed across his back and he jerked at the pain, gritting his teeth. How long? How long had he been here?

"Is that all you've got?" he said as the lash landed even harder. "You won't break me!" he screamed. He shivered uncontrollably, his empty stomach protesting.

But he wasn't so sure they weren't close. He was

shuffling between delirium and such clarity of mind it almost hurt.

When he raised his head everyone in the room looked so familiar that he was close in identifying them, but then the knowledge would slip out of his mind like water running off a roof.

Finally they cut him down and dragged him away. Threw him into a cell. He brought his hand up and wiped it across his mouth. The cramped cell in the cold rocky earth was the only thing that cradled his bleeding body, his spirit hanging by a thread.

The guy next to him was continually screaming as if he were being flayed from the inside out. The grating noise scraped his own nerves raw. As if his mind had just broken and he couldn't stop screaming. His voice was hoarse, but it was still audible. He prayed every day it wasn't Mike. Because if they got Mike to scream like that, Sam didn't have a chance of holding out.

The filth, the smell, the shackles, that was his only reality. That and the excruciating pain.

It was as dark in that place as the depth of hell without the fires. He shook and shivered with the cold—so cold. But then there was the white and the bright light, that room they took him to, and it hurt to even think it. How bright that place had been, the light almost blue, searing his brain and making time stop.

There had been nothing to hold on to in that place, no foothold for reality, and maybe there hadn't been any reality at all. Maybe the white place had been a drug-induced hallucination.

Because there had been drugs. God only knew what.

And he was afraid that was where they finally broke him and that was where he'd picked up the blackouts and the lost time and the memory loss. That was where they took what was left of him and…and…what? What did they do? What did they want? What did they take?

And in that white place was suddenly filled with color that burst and danced in such a beautiful way he was mesmerized by it.

There was golden brown…no, caramel and chocolate-brown, soft white skin and sensual pink lips and curves that went on for days. He held on to that vision until he blinked and then blinked again and she came into focus.

"Olivia."

"Sam." She was lying down next to him, her head propped on her arm. Both weapons within easy reach. She'd been crying. The tracks were on her face, and something cool and dry was against the back of his neck and across his forehead. Terry cloth towels with ice nestled inside.

He went to move and he couldn't. He realized she'd zip-cuffed him and his confusion was probably clear in his eyes when he looked up at her.

"You told me to."

"Shit!" His heart jerked hard and went into his throat. "Did I hurt you?" he said, trying hard not to sound even half as panicked as he felt.

She set the towel down and scooted forward and wrapped her arms around him, pressing her hot face against his. His heart tumbled over and over. He closed his eyes as something he'd never felt in his life consumed him.

He couldn't do this. He couldn't feel this way about her and function.

His tough, vulnerable, direct sweetheart.

"Are you back? Are you okay?" Her voice was

clogged with emotion and he could only feel relief broadcasting loud and clear that she cared about him, too.

"I'm back. I don't know what happened."

She clung to him tighter. "You had a massive blackout and you told me to cuff you. Then you looked at me like you didn't know me. Then you collapsed. You've been out of it for four hours and mumbling and then you started yelling really loud."

"I'm so sorry. Cut me loose, babe."

With just a slight pause and a little apprehension in her eyes, she pushed away from him and reached down and pulled a wicked knife out of her boot. His eyebrows rose and she just gave him a don't-mess-with-me-now-while-I-have-a-knife look.

He kept his mouth firmly closed.

As soon as his hands were free, he sat up. "Come here," he said, and pulled her across his lap. He was a U.S. Army Ranger and he didn't remember anywhere in the regs where he could haul his teammate across his lap and kiss her like there was no tomorrow.

Nope, not once had he done that in all of his military service.

But he did this time, hauled her to him and kissed and breathed her in.

"I have money, a lot of it, Olivia. I can put you on a plane and get you out of here now. Hide you away for a long time. Go to the airport right now and get you away from here."

She sighed. "I knew that as soon as you came out of whatever it was you were in, you were going to say that."

"I'm serious."

"I know you are, Sam, and so am I! I'm *not* leaving you. But when this is all over and since you're such a rich guy, you can take me to dinner."

He pressed his face against her hair and laughed. "What am I going to do with you?"

"I have a few suggestions."

He laughed again. Unbelievable. "What if I order you?"

"You're not the boss of me." She pulled away from him so that she could make eye contact. "I'm not going to say this again. This is the last time. I couldn't live with myself if I abandoned you now, knowing the challenges you have. I won't do it and you cannot make me."

"Are you done?" he said, tight-jawed.

She lifted her chin and dared him to contradict her. "I think I am."

He took a breath, trying to get a hold of himself. "Fine." He hauled her against him again and took her mouth, but more gently, softer because he needed to. He was furious and frustrated and trying not to freak out, but he really wished she'd made the choice to go. *Damn.* No, he didn't. How could he explain to her that he needed her when he was so torn, that she go for her own safety? But that wasn't going to happen. He finally let her go, combing his fingers through her hair. "You brought me out."

"I did?"

"Yes, you. You brought me back to myself."

She cupped his jaw, her thumb running along his cheekbone.

He glanced behind him to the closed door and inclined his head. "I take it our guest is still inside?"

"Yes, he started yelling and I put a gag in his mouth. He's not very happy with me."

Sam rose. He was still a little shaky, but that would pass. "Let's go get some answers."

"I brought those hypodermics they were going to shove in my neck. I thought they might come in handy."

Sam took them from her and sniffed. "Garlic. This is sodium pentothal. Looks like they wanted answers from you and they were going to make sure you gave them."

"Truth serum. Who do you think they are?"

"I don't know."

"I'm sure ready for this to be over."

He hugged her. "So am I, sweetheart."

Sam opened the door and the guy's head swiveled to his. He had mean eyes. Professional killer eyes. Sam knew he was either CIA or former. He was pretty sure this guy or a guy like him killed Dr. Owens. Thad had already come up empty on the facial recognition for this guy. Trying to find out who he was through an official channel wasn't going to work. So it was going to be the hard way. Sam clenched his hands and the killer looked at him. His face tightened, until Sam brought out the hypodermics.

"What's in these?" He used all his training to control his anger. The bastard had planned to inject this substance into Olivia. Sam glanced at her, and the sight of her, so steadfast, so tough, made that cold anger freeze his guts. She'd stayed by him even though they were in peril. Even though she was unsure what he was capable of. Everything from this moment forward was a crapshoot.

The man's lips tightened, but he didn't answer.

And Sam's control snapped. "Well, I guess you won't mind if I inject them into you."

Sam walked up to him and shoved first one needle, then the second in his neck and pushed the plungers until the chambers were empty. Then he pulled off the gag.

"If I say one word, they're going to kill me."

"Do you think just because we kept you alive that we're any less tolerant? We've had enough of this crap. I'm going to ask you some questions. You're going to give me some answers."

The guy remained mute.

"Yeah, and if the drug or brute force doesn't work, I have some other persuasion techniques. Remember those street tricks, Sam?"

She raised her hand. She was holding a black device he recognized immediately. She depressed a switch and it buzzed, crackling electricity arcing between the two protruding electrodes.

"It involved a Taser and the male anatomy."

"A woman after my own heart. Damn, are you *sure* you weren't a commando in another life?"

She smiled and this time, the guy paled.

Chapter 11

"Did you kill my brother?"

The man said nothing, but his eyes were beginning to glaze over.

Sam had felt it enough, more than enough to know. He could smell it, too. Fear. The guy was beginning to sweat. Whatever was in those hypodermics was something that was going to make him start talking. Sam was watching and waiting for that moment.

"The trouble with people is that they are much too interested in things that they would be better off not knowing," the guy said, his attention fully on Olivia.

"What's your name?" Sam asked.

"Lenny Jeffers is the name I use, but my real name is Jesse Carter." The man's head swung in Sam's direction and when he realized what he'd said, his eyes narrowed and he swore.

"You've been watching me."

"Yes."

Sam was going to start slow. Ask the guy things that he already knew to be true and Sam would have clues deeper into the interrogation whether or not the bastard was lying.

"Why?"

"Just watching. That's all we were supposed to do. Then I saw her." He swung his gaze back to Olivia. "She was watching you, too. The people I work for didn't like that, so they told us to snatch her."

"Us?"

"I work with other people. I think your face met up with one of their fists."

Sam chuckled and unfolded his arms, pushing away from the wall he was leaning against. "Funny guy, huh?"

Lenny/Jesse was beginning to sweat and looked as though he was moving deeper under the influence of the drug.

"So, Jesse, why don't you tell me what you know about me?"

"You're just a means to an end, Winston. You shouldn't fight it."

Olivia moved forward, her hands fisted at her sides. "Did you kill my brother?"

"I was ordered, lady. It was just a job."

Sam moved faster than she did and grabbed her around the waist, carting her out of the room while she screamed for him to let her go. He shut the door and she kicked him in the shin and he released her. She moved a few paces away from him, then rounded on him, her eyes blazing.

Angry, hurt tears filled her eyes, and Sam went all gooey inside. He could take on a million tangos and not falter, but the sight of Olivia standing there brokenhearted about her brother, probably wanting to put that gun up against the back of that bastard's brain stem and pump a bullet into his head, was too much for him.

She flew at him, her frustration level too high for her to calm down. The night had been stressful and his episode had just added to it. But it was now his turn to help her.

He caught her against him, her small fists pounding on his chest, but he took it, letting her vent her frustrations; then he folded her against him as she sobbed softly against his neck.

He cupped the back of her head and held her. With each intake of breath, each touch of her salty tears, each movement, he only felt more tenderness for her fill him up. She was a marvel. When she curled her hands into his shirt and held on, he knew most of the storm was over. He had a dangerous operative tied to the chair in the next room and he couldn't seem to let go of her until she was ready to let go of him.

When she started to protest, he held her tightly against him. "Take a breath, babe. I know what you want. I understand your pain. But this isn't going to help."

"My brother was murdered trying to help you, Sam. How can you say that?"

"If you think this is easy for me, think again. I lost someone, too. I want these people to pay. I'm not diminishing what happened to your brother. I would never do that, but it's counterproductive to attack this guy when what we need are answers. If there's any punching to do, I'll be doing it."

"I want him to pay for murdering my brother."

"Don't you think I want that, too?"

She stared up into his face and the pain and anger in her eyes softened. "Yes," she whispered. "I do."

He cupped her face. "I want to get everyone who was involved, not just the guy who made it his job to kill your brother. Do you understand?"

She closed her eyes and nodded, pressing her face into his hands. His heart contracted and he was desperate to keep this woman safe. The light washed over her skin, deepening shadows, highlighting her curves, like the curve of her mouth, the soft fullness of her lower lip, the sweet dipping curve of her upper lip. His tie to her was strong. At first he was all hot and bothered for her. But tonight the need was deeper. She'd been there with him through that firefight and his subsequent meltdown. He wasn't sure he understood why, but she'd twisted him up inside and he never thought it would feel this good.

Her mouth was soft, sad when he met it, but she made a low sound in her throat and opened her eyes. Those warm chocolate pools he wanted to bathe in and get all sticky. For a moment their eyes met as their mouths moved together and she wrapped her arms around him and gave herself up to him. He hoped he hadn't taken the fight out of her. He rather liked what had happened last night.

And he wasn't giving up the idea of getting her naked and keeping her that way.

He broke the kiss and then pressed his mouth against her temple. "Trust me, sweetheart. Trust me in this. He might have been the triggerman, but the person who's responsible for your brother's death is the one who gave that order."

Everything in him went hard and tight. "I *want him.* He's the one who also gave the order to have my mother killed and I think he used my best friend to carry out that order."

She nodded once and when he turned to go back inside, Olivia started to follow him. He stopped her with his hand on her arm. "Olivia, it's going to get ugly in there. You stay here."

"But I'm not squeamish about this, Sam."

"Spare me you witnessing what I do. It'll be brutal and I don't want you to see me like that."

She took a breath. "Sam, I wouldn't judge you or hold it against you. We have to have answers. I understand what you have to do."

"I hear all that, but it still doesn't matter. I don't want you to see it."

"You are such a man…such a man…."

He smiled and chucked her under the chin. "And you, sweetheart, are all woman."

He went through the door, resolved to do what it took to get his answers.

Before he closed it, he held out his hand. "I'll take the Taser."

She handed him the device and he pulled the door closed. The guy was hurting. Whatever was in those drugs caused pain. Spasms. He would have had no regret shooting up Olivia with that stuff. Sam wasn't going to hold back.

Sam picked up one of the doctor's chairs and sat down in front of the man. The sheen of sweat and the grimace on his face left Sam unmoved as he thought about the blood on his mother's clothes, her pale face, the horrible, aching feeling in his gut when he thought he might lose her. He thought about Dr. Owens. His care, his patience, his skill. He thought about how he'd helped him through so much, using his skill to alleviate some of his mental anguish. Sam let the guilt of his death wash through him. He would have to live with it for the rest of his life. He didn't care what Olivia said. Her brother would be breathing right now if he hadn't become Sam's therapist. Now his beautiful sister was all tied up into this. No matter how much he wanted her safe, she wasn't going to go. He would have to work around that.

Finally he thought about Mike. His ribbing, his pushing, his friendship. The many nights after what happened to them weighed on them so much they'd begun to talk about it. He remembered the many, many firefights where Mike had his back, saved his life without comment, without thanks. It was just an unspoken and unbreakable code.

And here, even in death, Sam had Mike's back. He'd been forced to do this, Sam was sure. Sick sure that Mike had been coerced in some way. Now he had to have answers about what they wanted Sam to do. Mike should have been buried with honors.

"Jesse, I'm going to ask you a question. If I don't like the answer, there will be some kind of repercussion. As long as you keep answering, you'll live through this night. If you don't…"

"Go to hell, Winston. I'm already a dead man. Do you think after this screwup they're going to let me live?"

"Well, then, it's all about how much you can take, Jesse. You as tough as my buddy Mike?"

"Yeah, I heard your brother iced him. That must have hurt," he taunted with a grin.

Something raw and mean came out of the locked place where Sam kept it. The part of him that had battled and survived months of torture. The part of him that was cold and ruthless.

He shoved the Taser forward until it connected with the guy's groin and pressed the button. He jerked and screamed at the unexpected attack.

It took everything Sam had to pull back.

The guy leaned his head back and sucked in air around the pain.

"I bet that smarted."

The guy swore at him. Sam showed no emotion at all.

"I guess you didn't like that answer. Too bad."

He shoved the Taser toward him again and this time held it just a bit longer. This time the guy's head dropped forward and his chest heaved.

"Was my kidnapping planned?"

The guy looked up and his lips tightened as Sam held up the Taser and pressed the button.

"Yes. It was planned. They wanted both you and Harris. Everyone else was dead meat the moment they hit that ambush."

"Who planned it? Who's in charge of this?"

"You are so out of your league here. They have resources you can't even imagine. I don't know their damn agenda. They didn't tell me that." He had the same look in his eyes as when he'd told Sam his real name.

"What was the purpose of my kidnapping?"

"I don't know. I'm just hired muscle."

The right cross caught the man on the jaw and snapped his head back, blood blossoming on his cheek.

"Okay, okay. What does it matter, you can't stop it and I'm not getting out of this alive. They wanted you and Harris for something specific. Apparently, since Harris tried to kill your mother, that's what they wanted him for. You? I have no clue."

Sam squatted down, his knuckles stinging. He stared into the guys eyes and reluctantly felt he was telling the truth. "Who do you work for?"

The guy was sweating profusely now and every ten or twenty seconds he would jerk as his muscles spasmed. A faint memory sent chills crawling down Sam's spine. The white room, the drugs. The pain and the fear. He remembered and he shook his head. He couldn't lose it now. Or had it been real? Was this the drug they used on him?

Sam sent another blow against the guy's face, and when his head snapped back it stayed there for a moment, blood trickling from his mouth.

He exhaled and sucked in a mouthful of air.

"The Cartel. They're called the Cartel," he mumbled through his swollen lips.

"What do they want?"

"I told you. I don't know!"

"I think you do." This time Sam delivered several blows. When he stopped punching, Jesse swore at him.

"They were right about you," Jesse said, spitting blood. "You are a dangerous son of a bitch."

Sam got into his face. "Answer the question!"

"The Cartel's plan is to assassinate several key people who may run for president in the next few years.

Like I said, Harris was programmed to kill the former vice president."

"I was programmed to kill someone. Is that what you're saying?"

"You don't get it. Yes! That's what everything was about! Do you really think insurgents kidnapped you? You weren't in an Afghani prison. You were in a compound specifically designed to look exactly what you expected it to look like. They're smoke and mirrors, man. They live in shadow and they have some scary dudes working for them. You and that hot babe don't stand a chance against them."

"But I was rescued." Memory came flooding back as sharp and clear as the man in front of him. "She rescued me and took me to a CIA compound." He closed his eyes. He'd been tricked. These bastards had kidnapped two U.S. Army Rangers, murdered two others and tortured them so they would believe they were captured by insurgents. And Sam had swallowed it. Everything had seemed so real. He realized that the torture wasn't just something they had planned to stage. It *was* real. They tore him and Mike down, broke them. Sam knew that was what they did. He couldn't remember it, but he felt it in his nightmares.

"CIA. That wasn't the effing CIA. They screwed with your head and they're good at what they do. They snowed you and they snowed you good. You're a ticking bomb, Winston!"

With a growl, Sam kicked out and both the man and the chair hit the wall. The chair shattered. Jesse, loose, came up swinging and hit Sam with a hard blow to the jaw, then rammed into him. They crashed into the doctor's desk, rolled off as they fought for supremacy.

The guy was good, and though he was fighting for his life, he was under the influence of the drug and, as a result, weaker. They broke apart and he picked up one of the chair legs. Sam blocked with his forearm as it cracked against his skin.

He ducked the second wild swing and punched the guy right into the kidney, sending him flying.

"Sam!" Olivia came through the door and Sam was momentarily distracted. The guy swung the chair leg and hit Sam with a stunning blow to the side of his face. He then bolted out the open door.

Sam scrambled up off the floor and chased the guy to the front door of the office, his rage making him out of control.

He caught him and shouted in his face, "Who was I programmed to kill!"

But the guy was ready and fought Sam off. Rushing frantically out the front door with Sam in hot pursuit, he made it to the road, but as he dashed across, a car struck him so hard he flew into the air. When he landed, he lay still.

Sam could see from where he was standing that his eyes were open, but Jesse Carter was dead. There was no getting any more answers out of him.

Sam backed into the shadows, his chest heaving from exertion and his anger that still burned through him like a brand.

When Olivia came out the door, he grabbed her and pulled her back inside, dragging her to the truck in the back parking lot. He heard the sirens and drove away as the police arrived along with an ambulance.

For once, Olivia took one look at him and didn't say

a word. She just pulled the seat belt across her lap and settled into the seat.

Sam was reeling, terror running through him like electricity.

You're a ticking bomb, Winston!

The impact of the guy's words was like the impact of a bullet tearing through muscle and bone.

Oh, God.

Who was he programmed to kill?

Back at the house, Sam sat down on the couch and set his weapon in front of him and stared at it. Olivia hovered, but again she said nothing. Asked no questions.

He'd been living in denial. He knew he'd been compromised after what happened with Mike. It was hovering around in his head. That had to have been what Dr. Owens found out. That Sam had been tampered with. His mind had been altered. *Brainwashed.*

Everyone breaks under torture. He'd been no different, and the feeling of betraying his country washed over him like a huge wave, sending him into a free fall.

He was a warrior, a damn tough one, but everyone broke.

Everyone.

He was so tight. Just barely holding himself together by sheer will. All this time he'd been a walking time bomb.

For a man who was always in control, it was frightening. The feeling of absolute, utter helplessness transfixed him. The dread from the guy's words compounding into something cold and heavy, his heart laboring as if it were encased in wet cement.

Olivia watched him intently

That guy had been tough. Olivia would give him that. She couldn't feel sorry that he was dead. He killed her brother and got what he deserved.

These people, if they got their hands on her, would most likely kill her. She really didn't doubt that. She knew they had killed her brother, so she had no hesitation about taking the Taser and using it to get all the information out of him that they could.

She watched Sam. Looking for any signs that he might be close to another episode.

Close to the edge. It was the only way she could describe him. But there was more than that. A hard male force radiated from him; it was in every movement, in his posture, how he carried his head, the glint of steel in his eyes. Olivia had never *felt* his strength and size the way she did in this moment.

His hair dark with sweat, his face set and determined. Olivia stared at him, a strange flutter of awareness slicing through her when she identified the tone of his whole bearing; it was a silent warning that no one, absolutely no one, better challenge him.

There was violence in him.

And that made her shudder.

Not for the sake of the man in the chair when Sam had done what he had to do. That was his life in the Rangers. He did what he had to do. That man had been a killer, a contract killer. Whoever he worked for was somehow holding Sam hostage. She and Sam just didn't know how.

In the cab of his truck, the silence had been strained and alienating. As if Sam's own perception of himself had shifted her own. She wanted to know what had happened, what he had found out, but she didn't think pushing Sam right now was a good idea. He was hovering on the very edge. She could see it and she didn't know what to do. A frisson of fear shivered down her spine as she remembered how he had looked at her as if he didn't know her right before he blacked out. His mouth was set in stern lines, the fading light in the room softening the tautness in his expression. Experiencing a strange little flurry in her chest, she folded her arms across her abdomen, clenching her waist, and just stood there feeling totally ineffectual.

Could it have been only three days since she'd had her "date" with Sam? She felt as if she'd been walking some kind of emotional tightrope ever since.

Maybe she should try to get him to talk. Her brother had once told her that keeping things inside was counterproductive to dealing with them.

The wrenching, shell-shocked look in his eyes broadcast loud and clear that whatever he'd found out, it was bad. Very bad.

A tight ache settled around her heart.

She noticed the back of his hand was raw and he had a cut on his temple and one on his arm. She went and got antiseptic and a small bowl of water. Sam didn't even move when she sat down next to him. When she touched his knuckles, he drew a sharp intake of breath. She dabbed them clean and put on the ointment, then handled the arm wound and the cut on his temple.

He was so silent. Getting up, she went into the kitchen and dumped bloodied water into the sink, the feeling of being isolated from him making her unsure.

She took a deep breath and went back out into the living room. Her heart pounding in her chest, she sat down beside him, feeling shaky and afraid. Not of him, but of the weight of what he carried.

Gathering her courage, she tugged at him until he moved enough that she could get her hands on his back muscles. She bit her lip. They were so tight.

He made a sound between despair and agony, dropping his head down and clasping his hands around the back of his skull. He folded into himself, and Olivia felt her heart break.

"Oh, Sam." She swallowed against the tears that threatened and the panic that spiraled, wanting to touch him so bad, unsure if she should.

Deciding to retreat and give him some space, she rose and headed toward the front door to make sure it was locked. She would give him a little time, and once he'd gotten his feet under him, she'd start asking her questions. She knew this much about Sam. When he was ready, he would talk.

But she didn't make it to the door. Sam came up behind her, wrapping one of his arms around her waist, burying his face into the back of her neck, sending spiraling shivers in every direction.

"Don't leave me, Olivia. I should let you go, but I can't...."

His free hand slid sensually down her arm, his palm against hers as he gripped her hand.

The instant his fingers slid through hers, she understood, and she closed her eyes against the wild surge of emotion that made her shiver. She turned against him, keeping the close body contact.

He stared down at her, her wounded warrior, the muscle of his jaw tensing, his expression so rigid he appeared angry.

Her tone was gentle. "I won't leave you. I promise. Do you want to talk about it?"

He shook his head, his eyes bleak. "Not now. I need you, babe."

"You have me." She wrapped her arms around him, trembling at the basic, elemental, raw way he looked at her.

With a low moan, he folded his head down against her, his temple settling into the hollow of her throat as he clasped her butt and pulled her against him. His coffee-hued stubbled jaw grazing against her collarbone. For several seconds they stood like that. Delving under his T-shirt, needing the skin-to-skin contact, one of her hands went around the thick muscle of his shoulder blade to hook over his collarbone; the other curved over his buzzed head, holding him against her, giving him as much comfort as she could.

There was an instant, just a heartbeat, when he remained rigid; then his resistance buckled, and he caught her against him in a viselike embrace, emitting a ragged groan as he found her mouth with a kiss that shattered her senses.

Crowding her against the wall with his big body, his chest heaving, he whispered against her lips, "Need you." Then more raggedly, he choked out, *"Need you, Liv."*

The words felt thick in her throat. "Take me, Sam. I'm yours. All yours."

Their eyes met as he brought her face-to-face with his bold, masculine features, his desperate blue eyes, achingly intense, his chest grazing her throbbing breasts with each deep breath he drew.

His hand supporting the back of her head, he locked

his other arm around her hips, hauling her up against him. He kept his eyes on hers as his mouth opened hungrily against hers, seemingly feeding something essential that raged in him, and Olivia sagged in his arms, the frenzy in her chest making it impossible to breathe. He bracketed her face, asking for more, desperate for more, and she yielded, giving access, drawing him deeper and deeper into her as he probed the moist recesses, as if he were famished for the taste of her. Another guttural sound was torn from him as she moved against him, and he widened his stance, pulling her hard against his groin, thrusting against her with a thick, heavy need. Olivia cried out, and he drank in the sound of her response, the feel of his hardness making her heart pound and clamor as a rush of hot, pulsating desire slammed through her. Caught up in a delirium of need, she twisted against him, and the passion in him exploded, his hunger turning desperate, his need ranging out of control.

She grasped the hem of his T-shirt and pulled it over his head, the metal of his dog tags jiggling softly, gleaming in the light. They settled against the thick muscles of his pectorals. She sent her palms over his erect nipples.

His eyes flared wide in response, giving her a brief glimpse of passion, heat and something else warring in their hot blue depths. Before she could analyze that last emotion, before she could release the air trapped in her lungs, he dragged her top off in one smooth motion. His hands caged her ribs, traveling up until he cupped her breasts through the black lace of her bra, squeezing her just shy of pain. His hands branded her through the sheer mesh, his thumbs pressing and rolling her nipples.

"Come closer, Sam."

Chapter 12

He took a ragged breath and bent his head and she cupped his face in her hands, sending her thumb over his mouth. The sensual assault on her breasts and the feel of his mouth beneath her thumb was ramping up her desire into a tightly wound ache between her thighs. "*Closer,* babe," she pleaded. He brought his mouth within a hot breath. Openmouthed, she brushed his lips. He was panting against her mouth, his body vibrating. The teasing was torturous as she held back firm contact each time he tried to press his mouth.

"You make me crazy. Beautiful, beautiful, Liv."

"I love your mouth, Sam. I want to devour you." He rolled his head and groaned as she traced his mouth with the tip of her tongue. He let her play with him, tolerated her tasting him the way she wanted to. But then he lost his patience and pressed forward, brushing his mouth against hers. When he slid his tongue against her lower lip, she opened her mouth and eagerly let him inside. He deepened the kiss, voracious and hungry, and she answered by sliding her body sensually against his in a rhythm that matched the thrust of his tongue.

Without warning, he broke the kiss and lifted her breast to his mouth. Holding her ruthlessly, he took her nipple with his teeth and she cried out, arching her back away from the wall. The sound of her bra snapping in the middle made her stomach jump. When his lips brushed across the beaded knot of flesh bared to him, she nearly wept with relief. His tongue swirled until he finally drew a nipple into his hot, wet mouth and suckled her. He tugged at her nipple. "Sam, please," she whispered.

Inhaling deeply, he groaned like a dying man, his mouth coming back to hers, open and hot, pinning her between the wall and his hard, fierce body. His silky tongue thrust deep and tangled with hers, and he crushed his smooth chest to her breasts, the heat of him setting her blood on fire. Widening his stance so his knees bracketed hers, he rolled his hips, grinding his rock-hardness against where she needed him.

She moaned into his mouth and flattened her hands on the wall behind her, needing the connection with something solid because Sam was consuming her.

His eyes gleamed. Tearing open the button on her jeans, his hands pushed into the waistband of the denim and underwear, slid them over her hips and around to her buttocks. He shoved the material down her legs. "Step out of them."

When she obeyed, he kicked them out of the way.

"I'm not sure I can be gentle…" he rasped.

She didn't want *gentle*. A tiny thrill shot through her. Sam was at his most virile, his sexiest when he took her roughly but not enough to hurt her. He seemed to know exactly the right amount of pressure— powerful but just short of pain.

"Bring it on."

Reaching for his own fly, his movements frantic, she pushed his hands out of the way and did it herself. He braced his hands on the wall and bowed his head. His chest tightened through his arms, his biceps bulging in hard relief. That powerful male stance, his hips slightly cocked, his rippling washboard abs drawing her as she palmed him all the way to the waistband of his jeans. He trembled and groaned when she helplessly reversed her hand and cupped him through the fabric, heavy, hard and hot in her hand.

His eyes went dark and fevered with desire, his mouth so gorgeous she ached to kiss him. "Sam," she said softly. *"Sam."*

"Take them *off,* Liv. *Now.*"

His demanding tone only made her blood pump harder. Her mind slid into a long, slow spin and she pulled down the zipper, unable to resist palming the tip of his erection. He thrust powerfully into her hand, his head twisting, his throat vibrating from a powerful growl in his throat. She peeled his jeans back, delving between his smooth, hot skin and the soft cotton of his underwear and pushing. He thrust his hips again as she brushed against his groin.

She pushed them all the way off him, and he stepped

out of them and kicked them away. He pressed his naked body against hers

He pushed off the wall. One of his hands grasped her hip while the other slipped over her bottom, past her thigh, and he hooked his long fingers behind her knee. He lifted her leg up to his waist, wedged his thighs tight between hers and pressed his hard-on to her intimately. Every hard inch of him.

It was all the pressure she could handle against her moist, swollen flesh as a white-hot burst of pleasure rippled over her in fierce waves.

Then he grasped her other leg as he lifted her, using the wall to brace her against his hard hips, effectively trapping her with the weight of his body.

Staring into her eyes, he said, "Wrap your legs around my waist." As she continued to ache for him, he drove into her strong and deep, penetrating her to the hilt with that first unrestrained thrust, and she came with a stabbing, exquisite sensation, her hips bucking against his.

Her reaction elicited a low, throaty, on-the-edge moan from him, and he crushed his mouth to hers, kissing her with a desperate, fierce passion that caught her off guard. His tongue swept into her mouth, matching the rapid strokes of his hips and the slick, hard slide of his flesh pumping into hers.

Tremors radiated through her right where they were joined. She felt possessed by him, body and soul, in a way that defied their short time together. In a way that aroused feelings that had no business being a part of this temporary relationship.

Then she lost her mind, holding on to him, the pleasure so delicious, so intense, she gasped against his neck, biting him. She locked her legs around his waist more firmly to pull him closer, deeper.

It was clear Sam could no longer hold back. As she reached the peak of her climax, he groaned, broke their kiss and tossed his head back, his hips driving hard, his body tightening, straining against hers.

"Liv." He hissed her name out between clenched teeth as his body convulsed with the force of his release.

Olivia was his lifeline, his connection, his touchstone to keep him from going off the deep end. He still needed her. Still semihard, he pulled out of her, even as she was gasping. He held her tightly to his body and headed for the bedroom.

"Sam," she said softly, her voice so tender his heart ached. When he hit the bed, he folded down on top of her, his dick already tightening, hardening fully again.

He looked down at her, caressing her with his eyes as they ran over her beauty from her mussed hair to her polished toes.

He trembled with the realization of what he'd found out, but he pushed that away. He would deal with it. They would deal with it because he knew she was going to be there every step of the way with him.

He relived the panic when he'd thought she was going to leave. The thought of being alone with this knowledge and the fear of not being in control of himself shuddered through him.

He closed his eyes and the panic twisted and gouged at him until he felt her hands on him, sliding up his thighs to his hips.

Slipping his arm around her lower back, he jerked

her hips against his throbbing erection. He caressed her cheek with his palm, felt her tremble with a renewed urgency, and lowered his mouth to hers. He smoothed his hand over her breasts, pinching her nipple until she cried out into his mouth.

Despite her attempts to quicken the pace, to devour him, he controlled her response until she softened against him.

When he finally felt her relax, he loosened his hold.

He glided his lips along her jaw and her hands pressed against his chest, her nails lightly grazing his taut flesh. He swirled his tongue down the side of her neck and filled his palms with her generous breasts and she released a soft groan. Dipping his head, he laved her nipples with his tongue, drew them into his mouth, sucking first one, then the other stiffened crest.

She cried out hoarsely and moved restlessly against him in a silent plea for more. She dragged her palm over his short hair, holding him in place, encouraging a deeper pressure of his mouth on her breast. He gave her everything she wanted, but at his own leisurely pace, which increased her excitement, her need for him, just as he intended.

But when she thrust her hips against his and whispered his name like a prayer, he lifted his head, fitting his length between her spread thighs and braced his arms on either side of her head so that they were face-to-face. Refusing to let her look away, he stared into her eyes, watched her expression as he slowly pushed into her. Without the barrier of a condom, she enveloped him in a tight, slick heat that made him suck in a quick breath at the exquisite sensation of being one with her, without anything to separate flesh from flesh.

She gasped when he grabbed her wrists and raised them over her head, pinning her down as she writhed beneath him. "You feel so good with nothing between us. So hot and so damn tight."

She closed her eyes and moaned as he thrust into her—long, slow strokes that increased the building pressure, the incredible, delicious friction. He bent his head, brushing his mouth over hers. Kissing her lips, he chased her tongue with his and arched his hips high and hard, forcing her to wrap her legs around his waist as he rocked against her over and over.

He trembled inside and had never felt such emotion for any woman he'd been with. Nothing had *ever* felt this good.

Then he pushed into her hard over and over, slipping his hand between them and stimulating her. Her breath hitched with each thrust, her hips meeting his. "Come for me, Liv."

And she did, dropping over the edge, her eyes glazing over, her eyelids fluttering closed, her powerful contractions pulling him over with her into that sweet, violent release.

With him every inch of the way.

Dan Henderson was just going off duty after being relieved by a fellow agent for the night. As he came down the stairs, heading for the guesthouse, he saw Robert D'Angelis. The veteran agent had been with Kate's detail since she was vice president.

But something was obviously wrong with him. He was talking on the phone, his face screwed up in anger. Although Dan couldn't hear what he was saying, he was definitely shouting. Concerned, and mildly curious, he stood on the pool deck and waited.

D'Angelis saw him there, and something flashed across his face and he barked something else into the phone and hung up.

He smiled affably when he turned and crossed over to Dan. "Henderson," he said. "I was just heading to the guesthouse. You done for the night, too?"

"Yes," he responded, falling into step with Robert. "Is everything all right?"

"Kids. They're always trying to push the boundaries."

"Ah, I was not much of a rebel when I was young." Dan shrugged. "Pretty boring, in fact." They walked along the stone path, lush with greenery and flowering plants, the scent of spring in the air.

"Well, daughters can be trying, especially teenagers. Really get you worked up." When they reached the front door and stepped inside, Robert said, "Well, good night, Henderson." Then he disappeared into his appointed room.

Something about the man's hurried explanation just didn't sit right with Dan. He had to wonder if he was now starting to get paranoid.

He shook his head and headed for his own room.

The Suit slipped into the apartment without a sound. There were two silenced shots. Burroughs and Hempstill were nothing but liabilities, and he'd been smart enough to clean up his mess. He was a shadow as he slipped back out. Now if he could get close enough to Olivia Owens. She had been nothing but a pain in the ass since she showed up. If he got an opening, he wasn't going to worry about questioning her anymore. Winston's job was fast approaching, and even through Jeffers might have given him information, it didn't matter. Winston's will had been broken. Once he carried out what the Cartel wanted, he'd be either dead or imprisoned. It would be up to the Suit to take out Kate Winston. The leader of the Cartel realized they were already compromised with Harris's failure. Once the Winstons were taken care of, that would just leave Owens, unprotected and alone. He could bide his time.

Sam shivered in his sleep, a deep tremble, and shifted. Olivia opened her eyes. It was still dark. He was breathing strangely, as if he was running a mile instead of lying on his mattress. When she raised herself up on her elbow, he was covered in sweat and with surprise that rumbled like a shock wave through her, she saw that his blue eyes were open.

But he wasn't here in this room.

He was back there.

Back in the compound in Afghanistan.

He rose out of bed and started to walk until he was in the middle of the room. He stood there, his fists clenched, his whole naked body rigid.

In a broken voice, he kept repeating, "No, no, no...."

She snapped on the light, but he made no indication that it registered. He didn't flinch or blink or look at her.

He looked worse and worse by the minute. His chest heaved, sweat running in rivulets off him. He closed his eyes tightly and whimpered, then cried out in pain, twisted and fell to his knees. The sounds he made were like an animal in pain.

Olivia scrambled out of bed and ran over to him, thinking that waking him up would be the best thing that she could do.

But before she reached him, he lifted his head and screamed in horror. Then he gathered his breath and screamed again, over and over.

This was a bad episode. She instinctively knew that something from the interrogation of that man had to have set him off.

She couldn't stand there and watch this. Without thinking about her safety, she grabbed his shoulders and shook him. "Sam! It's a nightmare. Wake up!"

His eyes went wild and he looked at her as if she were the most hideous monster on the planet. He broke her hold and shoved her, knocking her back and away from him. He was shaking and dry-heaving, moaning.

"Sam," she said softly. He backed up on all fours until his back hit the wall. His face crumpled and his painful cries tore at her. She took a deep breath and pushed up off the floor and rushed to him before he could react. She straddled him and wrapped her arms around his neck, burying her face into the hollow of his throat.

He sagged and then she felt the change in him.

"Olivia," he said, his tone confused and shaky, his voice hoarse.

"You had a nightmare," she said, but when she raised her face to his, his eyes filled with tenderness.

"Why are you crying? What did I…" His eyes zeroed in on the scared look on her face. "*Dammit,* did I *hurt* you?"

She said in a rush, "You didn't know it was me. I wasn't crying because you shoved me. It was the pain and agony you were going through in that nightmare. It hurt so much to see you like that. I wasn't letting you go through that if I could help in any way. I couldn't stand by and watch that and do nothing."

Cupping his jaw, she brushed a kiss against his mouth, then she eased back and looked at him. His face was ravaged by strain, with lines of soul-deep weariness around his eyes and mouth, but what made her heart contract was the tormented look in his eyes, as if he was so raw he simply couldn't handle much more. And she realized Sam had never been vulnerable like this, and that only made her heart hurt even more.

Desperate to soothe that horror off his face and in his eyes, she placed soft, tender kisses on his temples, brushing her lips against his forehead, the hollow of his cheeks and his mouth. He stirred and pressed his mouth against hers.

"Sweet, sweet, Liv." His voice choked with the rawest kind of emotion. He kissed her and she pressed her hands against his wide chest.

In that moment, she knew she loved him with everything she had. She was in love with Captain Sam Winston. Oh, God, how had it happened? How had she let herself get in so deep?

Drawing in a breath, she slid her hand up the back of his neck, cradling his head against her with infinite tenderness. Sam shuddered and tried to get out from under her, but she held on to him, refusing to let him go. He turned his head away and massaged his eyes, but she had already seen the glimmer of moisture along his lashes. Her own face wet, she caught his wrist and tried to drag his hand away, the love and compassion she felt for him so big, so consuming, they were unbearable. "Don't," she whispered, her voice breaking. "Don't hide your feelings from me, Sam. I'm here for you completely."

He shuddered as if she'd touched an aching nerve, but he yielded to her and lowered his hand, his gaze dark and tormented. He tried to speak, but his voice gave out on him. His face contorting in agony, he shut his eyes tightly and pulled her against him.

He was raw and hurting, but she'd be damned if he withdrew from her. He had every right to her compassion.

"Olivia," he whispered, his hold on her tightening. "I'm so sorry." He met her eyes. "I should have made you get out of town, away from here, away from me."

She closed her eyes, waiting for the ache of emotion to ease a little, then she stroked his head and pressed a kiss against his cheek. "I'm not going anywhere, Sam. I'm sticking with you through it all. I'm not leaving you."

Sam's chest expanded raggedly. He dragged his hand over his face, a wild gleam of pain in his eyes because he'd lashed out at her in the throes of his intense and terrifying nightmare. Or was it something else?

She cupped his face. "Sam, you are one of the most honorable, courageous and beautiful men I have ever met. You have been *so* wounded and so *alone* in this. Well, you're not alone anymore. You shoved me. Big damn deal. The shock will fade, but my admiration for you won't. Do you understand? I know you. Don't internalize this."

He shook his head. "How did I get so lucky to have met you?"

"You *are* lucky," she said firmly.

He gazed at her, his expression softening into a near smile. "I wish…everything was different, Olivia. Normal."

Through her tears, she smiled at him. "Shhh, Sam," she whispered unevenly.

His face crumpled and he pressed his forehead against hers. "But it's not." His chest expanded and he slid his arms around her and held her fiercely, protectively. "What I found out… I'm afraid, Olivia." His voice was hushed.

"Oh, Sam." So full of emotion, she held him as fiercely, as protectively as he was holding her. "Tell me now and we'll get through it."

He told her everything, about the ambush and the torture. She rocked him in her arms as his flat voice relayed all that he'd endured. She wanted to kill someone with her bare hands. He told her about who was involved, including the chief of police. The lengths these people had gone to sent alarm ringing along every nerve ending.

He left the white room for last and Olivia could barely breathe around her horror at what little he remembered they had done to him there.

"I think that's where they broke me. Took my identity and did something to my mind. I have no memories until only recently. I've been having this dream over and over about Trey. I dreamed we were at Yellowstone, but Thad doesn't remember going to Yellowstone. My father was there and, Olivia, he was so busy he barely had time for us. It was so vivid. But when I looked at Trey, he had no face. It was blank. I don't know what that means."

Those details chilled her blood and she realized

why they had killed her brother. He would have helped Sam to discover what his memories meant. Decipher the real from the imaginary.

Then he dropped the bomb, a sick, hollow feeling welling up in her at his next words.

"They programmed me to kill someone, Olivia. That's what that bastard told me. I'm terrified that it's my mother. I would say it wasn't possible to make me do something against my will, but then I think about Mike. He was a tough son of a bitch and he buckled, betrayed his country and tried to murder my mother. I invited my mother's assassin into my home. But I *knew* him. He was my friend, my teammate. He would never have betrayed me. He would have died first. They took everything from him. Mike was dedicated and decorated. He had my back and saved my life so many times. He proudly served his country and now he doesn't even get the benefit of a hero's burial.... He didn't deserve that or to die like that. I don't deserve to die like that."

Trying to keep the panic out of her voice, Olivia said fervently, "You're not going to die. Don't say that. I'm going to make sure of that, Sam. I'm sticking to you until we figure this all out. Those people didn't take your identity. If they had, you wouldn't have cared if you'd hurt me. You wouldn't have argued with me to go, or been so livid when I was shot. You are you, Sam. Every tough, gorgeous inch of you."

He stared at her for a moment, then smoothed his hands through her hair, his expression somber. Then he swallowed hard and met her gaze, a flash of bleakness in his eyes. "God, Livvy, I don't know what would have happened if I hadn't met you. I might have gone insane, spiraled down into madness. You keep me grounded. You're very special to me."

A knot of hope formed in her chest. She traced his soft mouth with her finger, aching to give him comfort. Then she brushed her mouth against his. Her voice husky with an overload of feelings, she whispered, "Let's go to bed."

Chapter 13

Olivia woke up and the first thing she saw was Sam's handsome face. She could get used to this for the rest of her life. But no. She couldn't have thoughts like that. There were no guarantees where Sam was concerned. He was going back to the army. Damn him.

She just watched Sam sleep for a few luxurious minutes as she absorbed his heat, watched the soft beat of his heart in his throat, his jaw sexy and stubbled.

She slipped out of bed and took a shower. Dressed in her robe and a towel twisted on top of her head, she walked toward the kitchen to brew some coffee.

There was a knock on the door, and Olivia whipped around. Sam's weapon was still on the coffee table. She rushed to it, thumbed off the safety and walked to the door, her heart pounding.

When she took a quick look through the peephole,

she saw it was Thad. Breathing a sigh of relief, she unlocked the door and let him in.

"Good morning—whoa," he said when he spied the gun she was holding. "Expecting company?"

She looked over her shoulder to Sam's bedroom. "Maybe. Sam's still asleep. He had…a bad night."

"Damn."

"Come in. I was just about to make some coffee."

He nodded and then glanced over, his eyebrows raised. Puzzled, she followed his line of sight and saw their discarded clothes and, even more telling, her torn black lace bra lying close to his shoe.

She bent down and snatched it up as a wide grin spread across Thad's face.

"Stop smirking, Detective."

"Yes, ma'am," he said, the grin still there.

She shoved the ruined bra into the pocket of her robe. This was an expensive bra. Sam owed her some money. But then she thought about them up against that wall. Maybe she could give him a pass.

Thad gave her a nudge and she shoved him back. Chuckling, she walked into the kitchen.

As the coffee was brewing, they settled at the kitchen table.

"I came by because we found these two guys dead this morning. Head shots from a silenced nine mil. They look familiar?"

"No, but—" She tapped the picture of the taller man. "His build looks familiar. I think he was one of the kidnappers. The one in the van. I didn't get a look at the driver."

"Someone's cleaning up their mess." He gave her a knowing look. "This guy was hit by a car last night right outside your brother's office. He's the guy Sam asked me to run for facial rec. Know anything about that?"

"I used a Taser on him and beat his face until he gave me the information I wanted," came Sam's voice. "He got away and the rest you know."

Olivia's gaze went to Sam standing in the doorway. He was dressed in just jeans, his dog tags flat against his broad chest, winking in the morning light streaming in from the kitchen window.

He looked exhausted and tense, tough and so very sexy. He also wasn't looking at his brother when he spoke. He was staring at her. There was a raw tenderness in his eyes, an intense look that made her stomach tumble over and over. The love she felt for him welling up in her.

"Well, good morning to you."

Still staring at her, he said, "I'm not in the mood, Thad."

"I guessed as much from your sunny disposition."

Sam walked over to her, pulled her up from her chair and captured her mouth, giving her a deep, drugging kiss before letting her go and looking down into her eyes for a moment. She smoothed her hand over his shoulder and down his arm to his hand, squeezing it.

"Next time don't let me sleep," he whispered for her ears alone. "Why don't you get aggressive? I like waking up with you wrapped around me. If I had my way, I'd keep you naked for as long as I possibly could."

These weren't exactly sweet nothings, but okay, sweet was way overrated…hot nothings. She was all for that. Her sharp intake of breath didn't do anything to help her compressed lungs.

"Breathe, Liv," he said, giving her a lopsided, wicked half smile.

After a few more heated seconds, he broke eye contact with her and gave Thad a sidelong glance. Olivia noted that Thad's grin was back.

Sam poured himself a cup of coffee and sat down at the table. "Thad, his alias is Lenny Jeffers, but his real name is Jesse Carter. I doubt you'll find either name in any database. He was part of the three men that tried to kidnap Olivia, shot her and is part of that political organization you unearthed after Mike died. It's called the Cartel."

Thad sat up straighter. "Dammit, I knew it. The chief said this went higher than any of us could imagine."

"It's even worse than that." He looked at Olivia, his face grim. "I think I've been compromised. He told me I was programmed to kill somebody."

"What? Are you talking *brainwashing?*" Thad's concern was in his hazel eyes when he looked at his brother along with a fierce dose of protectiveness. Olivia felt the same way.

"Yes." He shuddered and closed his eyes. "It's definitely possible. I remembered some things when I was interrogating this guy. The Afghani camp was bogus. It was the Cartel who kidnapped us, programmed us and let us be rescued by a bogus CIA."

"Sam, if this is true, you need to get yourself back to D.C., back to Walter Reed."

"I can't, not until this threat is neutralized. I can't risk another innocent therapist's life, Thad. I won't. Dr. Owens was murdered because he recognized the signs in me. I'm convinced that's what was on the tapes they took. He knew how to treat me. He was helping me. That's why I was having so much recall. The nightmares were a way for my brain to help me remember. It was just in a twisted way of nightmares."

"What makes you think you didn't resist the torture, the brainwashing?"

Sam shook his head; his mouth tightened. "No one can resist torture, Thad. They teach us miscommunication. Believe me when I tell you that I gave up everything and then some."

"Maybe you did and maybe you didn't. It doesn't matter to me, Sam. Not one bit."

Sam closed his eyes and took a deep breath. "Thanks, Thad."

"So, what are you going to do?"

"Ride it out, hope if and when the time comes, I will do the right thing. Hope I'm capable of it."

"What about Jeffers?"

Sam took a sip of his coffee. "I trust you. Use your judgment. He was a ruthless killer, the triggerman for Dr. Owens. He got better than what he deserved. I know it wasn't exactly within the letter of the law, but I needed answers and they were after Olivia with hypodermics. As far as I'm concerned, they moved the battleground from Afghanistan to here. I responded with deadly force."

"I'll keep your involvement out of it. I'm not keen to turn my brother over to the Raleigh Police Department after the chief's betrayal. I still don't know if we're compromised." He rose. "I've got to go. Got a heavy caseload with three crime scenes and three bodies to deal with. I'll see you at Mom's birthday party this weekend?"

Sam looked away. "Do you really think that's a good idea?"

"Are you kidding? Of course, Sam. You wouldn't hurt any of us. I don't believe that for a minute." He looked at Olivia. "Why don't you come, too, Olivia? I know my mother would *love* to meet you."

Sam groaned.

"Yeah, wait until she gets a load of her. And the way you look at her, brother, Mom's going to be all over that."

Rolling his eyes, he said, "He's right, Liv, she's going to be intense when she sees us together. You up for that?" He let his breath go in a rush.

Olivia swept her hand across Sam's shoulders as she passed him. "I can handle assassins. I can handle a little mother scrutiny. I'll see him out."

At the door, Thad glanced toward the kitchen, Sam sitting still and contemplative at the table. "Thank you, Olivia, for being here."

She nodded, her emotions really too close to the surface to answer, so she just nodded.

When she got back to the kitchen, she was about to ask Sam if he wanted some breakfast. But before she could get the words out, Sam grabbed her around the waist, pulling her onto his lap. He buried his face into her neck and breathed deep.

His voice muffled, he said, "Will you come with me to the party? I need you there, Olivia. I'm still not sure.... Dammit!"

She understood his frustration. This whole Cartel thing had made him uncertain, which she was sure Sam hated.

"I told you I would stick to you, so try to keep me away, even with the threat of your mother's inspection."

He raised his head and met her eyes. "She's pretty formidable when it comes to her sons. Olivia, I have to be honest here with you. You are very special to me, but you know I've got to leave, right? You know I can't make a commitment to you. I'm so messed up and I have to put everything right before I could even think about something else. I've never been an indecisive man. But in this case, I really don't know what to do or say. Other than I'm so glad you're here."

"You are very special to me, too, Sam. Whatever happens, know that. And we will take each day at a time. We'll go from there."

He nodded, his eyes so blue and earnest.

"Can we talk about what happened last night?"

He shuddered, obviously still feeling the guilt over shoving her while he was still in his nightmare.

"Not about that, Sam."

"What, then?" he asked.

"About what you said Jeffers told you. Being programmed to kill someone."

"What about that? I think that's pretty straightforward."

"You're acting like it's a given. That you will do this thing they want you to do. Who do you think the target is?"

He closed his eyes and took a breath. "I'm worried that it's my mother. That I might have been some kind of backup if Mike failed."

She stroked his face. "I know this is tough, but I think that if we talk about it, if we have a plan, when the time comes maybe we can somehow prevent it."

Some of the heaviness left his expression, his eyes roving around her face. "You really are a pistol, sweetheart. Your optimism humbles me. I'm as gung ho as the next soldier, but since I can't remember what they did to me, it makes it difficult to counteract it."

"Well, maybe we should do that. Try to get you to remember."

"What are you saying? You want to try some kind of therapy?"

"Bear with me. I've been thinking about this a lot and I did some looking on the web last night after you fell back to sleep. I don't think your memory loss is tied just to the drugs they might have given you, Sam. I think your blackouts and memory loss are all about who they want you to kill."

"I'm listening."

"My brother once told me that the human mind was extremely complex and people did a lot of mental gymnastics to avoid really unpleasant thoughts. I think you have something called memory inhibition."

"What is that?"

"It's when something is such a shock to your mind that you have to forget it because it's much too horrific to be a conscious part of your aware mind. I think a lot of what happened is that you repressed some of those memories instead of them being actually forgotten."

"You think that I had some kind of psychotic break?"

"Not exactly a psychotic break, more like dissociative amnesia. I think they pushed you, Sam. Pushed you beyond your endurance because of who you are. Because of your dedication to your country to your service of it, breaking you was actually the action that caused you to resist even more. I think you were so strong mentally they had to take it up a notch. No one can predict how anyone will react under torture. No one can really predict how anyone's mind is going to react to stimulus. So, in your particular case, I think that when they tried to program you to kill someone close to you, you rebelled, but the torture and the drugs they used made you helpless against the programming. Therefore, you forgot *everything* associated with the whole episode. It was the only way your strong character could accept and process everything they were feeding you. Does that make any sense?"

"I think so. So do you think there is a way for me to remember?"

"I'm not sure. I'm certainly not my brother. But take this Yellowstone trip that you're remembering, for example. I find it peculiar that Trey is the only one whose face is blank. Maybe we should talk about that and see what that could mean."

"All right," he said, looking like the Sam she knew. The man who was willing to fight, the man who could overcome any obstacle, take on any enemy. "How do you want to go about doing this?"

"By taking you back."

"Damn, Liv."

"I know this is going to be painful and scary and if there was any other way, Sam, believe me, I would take it. But we've got to try to access as many memories as we can. The Yellowstone memory was obviously planted. What do you remember other than Trey's missing features?"

"Being really angry with my mother that she wasn't with us. It was beyond anger, you know what I mean? It was out of proportion. It's so odd, because my mother was the one who was always going that extra mile. It was my father who was always too busy to have any time for us."

"That's your reality Sam. When planting false memories they have to use what's available to them. But it's scary that they have all this information on your family. That they know so much about you."

"Mike knew a lot about me. Maybe they pumped him for information about me before they programmed him to kill my mother."

"That's certainly possible. Still, do you think the chain of command on your unit was compromised by the Cartel?"

"Very few people know about what we do tactically. All my missions are top secret. They have to be. If the enemy gets wind of what we're doing, we could be landing ourselves right into an ambush. Those two other Rangers who dropped into Afghanistan with us were already dead before they even hit the ground. That's what Jeffers said. Something else I have to process and the Cartel has to answer for."

She wrapped her arms around his neck, sliding her face along his. "Oh, God, Sam. You are so amazing. It's no wonder you're not in a padded cell right now with everything you've had to deal with."

He hugged her tight and kissed her neck. "I think that has more to do with you, Liv, than it does with me."

She pulled away from him slightly enough to look at him. She smiled. "I'm certainly not going to argue with that, you beautiful man."

His gaze dropped to her mouth, then back to her

eyes. His mouth slid over hers, his blue eyes intense and warm. She didn't think there was any way she would ever get tired of kissing that mouth. She deepened the kiss, pressing harder against him, moving over his lips and just being in the moment kissing him, enjoying the sensation as it tingled through her. Sam was easily the most potent man she'd ever met. Their chemistry was off the charts.

He moaned softly and opened his mouth, giving her his tongue. She sucked on him. Changing position, she straddled him, the ache in her flaming up so fast it left her breathless.

"Undo my jeans, Liv," he pleaded against her mouth. "God, I need you."

She wore nothing under her robe, so it was easy for him to part it and cup her bare breast, rubbing over her nipple, pinching it, adding to the shivers his soft, sexy mouth were already producing.

Reaching down, she undid the button and he groaned as she pulled down the zipper. She felt the hot, pulsating heat of him beneath her fingers. She pulled down his boxers and he sprang free.

The raw truth was she was craving the feel of him deep inside her, thick and penetrating. As soon as he was free, he was jerking her down on top of him.

She pushed down as hard as she could, frozen at the impact of the moment. He caught her gaze. She was drawn into those deep pools of blue until she felt swamped, overwhelmed and drowning in him. Neither one of them moved, caught and just hovering on the exquisite moment of not only powerful pleasure, but deep intimacy as if she was pulled into his soul and he was pulled into hers.

"Sam," was all she could manage, her love for him evident in the way she said his name. She cupped his face in her hands, unable to get enough of the feel of his skin. *"Sam,"* she whispered again, moaning and struggling with the breath trapped in her throat.

"You are so beautiful, Livvy."

"You feel so good, Sam. I feel so close to you."

"I want you all over me."

He moved his hips, their eyes still fused by such an elemental bond she couldn't look away. She slid her hands down to his thick chest muscles, brushing over the dog tags that were warm from his body heat, and pressed her palms flat. She thrust her hips forward, their long groans of satisfaction mingling. She was practically vibrating with need for this man. Maybe it was the uncertainty of the situation; maybe it was that she realized she only had so much time with Sam and it had to matter because he mattered so much to her.

The sensation of him pushed her to ride him help-lessly, with abandon. She'd never experienced anything like it with any other man. She came fast as he cli-maxed, his hips jerking against her pelvis and the chair.

She clung to him when it was over, and he clung just as tightly to her, surrounding her with his male scent. She struggled to stay upright in his lap, her hand open against the back of his neck, her face buried in the slope of his shoulder. Their breaths came in heavy pants.

The ferocity of what they'd just experienced couldn't be categorized. Sam was hers now and it felt as though it would last forever. Of course, the risk to Sam cer-tainly heightened the act, but that didn't explain the hot tears that gathered behind her closed eyelids or her reluctance to let him go, to look him in the eye. The emotion was too raw, and if he didn't already know, he would see it in her eyes. She wasn't even sure she could hide it from him. Sam was perceptive and intelligent. But the circumstances of his life were prohibiting any kind of promise.

He was still holding on to her, his face buried in her hair, as if he wasn't ready to let go, either. Could it be possible that he was in love with her, too? Not that it mattered. Sam had to go, no matter what. She willed herself to move, to gather herself and not lean on his shoulder. But even as her muscles refused to move, his arm tightened around her, his fingertips dug more deeply into her hair. Oh, God, how was she ever going to let him go for real? She pressed her lips against the damp, heated skin of his neck, a tender kiss that came from the very core of her. And when she felt him kiss her hair, she kissed him again, dragging her mouth against the hard edge of his jaw, before nuzzling against his cheek, until he turned his face and met her lips with his. She kissed his sexy mouth, his so, so sexy mouth, something warm and tight and stunning spreading out from that physical connection, something more profound and beautiful than any physical release.

"I told myself that I should keep my hands off you. But I can't. I just can't." His voice was raspy and sounding gruff.

"I don't want you to stop touching me, wanting me, Sam. Time is…"

"Running out," he said with finality, and she felt the impact of those words as if she'd been punched in the chest. She did move then, but he captured her face between his palms before she could slide completely off his lap. His expression tortured, his gaze locked on to hers so intently that it was as tangible a connection as the kisses they'd just shared.

The bittersweet silence between them intensified. This was a man she could spend the rest of her life with. She knew it as well as she knew her own name.

He said nothing, just held her gaze for the longest moment. Then he took her hand and put it over his heart, covering it. "I've got you, sweetheart. Right here. It's all that's keeping me going. Keeping me in this game this organization has put in motion, trying to play me like a pawn. You make me feel like it's possible to overcome it all."

Covering her hand with his other hand, he pressed it against his warm skin. She slid her hand down and threaded her fingers through his and brought it to her mouth.

"I've got you, too, Sam."

He closed his eyes when she brushed her mouth against the back of his fingers.

She would do anything for him. Anything. They would go into battle together.

The Cartel didn't stand a chance.

Chapter 14

After their fierce joining in the kitchen, Sam was totally aware of how Olivia felt about him. But his hands were tied. He could make no commitments. What he felt for her threw his whole future plan into a tailspin.

This whole ordeal had been taxing on him in more ways than one—physically, mentally and emotionally. Especially the emotional part. Being a man and a soldier, he rarely acknowledged that part. But things had to be done. He'd signed on to do them.

But he was burned out, disillusioned and he realized that wasn't just now, not only because of all this business with the Cartel. It went further back. He'd been gone from his family for almost ten long years.

His reenlistment was coming up in a couple of months and he truly didn't know what he wanted to do for the first time in his life.

Maybe he wouldn't have a life to live after what the Cartel wanted him to do.

Currently Olivia had decided the best thing to do was try to work backward. Use the bits and pieces of his memory to try to make it whole.

He looked at her earnestly. He wanted to protect her. No matter who came after her, no matter how hard they came after her. He would do his best.

To his very last breath.

He knew all about being broken. He accepted it, gained strength from it. He'd been there and done that. It was now time to try to get back what he had lost.

She was behind him, tucked right up against his back so that her mouth was right at his ear. She sent her fingers down his arm. "Just talk, Sam. Go back to right before you jumped into that ambush. Remember what happened and just let it form in your mind."

She trailed her fingertips down his biceps and his forearm all the way to his fingertips. And Sam went back. Back nine months.

"Mike and I were getting ready to go on the mission. I said to him, 'Who the hell are these wet-behind-the-ears kids they're making us take into this cluster?' He grinned at me as we assembled the items we needed while gearing up, checking out our weapons, and getting into the kick-ass mind-set. He laughed. The memory of it feels alien now. He said, 'Cut them some slack, Winston. We were once those guys.'

"I grinned like the devil. 'Not me,' I said. 'I was born a badass.'" Sam blinked at the sting in his eyes and heaved out a breath.

"I know this is painful, Sam, but keep talking."

"We loaded into the helo and it was pretty quiet on

the trip. I was going over tactical stuff in my head. When it came time to jump, it went very smoothly. We hit our spot almost to the degree. They took out the two kids. *Bam,* they were dead, and I...saw Mike. He never even got off a shot. Three of them took him down, shoving a needle into his neck.

"They came for me, too, but I opened fire, hitting two of them. The three after me, plus the fourth guy, took me down hard and I got the needle, too."

Sam stopped talking; he knew the next part was bad. The part he remembered. But her soothing touch seemed to take him into the memory easier.

"I'm with you, Sam, in the here and now. That was the past. It's past and can't really hurt you. Tell me and let it go."

He took a deep breath. "This is the part that's hazy."

"Is there some way for you to make it clear? Try to free your mind. You're safe with me, Sam. You can tell me anything."

He leaned back, resting his head against her.

"Focus," she said softly as she cradled him against her.

He relaxed, breathing in her scent, and let himself float, not thinking about anything in particular.

"It was wet. Cold. I felt sick and I heaved. It was a cell, rock all around. I was groggy and stumbled when I tried to rise. I was angry... I was..."

"What Sam?"

"Scared. It was the first time I felt like that."

"Weren't you ever afraid in battle?"

"It's different. You can be proactive in combat. You can move and do your job. There is adrenaline and chaos and action. Here I was, trapped with an unknown enemy. No buddies, no backup, no support. Utterly alone."

"Oh, Sam." Her arms tightened around him.

He made himself recall the memory, made himself bring it out of the dark recesses of his mind where he'd pushed it. He used the remnants to construct what had happened to him. Because she'd asked him to, because she was trying to help him.

He shuddered with the ugliness, the pain, the fear, but her presence helped.

After a while he spoke. "I'm not going to go into detail here, Olivia. I'm not going to give you those images to torture you, because…you care about me."

"I do care about you, Sam."

"They beat me for days, weeks, starved me and kicked me. I was so thirsty I think I would have tried to suck the water out of mud."

She rocked him against her then, both her arms coming around him, one hand curving over his shoulder to rest on his chest, the other around his rib cage. "Then when I was losing my grip, they used the water board."

"What—"

"No, Olivia. No details. Suffice it to say it was a very effective way to make a man spill his guts. But I held out, for days. It was shortly after that that the screaming began. It went on for a long time. Day and night. The guy just kept at it until he finally lost his voice. I think it was Mike."

"Oh, God."

Panic crowded his throat as he probed at the memory he most feared. He took a breath, but he couldn't speak about it. "Olivia. I don't think I can…"

"You can, Sam. You must."

He was a Ranger. He let the fear wash over him, let it take him, and he rode it until the end. "The white room," he whispered.

"They strapped me into this chair and this doctor came in and administered these drugs to me. They burned as they went into my veins. And I started to cramp, my mind reeled and I…" He choked and clenched his teeth, fighting off the memory, so wanting to let it go back into the blank recesses of his mind.

"I…I…"

"Sam, that's enough."

He didn't even realize he'd broken away from her and was in the middle of the room kneeling on the floor. He understood, the middle of the room was open, unrestricting. That's why he went there. He needed the freedom of nothing around him.

"Oh, God, oh, God," he panted. He tried to breathe around the sickness inside him, tried to control the panic that made him want to run away.

But it was as if the floodgates had been opened and all the pain and agony of the time he'd spent in that room surged out of his subconscious. He doubled over, his breathing ragged, his heart racing. "It hurt so badly. I was seeing things. Hideous things. Hallucinations. All my combat experience dumping onto me, crushing me. The horrors of war…the images I'd locked away. Dammit!" Hot tears burned behind his closed lids, squeezed out between his lashes and ran down his cheeks. "Like I was being consumed by fire from the inside out. I spilled…everything I knew. It came out of me in one long stream. I gave away coordinates, every scrap of information. At the end there, I was making shit up. I broke. They broke me," he whispered.

He felt himself disappearing, going away somewhere else.

"Sam. I'm here, Sam. This was such a bad idea."

He got up and stumbled away from her. "Don't touch me. Don't look at me. I'm sorry," he said. "I'm sorry, Dr. Owens."

He started to fall, but she was there, her face, her scent, the feel of her hands, and he knew he could let go for a little bit because Olivia would hold him safe. Then he floated in some kind of nowhere land, a blank soothing nowhere until he felt the pressure of her arms around him, holding him.

"Olivia." He took a shuddering breath. "Sweetheart."

He was lying on the bed, and her face was ravaged by tears and worry.

"Oh, thank God. I thought I had lost you. I was going to call an ambulance if you didn't wake up soon."

"How long?" His voice was hoarse from disuse.

"Twelve hours."

"What?"

"You were so still."

She slipped off the bed and came back with water. He sat up, feeling light-headed and starving. He drank two bottles, then wrapped his arms around her waist and pulled her against him, resting his face against her stomach. "Livvy, I held on to you. I think I just needed the rest. It's been so long since I've slept through the night."

He rose and pulled her in to his arms. It was his turn to give her comfort. "You ground me."

She clung to him and he felt her concern and fear.

"I was so worried, so afraid."

They stood like that for a few more minutes, and then she insisted that he eat something. Once his stomach was full, she looked at him from across the table and said, "Was the exercise helpful? Did you get anything out of it?"

"For my sanity, yes. As for remembering something that might help us, no. But you said the mind is a complex thing. Maybe whatever it is will surface after time. Maybe something crucial will come to me and counteract what they programmed me to do."

She nodded. "I'm sorry you had to go through all of that again."

"It was good to let it out. It was good to have you there. I wish you didn't have to see me like that."

"I think you're more of a badass now than you were before."

He laughed. Doing that felt good. She smiled.

"It didn't occur to me when we were ambushed that we were compromised. I didn't even entertain that possibility. It wasn't until later, at Walter Reed, when I was recovering that it occurred to me. But my doctor told me paranoia was part of the reaction of being tortured."

"How do you feel about going to your mother's birthday party now? Better or worse?"

"Still apprehensive, but you're going to be there. I'm hoping that's going to help."

She reached out her hand and he clasped it. "Is it formal?"

"Do you need to dress up? Yes, I guess you would. My mother always looks put together."

"Then let's go shopping. I need a dress that will knock your mother's socks off. We also need presents. We can't go to a birthday party without bringing presents."

"That sounds so domestic."

"Sam, you will never be domestic."

He laughed again.

With uncertainty and dread tearing at his guts, Sam approached the home that he'd always associated with comfort and warmth.

Olivia walked beside him, and when he hit the first step, she grabbed his hand and he held on to her as they approached the door.

He turned to look at her. She looked so pretty in her dress. He'd called it purple, but she'd corrected him and told him it was mauve. It had sexy black lace at the neckline and up the sleeves. The dress left her legs bare from midthigh all the way down to the half boots she was wearing. He remembered she called them fierce.

"You look amazing, by the way."

"Thank you," she said. "You look pretty good in that suit. Very sexy."

She smoothed down his tie.

"The black lace is nice, but I'd prefer it in lingerie. Something that comes off easily."

"Don't start."

"I'm just stating a fact."

"You already told me you want to keep me naked, so I'm not so sure purchasing black lace lingerie would be a wise investment."

"I didn't say that I didn't like looking at you in little nothings. Black, red, mauve. Just not for long."

She sniggered. "Typical man. I also never said I would be against wearing little nothings. Just I'd worry that it would go the way of my beautiful, expensive black lace bra that cost a small fortune."

"It was in my way."

"And, like the Ranger you are, you seek and destroy."

"Exactly."

She gave him a sidelong glance, a half smile on her lips.

He inclined his head toward the door. "You ready for this?"

"Do you mean your mother or that other thing?"

"My mother. I have a hope of at least controlling the other thing."

She chuckled.

She squeezed his hand a little tighter. "Let's go. We live life on the edge, right?"

He turned the handle and pushed the door open, pulling her inside. She stopped, tugging him back. "Wow."

"What?"

"Seriously, Sam. This place is gorgeous."

"It's home."

She was peeking into the living room and the dining room, leaning so that she could look up the winding mahogany staircase. "You so slid down that banister, didn't you?"

"I'm taking the Fifth."

She elbowed him in the ribs. He only laughed harder and dragged her into the backyard. There were a large number of people, some in the pool, tables laden with food and a bar. A huge cake sat by itself on a table.

As he hit the bottom of the stairs, Debra's eyes lit up when she saw him.

"Sam," she said, hugging him.

Olivia stiffened at his side, her eyes going narrow and dangerous.

He suppressed his grin. "Olivia Owens, this is Debra Winston, Trey's wife."

Olivia's stormy brown eyes cleared. "Oh, so nice to meet you."

"Owens."

"Yes, I was his sister."

"I'm so sorry for your loss."

Sam moved around the pool deck, introducing her to people he knew. Thad waved to him and pointed in the corner where his mother was conversing with the director of the Secret Service, Jed Kincannon. After surviving the attempt on her life, she finally looked so good and healthy his heart contracted.

She turned her head and saw him, her eyes filling with a joy that was reserved especially for him. He smiled. Then she saw Olivia and looked down at their clasped hands and her eyebrows rose. A gleam came into her eyes that Sam knew all too well. His mother was on the warpath for grandkids. Yes, that was plural. Even though Debra was pregnant, his mother was not known to settle for just one of something.

She made her apologies to Jed and walked over to Sam, hugging him hard.

"You look beautiful. Happy birthday, Mom."

"You look a bit more rested. Now please introduce me to this enchanting young woman."

"Olivia Owens. My mother, Kate Winston."

Olivia smiled and took the hand his mother offered. "Mrs. Winston, it's so amazing to meet you."

"Oh, please, call me Kate, and may I call you Olivia?"

The starstruck look in her eyes made him smile softly. When Sam finally dragged his eyes away, his mother's eyes were even more keen and speculative.

"I voted for you," Olivia blurted, and she blushed. She didn't blush when she'd told him an erection was perfectly normal on the table or when she'd kissed him that first night. Olivia was a big fan of his mother.

"Oh, I like her, Sam."

"Mom, I didn't know she was one of your constituents."

"I was trying to keep it on the down-low, you know, so that you wouldn't tease me."

His mother slipped her hand around Olivia's arm. "Sam, sweetheart, why don't you run off and get your mother some lemonade? Some for you, too, Olivia?"

Olivia gave Sam a sly sidelong look. "Yes, darling, could you get me a glass, too?"

He chuckled, sending her a now-you've-really-stepped-in-it look.

He walked over to the beverage table and poured two glasses of lemonade.

Thad sidled over and gave Sam a very direct look. "She's already got her claws into Olivia?"

"Yes, I'm sure she's getting the third degree right now."

"There is no doubt about it, man. So what is up with you two? After that heated kiss you gave her in the kitchen, I assume you're into this woman?"

"I…care for her a lot."

"Way to go, Sam."

Sam shook his head. "No, Thad. I'm still messed up and I'm going back to the Rangers."

"Sam, if you find someone like that and you click, you should do something about it." He looked over at Lucy. "After meeting Lucy, I was a goner. You're a goner, too. You just don't know it."

In this instance, he had to disagree with Thad. He knew he was a goner, but it was an impossible situation. He brought the lemonade over to the two women. But his mother shooed him away and he chuckled at the panicked look Olivia gave him.

He gave her an apologetic look and got caught up with one of his mother's friends who asked him a ton of questions about the army, since his son was interested in enlisting. An hour later, the luncheon was served and Sam made an attempt to extricate Olivia away from his mother.

"Olivia, you must be starving. I'm sure my mother has sweated at least ten pounds off you."

"Don't worry, Sam. She can hold her own. I like that. This one's a keeper."

"Yes, Mother. May she eat? Could I actually have some time with the woman I brought to the party?"

"Oh, all right, but I still want to ask you about—"

"Mom," he said as he quickly got her out of there. "I have had an easier time crossing enemy lines on a rescue mission."

Olivia laughed. "She is quite a formidable woman."

"You held your own, huh? My mother doesn't give compliments easily."

"If I can hold my own with you, Lone Ranger, everyone else, including your mother, is a piece of cake."

"Is that so?" he said, wanting desperately to kiss her. She saw the look in his eyes and smiled.

"You're going to have to wait," she whispered, smoothing his tie as an excuse to touch him. Unfortunately he had no excuse to touch her.

"Sam." Trey walked toward him, and Sam nodded to him.

"Olivia, I assume?"

She looked to Sam for an introduction.

"My brother Trey."

"It's nice to meet you."

Trey smiled and held her eyes for a second before he turned back to Sam and said, "Can I talk to you?"

"Sure."

"Privately. In the study."

Sam nodded, looking over at his mother, who was beginning to open her presents. He felt strange all of a sudden. It wasn't time. Time for what? Something was off, but every time he tried to focus on what it was, it slipped away. "Shouldn't we at least wait until the cake is cut, Trey? It's Mom's birthday."

"You're right. Just head for the study after she's done."

"He's got your mother's eyes," Olivia said.

He tried to focus on what she was saying, but her face kept getting fuzzy. That beer he had must have gone straight to his head.

When his mother opened his gift, she looked over at him, her face beaming. Season passes to the Hurricanes. She loved hockey. She gave him a thumbs-up and he smiled. As she grabbed Olivia's present, she motioned her over.

"Oh, no," she said softly. "Time for round two."

She squeezed his hand when she left, but Sam didn't notice. He suddenly had an urgency to get to the library as if he would miss something deeply important if he didn't get there in time. In time? In time for what?

He headed into the house, climbing the stairs two at a time. Then thought about going back to get Olivia. He turned away from the study, hesitating.

"Sam?"

Sam jumped and turned. Trey was standing at the door to the study. "Are you coming?"

Sam felt sweat trickle down his temple. His stomach felt jittery. He looked around for Olivia. He needed her.

"Sam," Trey said impatiently, and when Sam looked at him again, his face was gone. There was nothing there but blank flesh.

Sam was frozen in place as his brother's face dissolved and reformed, then dissolved again. Suddenly he was back in that white room.

Sam's chin touched his chest, the pain racking his body as he heard these terrible whimpering sounds. He realized they were coming from him.

"Sam. Look at me."

That was his brother's voice. What? How could he be here? It took all his effort to raise his head. When he met his brother's eyes, Trey smiled evilly.

"Who are you?"

"I'm your brother Trey. I'm the leader."

"Of what?"

"A new order."

"Sam!" He started back to the present, and that evil

face looked back at him reformed into someone Sam didn't recognize. Where was Olivia? But he was losing even that thought, the memory of her hair fading, her warm, alive eyes dimming.

Was he having another nightmare? Maybe that was what it was, just a nightmare, and he'd wake with her sweet, naked body. He had to remember this nightmare so he could tell Olivia about it. So he could hopefully understand it.

Trey turned around and walked into the study, and this time Sam followed. Trey was at the sideboard, mixing drinks.

"Thad told me about this business with Jeffers. I think we should talk about it."

Sam's phone buzzed. He reached into his pocket, and everything went white. Everything shattered inside his head like glass. Everything went completely white.

End game.

He walked over to the desk. Opening the drawer, he reached in and pulled out the nine millimeter he knew would be there. The grip fit his hand as if it had been custom built for him.

He faltered, his chest heaving suddenly. He whispered, "I'm on time."

Everything slowed down for him as he pivoted on his heel and turned toward his brother, bringing the gun up.

Trey had betrayed them. He was the leader just as he'd told him back in that compound. His was the face of his torturers. His was the face in his cell.

He was the leader.

Of the Cartel.

The one who had them kidnapped, tortured. He'd

killed Mike. His best friend. He'd ordered the death of Dr. Owens. Innocent, dedicated Dr. Owens.

Trey turned with the drinks in his hands. He was still talking, but Sam couldn't hear him.

Trey was trying to hurt his Liv. His beautiful Liv. No one was going to hurt her.

He pointed the gun directly at Trey's chest.

Chapter 15

"So, Olivia," Kate said. "Why don't you tell me what you think of my Sam?"

"I think I'm in love with him, Kate. I think that he loves me, too, but is worried about all the terrible stuff he's been through. He thinks he wants to go back to the Rangers, but I don't think he does. I think he's ready to take his life in a different direction. I would love that to include being with me. He's dedicated, beautiful, strong, courageous and stubborn. I can barely breathe when he walks into a room."

Kate just stared at her, blinking several times. "You are quite a direct and honest young woman."

"I don't believe in beating around the bush." A sudden chill went down her spine. She turned around immediately, looking for Sam, but then remembered he went into the study with Trey. Trey, the star of his nightmares. Trey without a face...

Her heart skipped a beat, then stopped. Trey didn't have a face in Sam's nightmare. Could it be because Sam was struggling with something that had been planted in his mind? That his brother wasn't someone whom Sam knew?

Without even saying anything to Kate, Olivia took off at a run toward the house.

Trey. He was the target. They wanted Sam to kill his own brother.

Please don't let me be too late, she prayed.

She hit the study at a dead run. When she burst inside, Sam had a gun pointed at his brother. There was no time for her to say anything. She ran into the room and planted herself in front of him.

Sam jerked back at her presence, his disorientation was clear. "Olivia…"

"No, Sam. No."

He pointed the gun straight down and flipped on the safety. She started across the room as his gaze rose to meet hers. His eyes were confused, wary and holding on to hers like a lifeline. "Liv…" Suddenly a man appeared in the doorway and he headed straight for Sam, yelling, "Secret Service. Drop the weapon."

"No!" Olivia shouted, as she tried to cut him off, but he pushed her out of the way.

"Henderson, stand down!" Trey shouted at the same time.

Sam went ballistic and was on the agent as Olivia stumbled away. He swept the man's legs out from under him. Three more agents burst into the room, and before Olivia could get to Sam, they were on him. Sam dealt with each one, his movements swift, deadly and effective.

She rushed over to him and grabbed his arms. "Sam," she soothed. His eyes were wild. She grabbed the back of his neck, and his vision cleared. "The target was Trey."

"His gaze swung to his brother. "Trey, I—"

"It's okay, Sam. I'm fine."

"Don't move, Winston." Another agent stood at the door with his gun on Sam.

Kate Winston fought her way through the men surrounding her. "Let me through. How dare you!" she shouted. "How dare you threaten my son?"

"He's under arrest."

Dan Henderson picked himself up off the floor. It was clear he was in pain. He pulled Sam's hands behind his back and cuffed him.

"No! You can't do this. His mind was tampered with. He's not to blame!" Olivia shouted. "Let him go!" She pulled at Dan Henderson's arm, but the man who'd had his gun on Sam held her back. She fought like a wildcat, but he restrained her. Sam started to struggle.

"Olivia," he said, his voice breaking. Her chest hurt as Sam kept eye contact with her all the way across the foyer.

"Sam." Tears pressed at the backs of her eyes, her throat constricting.

Kate glared at the man. "Let her go! Now!"

"When he didn't move, Kate said in an authoritative voice that sent chills down Olivia's spine, "Don't cross me, Robert. You will be sorry. You, in the hall. Halt!"

Her voice rang out with power.

"Go," she said to Olivia.

She raced out into the hall, straight to him. He couldn't hug her back because his arms were restrained, but he leaned into her. She broke down, sobbing.

"Sweetheart," he said, softly. "Babe."

Finally Kate walked out into the hall and touched her shoulder. "Olivia. Let him go now. We'll take care of this down at the police station."

She looked up at him feeling as if her heart would break.

"Go, sweetheart. Do as my mother says." He met his mother's eyes. "Mom, I'm—"

She cut him off, her voice soft. "This isn't your fault, Sam."

Thad walked over and nudged the Secret Service agent out of the way and took Sam's arm. "I'll take care of him, Mom. I won't leave him alone until you get there."

Kate nodded, the determination on her face giving Olivia hope.

"Sam," Trey said, his voice roughed with emotion. "It's going to be okay."

Sam's eyes filled with tears. "I'm sorry." The gruffness and regret in his voice made Olivia's heart contract. Feeling raw, at the exchange, she clenched her hands at her side.

Trey nodded once.

Then they took Sam away.

Sam couldn't sit still in the office where they'd placed him. Thad had reassured him that he wasn't leaving him alone. Even with all that had happened in the past hour, Sam couldn't help giving his brother a half smile. Just let anyone connected to the Cartel come at him now. He relived that moment when he'd pointed that conveniently placed gun at his brother. Tightening his hold on his emotions, especially the anger that burned in him, he knew how to channel it into something much more productive than railing at the circumstances he was in. That shit wasn't going to get him anywhere. That moment before he'd aimed the gun away from his brother, he'd never forget as long as he lived. Trey's eyes held his firmly without flinching. In them he was certain that Sam would win the battle Trey saw him waging inside him. He'd almost overcome the terrible compulsion to resist pulling the trigger, but when Olivia had rushed into the room, reality had overcome his fugue and he'd been released. She'd saved him in so many ways over the few days he'd known her.

They had tried to trick him into thinking that Trey was the leader of the Cartel so that he would pull the trigger. They had messed him up good, but there was no way he could reconcile what was planted in his head to what he *knew* about Trey.

Because those memories weren't real. Sam knew who his brother was.

His older brother, Trey, was dedicated to his family, had taken over Adair Enterprises and had handled their family legacy so that Thad could have his rebellion and follow his dream of being a forensic specialist and Sam could go running around the world keeping it safe.

Trey was a selfless, intelligent, caring CEO and would make a fine senator.

He wanted to run for office because he wanted to

contribute his expertise and time to making a better government and a better America. For that he had been targeted.

All of this, everything that had been set into motion from the moment that he'd had the hypodermic shoved into his neck, had been about killing his mother and his brother. Mike, another victim, he thought as Sam's hands clenched at his side, had been tortured and brainwashed, handpicked specifically because he was close to Sam. The Cartel had committed terrible acts, heinous crimes against humanity, and Sam was determined to see the Cartel destroyed no matter what it took.

But right now he wanted to be by Olivia's side. She was still in danger from that ruthless organization. Now that their plan had gone terribly off the rails, the Cartel would start cleaning up the loose ends. The leader, whoever it was, still hid in the shadows. All Sam cared about now was keeping his family safe, keeping his Liv protected.

Liv. That magnificent woman was everything he could ever want. He couldn't think long-term with her right now. There were just too many obstacles. He didn't know what the people in charge here would decide, but there was one thing for sure. He wasn't leaving her until he was certain she was out of danger.

The door opened and Sam swung toward it, ready for anything. When he saw the serious man enter, Sam relaxed slightly. "Who are you?"

"Be at ease, Captain Winston. I'm Dr. Collins. Your mother asked me to talk to you. The police and the army are also interested in assessing you and your mental health. They are going to turn you over to me, but the catch is we'll have to keep you contained until we work through this. The good news is you won't be held in jail."

"I don't like being poked at, Doc."

"I'm sure, young man, but have a seat and we'll discuss this for a bit and see how we can resolve this."

Sam huffed and sat down.

He spent several days relating everything to Dr. Collins at the psychiatric ward of Mercy Hospital. In the meantime, Thad traded off babysitting duty with his partner, Darcy, police protection against any Cartel reprisals. Sam was extremely thankful for Thad's support throughout his treatment. Being isolated from his other family members and Olivia took its toll. He wanted to talk to both Trey and his mother and reassure them that he wasn't a homicidal maniac. But Thad assured him they were well aware of that fact.

After the third day, Sam was ready to get out of there. He missed Olivia more than he wanted to admit to himself, his chest filling every time he thought about how ferociously she'd fought to get to him. Longing welled up inside him. He wanted to give her everything. Be everything for her. He'd come to rely on her support. He chuckled softly to himself, thinking that she'd infused her team spirit into him regardless of his intention to remain a loner.

After his most recent meeting with Dr. Collins, the good doctor currently sat back in his chair and thought for a few moments.

"Well, your lady friend, Olivia, isn't far off the mark. I think your dissociative amnesia was brought on by what the Cartel tried to plant in your head, and it backfired on them. False memories are a tricky thing. In a weaker-minded individual it may have been possible to coerce him into committing the act you have thwarted. In my expert opinion, what you suffered at the hands of the Cartel did indeed break you down, Captain Winston. But your love, your dedication to your brother and your mental acuity put you at such odds with the notion that he was the leader of the Cartel that you forgot everything. Because of that particular struggle, you sought out the excellent services of Dr. Owens. He was the one who started to unravel their plot and was murdered for it.

"But in all of this, and from what you have told me about Dr. Owens's sister, Olivia, it tells me that she played a large role in helping you to hold on to your identity."

"What is your diagnosis, then, Doc? Am I going to go off the deep end again?" Sam needed to get out of here.

"No, I don't believe so. Now that you are aware of what has happened to you, I don't believe you or your family are in any danger from you. But, Captain, I concur with the mandate from the army. You should go back to Walter Reed, where there are excellent psychologists that can thoroughly assess you. The mind is a tricky thing. You will want to process and work through everything that happened to you now that your memory has been restored."

"I'd rather go after the Cartel and kick some asses, Doc."

He chuckled. "You are a resilient young man, Captain. Please call on me or have your doctor call me if

I can be of further assistance. It has been my pleasure to work with you."

"So the mumbo-jumbo period is over now. I can get out of here?"

"Yes, I will recommend it, but with the stipulation that you are further assessed. Three days with you is not enough to see if you are handling the situation well, but for your health and well-being it's a trip back to Walter Reed for you."

Sam didn't say anything. He was well aware that getting more therapy couldn't hurt. His time with Dr. Owens had made that clear to him. He respected Dr. Collins, but there was only one priority now.

Sam rose and offered his hand and Dr. Collins shook it warmly.

After three days of torture, Olivia paced in the waiting room of Mercy's psychiatric ward for Sam. She couldn't sit still. Not until she saw him again, saw that he was all right. She kept telling herself that he was safe. She understood that he needed to be assessed, but she missed him terribly. Missed waking up to him, missed his sense of humor and his gruff ways. She even missed the way he ordered her around. Finally Kate walked out of the ward, looking satisfied. A dark-haired man in a white coat was standing next to her. She spoke to him briefly and he left.

Olivia rushed over to her as soon as she was alone.

"They're releasing him now, but, Olivia, there's a stipulation. Sam has to go back to Walter Reed and be reassessed. I've consulted with a prominent doctor here in Raleigh. He's been with Sam since the incident.

Sam's on his way up. They will process Sam out and then we'll get to see him in about twenty minutes."

"Oh, thank goodness." Her heart ached. Sam was going back to D.C. She didn't want him to leave, didn't want to lose him, but she had no choice. Sam had to have help. He couldn't rely on her lame attempts anymore.

A studious-looking man came out of the double doors and approached Kate, the Secret Service surrounding her. The agents were on edge. "Dr. Collins."

"Mrs. Winston. I'd like to have a few words with you."

"Yes, of course."

Olivia hung back, but Kate motioned for her to follow. Sam's mother was a rock. Tough, determined. Olivia liked her immensely. She had insisted that Olivia stay at the estate under the protection of the Secret Service until the threat against them all was neutralized. Getting to know Sam's mother and two brothers only made her fall in love with him more. They were all so different but still had one thing in common. They loved Sam deeply and were willing to do anything in their power to get him help. Olivia had even become friends with Debra and Lucy.

Once they were inside Dr. Collins's office and seated, Dr. Collins said, "This is only my preliminary opinion, you understand, but I think the crisis with your son has passed. But I highly recommend that he return to Walter Reed. I talked to the administrator at Walter Reed and the army is very keen to have Sam back. They are dedicated to working with him to help him put all this behind him. They are also sensitive to any publicity for your son and your family and would like to keep this all under wraps. This is for his own benefit."

"I understand. We want Sam well, too. And thankful for their intention to be discreet."

"I feel compelled to tell you that he is a very fine man, Mrs. Winston. His character is impeccable. He is very resilient and, in light of what he has endured very, very courageous. With the proper treatment and rest, he should weather this just fine. Torture and brainwashing." He shook his head. "It's extraordinary. If you need my further assistance, I am at your service."

After leaving Dr. Collins's office, Kate and Olivia waited for Sam. She ached to see him again, to hold him.

When he appeared her throat closed up. He looked so good. So solid, so gorgeous. She was struck again by the power of Sam, his blatant masculinity, his quiet and intense confidence, even in the face of what he'd gone through. Sam was his own man, a warrior through and through. And she ached because she wanted him for herself. Love and respect, honor and admiration were heavy on her heart as she met his eyes.

And best of all was their connection. It was silent. It was beautiful as everything he was feeling passed between them. He was thankful for her. He wanted to hold her, touch her. He wanted her to understand he was all right. He *missed* her. All those things he said to her without words.

Unable to wait until he got to her, she streaked across the room, slamming into him. His arms came around her, hard bands of steel, and she reveled in the feel of him, the scent of him.

Letting his breath go on a ragged sigh, he said, his

voice thick with emotion, "Babe, I'm sorry for all that I've put you through. So damn sorry."

"Oh, Sam, none of this is your fault. Don't internalize it."

He cupped the back of her head and pressed a kiss against her temple. "I'll do my best."

Wishing his lips were on her mouth instead of her face, she leaned back, marveling at how well he was handling everything. His chest expanded. "I was worried about you," he said softly.

"Ditto."

She knew that there was so much more he wanted to say, but it was private, not for the people standing around them to hear, even his brother Thad and his mother. He let go of her and swept his mother up into a hard embrace. She hugged him back and for the first time in four days, Olivia saw the mother in Kate instead of the tough former vice president who wanted nothing more than to protect and care for her son.

Sam was adamant that they go back to his own house, but the only way Sam's mother would agree was if Thad went with them.

When they arrived at the house, Thad headed to the sofa and pulled out his weapon and set it on the coffee table.

"Do you need anything?" Olivia asked.

Thad smiled. "No," he said, glancing down at his gun with a hard look. "I've got all I need. Why don't you two get some rest?"

Olivia wanted nothing more than to just be with Sam. She grabbed his hand and drew him into his bedroom. Once inside, he pulled her around and pinned her body against the closed door.

Sunlight from the waning day illuminated the room and the hard planes of Sam's face as he did nothing but hold her there and stare down into her eyes. His hand came up and, gently, he brushed the backs of his fingers across her cheekbone. His eyes traveled over her features, then lighted on her hair, and he admired the strands with both his eyes and his fingers. He rubbed his thumb across her jaw, his eyes returning to hers. She got a jolt. Instead of the passion and need she had expected to see there, she saw nothing but tenderness.

She pressed her hands against his chest, her fingers curling into his shirt, the material warm from his skin.

"There is so much I want to say to you, Liv."

"Say it, Sam. I'm listening."

He smiled wistfully, cupping her jaw. "Thank you for standing by me and believing in me when I was losing myself. I like to think I'm invincible, but I'm not. I was scared and indecisive. The nightmares affected me more than I knew. Before you came, I had all I could do to hold on to my sanity when I felt like I was fragmenting into the shattered pieces they tried to put together after Afghanistan."

"Oh, Sam. You had so much courage. So much. I'm just in awe of how you handled everything."

"I handled everything because you were there. Without your brother, I was worried and panicked. But I think if you hadn't been the dedicated sister that you are and stuck with the job your brother pushed on you for my sake, I would have—"

"Shh, Sam," she said, brushing her mouth over his. "You weren't a job, not after I met you."

He closed his eyes briefly at the feel of her lips. He smiled again, his smile warm and genuine. "You turn me on, babe. You make me crazy. You make me hot and out-of-control and I want…I so want to make promises. But there're so many unknowns. And Rangers do not act on unknowns."

She nodded, trying to alleviate some of the pain she saw in his eyes. "I know how you feel. I'm right there with you."

He nodded and pressed his forehead against hers. "I can promise that I'll keep you safe. I can promise that as long we're here together, I'll give one hundred and ten percent of what I have to offer, Olivia. I want to do that because, babe, you've given me more than can be measured."

His heartbreaking words made her throat contract and she let go of his shirt, slipping her hands under the hem of it.

Sam closed his eyes. "I can't get enough of you touching me."

The feel of his hot, smooth, silky skin over those rock-hard muscles made everything in her clutch tight.

She ripped the shirt off him and as the dog tags settled against his chest, she smoothed her hands over the symbol that broadcasted he was a fighter, and when she looked up into his eyes, she could see he was her battle-hardened soldier.

For now.

And that had to be enough.

He stripped her down with such ease of movement she gasped at his expert touch. She reached out and grabbed the waistband of his jeans and dragged him against her.

His eyes fired up as she undid his jeans and pushed the denim off him. As she slid her hands over him, a soft *ah* escaped his mouth on a heated breath. She knelt and pulled a hard, guttural groan out of him as she covered him with her mouth.

Sam pressed his hands to the door and pumped his lean hips. And with smooth strokes of her mouth and tongue, she brought him the pleasure she ached to see on his face. With single-minded determination she disarmed her lethal warrior and made him all hers.

The Suit stood in the shadow of the Winston Estate and tried to breathe around the fear the voice on the other end of the phone instilled in him. Words about failure and incompetence, issuing threats.

He knew it would do no good to try to placate the ruthless leader of the Cartel. There was nothing the Suit could do to escape his fate. One he ultimately knew was going to take his life. But that didn't matter. The people he loved would be safe. He had to believe that.

The leader told him what must be done, how the loose ends had to be tied up. Now that they were exposed, subterfuge was useless.

As he spoke, the Suit sweated more, his stomach tied up in knots. When the leader was done speaking, the Suit bent down and dropped the phone into the pool.

He looked up at the house again. He'd been on Kate Winston's detail since she was in the White House. He'd protected her and her family. In some twisted way, he figured she would understand what he had to do. She would do no less to protect the ones she loved.

Harris had failed in his mission to take her out.

Sam had failed in his mission to shoot his brother.

All that was left was tying up loose ends.

That included taking care of Olivia Owens and Sam Winston.

All of them had to die.

It was the only way.

Chapter 16

With Olivia snuggled up against him, Sam felt powerful enough to do anything. They still had some hard moments ahead, but his conscience was clear, even though his heart was heavy. He had decisions to make once he went back to D.C. and worked hard to get his clean bill of health. He couldn't seem to hold on to any thoughts about whether or not to stay in the army. His loyalty to Uncle Sam had been a bit shaken with all that had happened to him and to his family.

He also was well aware that just because everything had come to light, it didn't mean the nightmares would go away. Now that he remembered everything that had happened to him, those images and the pain he'd suffered at the Cartel's hands would have a lingering effect if he didn't deal with those memories.

Olivia had also made him think about the future and

a family of his own. Not something Sam had entertained even a week ago. It may have been in the back of his mind, but without that special woman, it hadn't been immediate.

It had just become immediate.

The thought of letting her go and walking away from her hurt more than a bullet to the heart.

She stirred against him. After her mind-blowing stunt by the bedroom door, he'd recovered enough to make slow, hot love to her. Then she'd dropped off to sleep, but he hadn't been able to relax. They were still in danger. Probably more so now that Trey was still alive and Sam hadn't fulfilled what the Cartel wanted.

He suspected they weren't just going to shrug their collective shoulders and go, "Oh, well, we missed."

Her hand smoothed across his chest, and his thoughts fragmented.

"Hey, there, sleepyhead."

She yawned and then smiled. "Hey, yourself. I'm starving."

He gave her a wicked smile. "For me?"

The hopeful look on his face made her laugh. "Later for sure, but your brother probably thinks were in here screwing like rabbits."

"My brother can mind his own damn business. And we *are* in here screwing like rabbits."

She laughed. "I just think it's a good idea to feed all aspects of the body. I need food."

"All right. Shower first, more screwing like rabbits, then food."

She laughed again as he dragged her out of bed and into the shower.

When they emerged from the room, Thad was

watching TV. He straightened and gave his brother an amused look.

Sam gave Thad a warning stare. "We're going to order food. You hungry?"

"Starving. I was wondering when you'd be done *sleeping* and we could eat. But I guess I shouldn't rush you since you have to be out of here tomorrow."

Sam looked at Thad and said softly, "I'm not going anywhere."

Thad looked at Olivia and she looked at Sam.

"What did you just say?"

"I'm not going anywhere until I make sure Olivia is out of danger."

"Sam, this is nonnegotiable," Thad said as he rose and came toward him. "Mom pulled strings to get you the rest of today, but they want you back in D.C. tomorrow. They'll send MPs here to get you. I know you want to avoid that."

"They can send whoever they want, but I'm not leaving Olivia, Trey or Mom until this is done."

"I know that voice," Thad said, and looked at Olivia. "You better talk some sense into him, and now, Olivia."

She huffed out a breath. "Sam, it is done. Your brainwashing has been identified and you avoided killing Trey—now you've got to do what was ordered or they'll just drag you back." Her eyes pleaded with him, but he wasn't moved. He simply wasn't leaving until he was satisfied. Even if he had to go off the grid.

"I might have been a bit bruised and battered after Mike and the shock of what happened to me. But I can guarantee you both I haven't forgotten a bit of my training. They can try to take me back, but they'd have to find me first."

Olivia grabbed his arm. "Sam, stop being stubborn about this. I'm not in any more danger."

He raised his eyebrows. "You have no intention of going after the Cartel to make sure that your brother gets justice?" he challenged.

She bit her lip and looked away.

"Now who's being the Lone Ranger?"

He saw the war on her face and in her eyes. He understood that war, and if he was honest and he was in her shoes, he wasn't sure he wouldn't go after the Cartel himself. She struggled with her own convictions and principles. Sam knew all about that struggle and he understood it.

"Olivia, you might be a very competent P.I., but these people are out of your league," Thad said, backing up Sam, who looked at him with gratitude.

"How is my brother supposed to get justice if I don't expose these people for who they are so they can be stopped?"

"By letting this situation be handled by people who are fully capable and trained to do that," Thad said.

Sam sighed and gave Thad a quelling look. "Olivia is very capable, but I have to agree with him. You need to leave it be."

Olivia looked away, her eyes bruised and sad. "Who's going to make sure my brother gets justice? Who, Sam?"

Sam dragged her against him and held her tight. She fought a bit. "Go ahead and use your superior strength, but no amount of sweet-talking is going to—"

He cut her off with a kiss.

"I'm…still waiting…for—"

He kissed her again, this time deeper and softer.

"Dammit, Sam," she said when he broke the kiss.

He watched tears well in her eyes.

"I know what he meant to you, and if it's even half of what my family means to me, I know I'd put on my gear right now and set up tactical to bring these bastards down. I swear it, Olivia. But I also recognize that sometimes, *this time,* you've got to let someone help you. That's what you taught me, sweetheart. Trust me."

He released his breath when he saw the acquiescence in her eyes. Tears slipped down her cheeks and he brushed them away.

"He was the only family I had left and they took him away just because he was a dedicated and caring man. Promise me, Sam. Promise me that whoever masterminded this whole thing will pay for my brother's death. If you can promise me that, I will accept that we at least identified the man that pulled the trigger."

"I promise you, Liv."

"Sam, this doesn't solve the problem of you staying here. I'll watch over her."

"No, Thad. Not because you're not good enough," he said, his gaze never leaving her face. "But because I'm better."

Thad huffed out a breath. "Why are you being so stubborn?"

"You know why, Thad. I told you and Mom. Someone planted a gun in the desk in the study so it would be there when I needed it to shoot Trey. There's a mole in the house."

"And I told you we'd flush the bastard out. You agreed—"

"I never agreed to go back. I know I need to and

I'll honor that agreement. But I never said I would go back tomorrow."

"Dammit, Sam! I will cuff you and take you to the airport myself, over my shoulder if necessary."

Sam let go of Olivia and faced his brother. "Thad, don't push me."

"You think you're tougher—"

"Oh, stop it, both of you," Olivia said, getting between them. "The level of testosterone is getting too high in here."

Thad let out a soft chuckle. "Maybe you should kiss her again, Sam. I'll have to remember that move. Lucy can really be a handful."

"How about we get something to eat and we'll discuss this later?" she said, giving Thad a quelling look.

"Nothing's going to change."

"Later, Sam. I'm going to go get my cell phone and call. What do we want? Pizza? Chinese? What?"

"Pizza," Thad said.

"Chinese," Sam said.

"Oh, for the love of God. Why did I give them any choices? I'm making the decision and you both are going to like it."

"Yes, ma'am," Sam said with a salute.

"Men," she said as she left the room.

Thad nudged him. "Tell me, man, that you're smart enough to hold on to that woman."

Sam gave him a nudge back. "Things are complicated, Thad. I don't know."

"Some things are worth fighting for, brother. She's one of them. Oh, and by the way, Mom loves her and so do Debra and Lucy. That's like triple estrogen coming your way and I don't think even Ranger training prepared you for that. No pressure, though."

He gave Thad a wry sidelong glance. "Right, no pressure."

"Sam!"

At the sound of her voice, he ran for the bedroom, Thad close behind, pulling out his weapon.

When they hit the open doorway, she looked up from her phone.

They breathed a collective sigh of relief when they saw her unharmed holding her laptop. "What is it?"

"The company who hosted my drive called and was able to retrieve some of the video I took and downloaded into your file. Maybe there's something on here."

They both walked over and Thad holstered his gun.

Both of them looked over her shoulder as she pulled up a file and opened it.

"Subject is Samuel Winston. I have been following him for two days now. Not sure what my brother was worried about, but so far he's just doing routine stuff. Running, going to the coffee shop—the guy likes his caffeine."

He saw himself in nothing but a pair of shorts stretching on his front porch. Then suddenly the camera zoomed in on his lower body, the thick muscles of his thighs. Then panned up his body in slow motion, getting a tighter shot of his chest. When he turned around, the camera panned down to his butt and stayed there.

Thad snickered and Sam elbowed him, but he couldn't help the grin that slipped across his face.

He heard Olivia say, "Oh, crap," so softly he almost missed it.

"Wow, Olivia, when you do surveillance on a guy you certainly cover all the bases."

"I was on stakeout and I was bored and Sam is... quite...spectacularly beautiful."

He curled his arm around her waist and pulled her to his chest. She leaned back and those guilty, sheepish eyes met his. "It's true, Sam. You are beautiful."

It hit him then hard how much he cared for Olivia. She was so direct, so sweet, so smart, and tough and every damn thing. He wanted to hold her and never let her go.

The scene changed and he saw himself at the coffee shop, waiting in line, then making his order. He looked preoccupied, tired and troubled. He wondered if he still looked that way.

While he was getting creamer, Olivia panned around the area, then pulled the camera back to him.

But he caught a glimpse of someone. "Wait, go back."

She rewound. And there he was as plain as day.

"I knew I'd seen that guy before, but I couldn't place him."

"Son of a bitch!" Sam said.

Robert D'Angelis, the Secret Service Agent who had been on his mother's detail from the beginning of her vice presidency.

And he was talking to Jesse Carter, aka Lenny Jeffers.

Trey rushed into his mother's room, clutching his arm. "We've got to move now, Mom!" He grabbed her arm and started pulling her toward the door.

"What is it? What's happened? I heard the gunshots... Oh, my God, you're bleeding." His shirt sleeve was ragged and soaked with blood. "Will this madness never end?" Her wide blue eyes met his and she tried to see his injury.

"There's no time for that," he said firmly, strain in his voice. "It's not serious."

"What is happening downstairs" Her son looked at her with sympathy in his eyes and she braced for the news.

"It's Robert D'Angelis, Mom. He tried to kill me, but Agent Miller, my detail…he saved my life by giving his own. Robert is busy downstairs, pinned down by two other agents, but I have no doubt that both of us are on his killing agenda."

She gasped, the man who had pledged his life to protect hers had been corrupted. Steadfast and true Robert. "Oh, no…that can't be. He's been with me from the beginning."

"They got to him."

She was trying to absorb the shock of being betrayed by one of her own people, stricken to the core. Just like Sam had to deal with Mike's betrayal. She had to deal with this. Would this ever end?

With her hand clasped in his, they moved to the door, but Robert had already dispatched the other agents and was coming up the stairs. Trey slammed the door closed and locked it as he opened fire on them.

Trey didn't hesitate. He grabbed her and pulled her out onto the balcony.

"There's nowhere to go, Trey. We're trapped here." She looked back at her bedroom door. Robert was trying to get through and that lock wasn't going to hold him for long; he was going to come through it at any moment.

Trey looked down at the pool and back at her.

"You can't be serious."

"Mom, we have to get out of here. Now let's go! Jump."

"I can't believe I'm doing this," she said as she flung herself off the balcony. When she plunged to the bottom, she immediately swam to the surface and got out of the way. Shortly afterward, she heard another splash and Trey rose to the surface and swam strongly toward her.

When she looked up at the balcony, she saw Robert. Her heart sank to think that these ruthless bastards had gotten to him.

Trey grabbed her waist and dragged her to the stairs. Pulling themselves out of the pool, they ran for the shelter of the pool house just as Robert opened fire.

"Robert D'Angelis. He allowed Mike access to the estate during the wedding reception. He was the one that planted the gun and alerted the Cartel when I was alone with Trey. He's their damn inside man."

Thad was on his cell, calling for backup, but when Sam reached the estate he didn't wait. As soon as Thad was done calling for backup, he was going to sweep the perimeter. This was not the time to take chances. There were other shooters around the estate or an ace in the hole—a sniper. He was out of the car, running for the house. When he heard his mother's scream from the pool house, he veered in that direction. When he turned to find Olivia there, he opened his mouth.

"Don't tell me to go back, Sam."

"We're in this together." He was just simply no longer the Lone Ranger. "Let's go, but be very careful."

Olivia pulled out her gun and Sam smiled, wishing

he had his own, but the cops took the guns at his house and hadn't returned them. "A gun-toting P.I. How did I get so lucky?"

She smiled. "Okay, let's go."

They inched around the house and a bullet whizzed by his head. "Dammit, he has some backup." He did a quick glimpse and the rifle discharged again. That was what Sam was looking for. He ducked back.

"I'm going to cover you. Make a run for the low stone wall bracketing the pool," Olivia said.

"All right."

"Ready?"

He nodded.

"Go!"

He ran and Olivia pulled off three shots. Then she was beside him.

"What now?" she said as he crouched down next to her. "He's heading to the pool house, Sam."

Sam's cell buzzed and he pulled it out of his pocket. "Thad."

"Two shooters down."

"Sniper on the ridge north of the pool house. Take him out, Thad."

"Got it."

He shoved his phone back in his pocket. "Thad's going for the sniper. I'm going for Trey and my mother. You keep D'Angelis busy."

"Sam," she said. She pressed her mouth to his. "I love you."

He met her eyes. He'd known for a while what he felt for her, but it was unfair to make that declaration when he couldn't make any promises. "Ah, sweetheart. You're killing me. You know how I feel."

"I know you, Sam. It's okay if you don't say it back. I just needed to tell you. To let you know. Just in case."

"No, sweetheart. We're getting out of this."

"You promise?"

"I promise. Be careful."

He slipped around the wall and headed for the pool house. Just then a man dressed all in black rose out of the nearby brush and pointed a gun directly at Sam.

Olivia rose and shot four bullets in him and he went down.

Sam looked back at her. "Hooyah, sweetheart."

"Go, Sam."

She focused her attention on D'Angelis, and Sam ran for the pool house. As soon as he tried to get a bead on Sam, Olivia fired, putting his ass back behind cover.

When he was almost to the pool house, he heard the unmistakable sound of an empty gun click. He was in the open, and exposed and Olivia was out of ammo. D'Angelis came out from behind the big planter he was using for cover, getting a bead on Sam. As he pulled the trigger, Sam rolled.

Olivia bolted toward D'Angelis. He was so focused on what he thought was the biggest threat, he ignored her. She hit him full out and they both went into the pool.

"Olivia!" He tried to get to her, but shots came from the hill. "Dammit, Thad, take that guy out," he muttered. When no one surfaced, Sam took his chances and sprinted for the pool

No shots. Thad must have gotten the sniper. He could see the bastard holding her down. Jumping off from the pool deck, he dived in.

He and D'Angelis grappled in the water and when

they broke the surface, fists flying, he was suddenly aware that Olivia wasn't moving. He let go of D'Angelis and dived for her as D'Angelis swam for the edge of the pool. Sirens wailed in the distance. And Thad was there, putting his foot right into D'Angelis's face as he fell back into the water.

As Sam hauled her up out of the water, Trey and their mother came out of the pool house and both of them ran to him. He was listening for her breath. "No, baby," he said, and started giving her mouth to mouth resuscitation. "Breathe, Liv. Breathe," he said through his gasps. "Come on."

The police arrived and Thad had already hauled D'Angelis out of the pool, cuffing him. Sam felt as if his whole world was ending.

Then she coughed and he turned her head to the side to get the water out of her lungs. When she stopped coughing, she looked up at him and he pulled her to him. He held her as D'Angelis was marched past him.

"You think you've won!" he shouted. "You'll never get anything out of me! I know if I tell, my family will be killed! I had no choice. *You* have no choice." Then he looked straight at Kate. "They're going to kill me soon enough. But, even now, Kate, other members of your family are in danger!"

With tight lips, Kate stalked up to him and slapped him across the face. "I trusted you, Robert. You betrayed us all, including your family, your oath and your country."

"None of that means anything to them, Kate. You have no idea who you're up against!" he shouted as they dragged him away. "No idea."

Sam had to disagree as he cradled Olivia in his arms.

He knew what they were up against.

And he suspected that Robert D'Angelis was just the tip of the iceberg.

Whoever was the leader of the Cartel, he was a powerful figure.

With D'Angelis identified, he was finally sure Olivia would be safe.

He closed his eyes and buried his face in her hair.

It was time for him to go.

Chapter 17

While Olivia and Trey were being checked over by the EMTs, Sam insisted that their mother sit down on one of the lounge chairs. D'Angelis and his thugs had taken out most of his mother's detail. Dan Henderson was the only one to survive because he was out of it on pain meds from his tussle with Sam.

Dan had reinjured a ligament in his ankle and was shocked and dismayed at the loss of so many men at the hands of one of their own.

He hobbled up to Kate to talk to her quietly, then handed her the phone.

"It's the director, Jed Kincannon," he explained.

Sam nodded. "Henderson, I'm sorry about what happened."

Dan waved Sam's words away. "Trey explained to me what you went through. I'm sorry that you had to endure that."

They shook hands.

Dan hobbled off and Sam turned to Trey, as he walked up to him, his arm bandaged. "This is some mess. What do these people want and why are they trying to kill us?"

"The Cartel's plan is to assassinate several key people who may run for president in the next few years. It's all about power." Sam took a breath. "Trey, I—"

"Sam, don't you think I know how you feel?"

"I almost killed you." All the tension of the past forty-eight hours drew into a tight ball in Sam's chest.

"No, you didn't." Trey grabbed the back of his neck and pulled him in forehead to forehead. They stood like that for a minute. "You trusted in yourself…" Trey's hand squeezed the back of Sam's neck, and he felt his brother's forgiveness and love. "…and our family bond. It's stronger than drugs and torture. We together are stronger."

The gravity of the situation the Cartel had placed him in made that tension tighten into something hard and determined. He would surpass this. He promised himself. He would be himself again.

He pulled his brother into a strong embrace and held him, unabashed at the emotion he was showing.

Debra's concerned voice echoed across the pool deck and Trey raised his head. "You take care, Sam. Focus on getting well, but stay in touch. If you need any of us, just call. We'll be in D.C. before you know it."

"I will."

He walked away and Debra clutched at him as he put his arm around her and drew her into the house.

His mother finished her conversation and rose.

"Sam, thank you for saving our lives." She wrapped her arms around him and he smiled into her hair. The familiar scent of her would always signal home to him.

When they separated, she asked, "You're going back to D.C. tomorrow, right?" She glanced over at Olivia, who was talking with the EMT, and Kate smiled.

Sam followed his mother's gaze, and his chest contracted. His mother looked up at him.

"She's a lovely girl, Sam."

"I know."

"I'm quite fond of her, and that doesn't happen often."

He met his mother's eyes. "I know where you're going with this, and if I could change things, I would. But I can't make promises I may not be able to keep. Do you understand?"

She sighed. "I understand I raised a fine young man. That's what I understand. But, Sam, maybe it's time for you to move on to something else. You've served your country and served it well. I'm so, so proud of you. Think long and hard about everything before you make your final decision."

"Once I get my head on straight, I will consider..." He looked at Olivia and she turned her head at that moment and met his eyes. "Everything." That's what she was. Everything.

"It was so good to have you home. I will want regular reports, Sam."

He smiled and squeezed his mother's arm. "Yes, ma'am."

He turned and walked across the pool deck. "What's the diagnosis? Will she live?"

"She will," the EMT said with an appreciative

glance at Olivia. And why not? Olivia was a fire-cracker.

Feeling proprietary, Sam slipped his arm around her and the EMT's eyes dimmed. "Take care, Olivia," he said as he turned and walked away.

Sam shot her a sideways glance. "You okay?"

She nodded, looking at him and then at the re-treating EMT's back. "He's quite attractive, don't you think?"

"Actually I'm more interested in someone a bit smaller, more feminine and too observant for her own good and with a damn smart mouth."

She was amused with him. He could see it in the sparkling depths of her eyes, in the way the corners of her mouth flicked upward ever so slightly.

Thad came across the lawn. "You two ready to go?"

On the short ride back to Sam's place, Olivia slipped her hand into his and he returned the pressure.

"You going back to D.C. tomorrow, Sam?" Thad said, looking back at him.

He nodded. "I'll get Olivia to drive me to the air-port."

"Okay." Thad was visibly relieved, but his eyes were sad when he looked at Olivia. "Hey, man." He twisted around so he could shake Sam's hand. "It's been great having you home. Don't be a stranger. Let me know how it's going in D.C."

"I promise. I'll let you all know."

He got out of the car with Olivia. They walked hand in hand into the house he'd shared with her for just under a week. But it felt as if it had been longer.

Then it occurred to him. He'd done what he'd al-ways done. Made the decision without even consulting her. "Olivia," he said as he turned to her after she shut the front door. "I wasn't thinking. I assumed you'd want to stay with me tonight. But if it's too much and you don't want to, I can have Thad take me to the—"

She covered his mouth with her fingers. "Oh, Sam, for such an intelligent man, you can be really dense."

She wrapped her arms around his neck and pressed her mouth to his. They had said everything, she had said everything, but he had held back the words. Instead he said it with his mouth and his hands.

Longing welled up inside him, and he reached out to touch her to ease the ache, to fill the hole in his heart if only just for now. He cupped her cheek, feeling raw at the softness of it. He pressed his mouth to hers, tasting her, starving for her. His palms framed her face. He slipped his fingers into the thick caramel hair as soft silk. He would never be able to look at that shade of brown without thinking of her. For a consuming moment he gazed down into her eyes, then bent his head again and took her mouth again, his lips trembling on hers.

She sank into him, pressed hard against him. So small, so strong, so exquisitely feminine. She was his for the moment, for the night, for a memory he could take with him and hold on to.

He soaked her up greedily and thought his heart would overflow.

He dipped down and picked her up, cradling her against him. He walked to the bedroom, his eyes locked with hers. Inside his room, he set her down gently and stripped them both of their clothes.

He kissed his way down her body, to her quivering belly and back up over her beautiful rose-tipped breasts. She lay back and stretched her arms over her head. His eyes locked on hers as he kneed her legs apart and settled his hips between hers.

Olivia's breath fluttered across his throat in a heated exhale. Then he filled her. Slowly. Inch by inch. His eyes still on hers. Giving her the essence of his maleness, being welcomed and embraced by the warm, tight glove of her woman's body. Pressing deeper, deeper until she gasped his name. When the joining was complete, he pulled her to him in a crushing embrace.

It went on forever. It could never have lasted long enough. They moved as one, body to body, need to need, heart to heart.

Sam lost himself in the heat, in the bliss, in the comfort she offered him without words. He gave himself over to desire, thought nothing of tomorrow or the future, only of his Liv. So sweet, so strong. He wanted to give her everything, be everything for her. He wanted to press her to his heart and never let go. She filled a hole inside him, flooded all the pain away and made him believe for a moment he could start over with her, have a family, have peace, find forgiveness.

They were wishful thoughts. But for this night he would cling to them as he clung to the woman in his arms.

Afterward he held her and neither one of them slept. He talked about his family, his childhood, his college years and his hatred of practicing law and becoming a lawyer. He spoke about his time in the army, the friendships, the ups and downs, the devastating deaths and the unbelievable triumphs. Olivia reciprocated with more information about her childhood, how her brother had raised her, how her marine biologist parents had died at sea during a storm.

"It's about time we talked more about each other," she said softly. "This has been such a crazy, adrenaline-filled few days with you, Sam. It feels good to just be together."

Sam absorbed her voice and the feel of her deep inside him, knowing it would carry him through the time ahead when he wouldn't have her comfort. Leaving her felt like having his heart ripped out of his chest.

Olivia slipped from the bed at dawn and dressed silently in the soft light that filtered through the curtains. The time had finally come to let Sam go. It was going to hurt—was hurting already. But Olivia could never force a man like Sam to change, and she would never try. He did things in his own time according to his own code of ethics. She could only admire him for his strong and steadfast convictions. It made her love him more. She fought back the terrible lump in her throat and quickly wiped away the tears that were forming in her eyes.

He was still sleeping. The nightmares, at least for the moment, seemed to have abated now that Sam wasn't struggling with those terrible false memories of Trey and trying to reconcile them with the brother he knew and loved.

She thought about John then, and her heart twisted for the loss of her brother, understanding how killing Trey would have left Sam a former shell of himself. It would have destroyed him, and these were the people his family were still continuing to battle if what Agent D'Angelis had said was true. She wanted to help them.

She'd simply fallen in love with his mother and Debra and Lucy and both his handsome and amazing brothers. But she was wise enough to understand that now that the Cartel was exposed, people with specialized training could take over. In all the mess and chaos of the past few days, she would trust Sam not only with her life, but with making sure that the people who had ordered John's death would pay for his murder. Even though Sam had so much to deal with, he had promised her and she trusted he would follow through.

For a long while she stood by the bed and just studied him, needing to hold him in this moment in time. The light of the early morning didn't quite penetrate the shadow of the bed. Sam lay sprawled on his belly, taking up most of the bed, his face buried in the crook of his arm. His bronzed back was a sculpture of lean, rippling muscle. The white sheet covered only a section of thigh and hips. One leg was bent at the knee, his thigh and calf strong, masculine and dusted with rough brown hair.

She remembered the first time she'd seen his body, the first time she'd touched him, in a way that was supposed to be in a professional nature, and how she'd failed miserably. The first time she'd kissed that beautiful mouth when she'd barely known him. Their relationship was completely new, but Olivia knew without any doubt Sam was the man for her. The only man. That if he didn't come back, if he decided that the army was his choice, she would forever feel as if a part of her had been lost with him. She would move on, most likely, but finding someone to measure up to him was going to be a challenge.

Olivia memorized the way he looked in that moment and she accepted that she was in love with him. She had no idea where these feelings would lead, but she wouldn't deny to herself that she felt them. She'd lied to herself enough in her lifetime.

She had to let him go. Her indrawn breath ended on a soft sob. She tried to catch her breath, force air past the frenzy of her tumbling emotions and her rock-hard obligations.

She wanted to wake him, grab him and run away from all this madness.

But in the end, she knew this was the way it had to be.

God, why now? Why did she have to go and fall in love with him now at this time in his life, when everything was in such flux for him?

Because he had needed her, and as dawn broke over the horizon with ribbons of soft color, her heartbeat answered in kind.

Unsure if her legs would hold her, she ran her hands over his shoulders and softly called his name.

His sleepy eyes opened and the moment he registered her face, he pushed up in bed and swung his legs to the floor.

"Sam…"

His gaze connected with hers, the muscles along his jaw tensing. He reached for her and caught her against him in a fierce embrace, crushing them together from shoulder to thigh. His chest heaved as he held her locked against him. "It's okay, Liv. It's okay, sweetheart."

She shook her head, barely able to take a breath, a hot thickness that was growing denser and heavier in her chest.

His rib cage expanding with a shaky sigh, he let her go and without a word went into the bathroom. She heard the shower come on and she sat down heavily on the bed.

When he emerged, he dressed and packed up his duffel, finally ready to go.

Outside, the sun was blazing in a glorious spring morning that could only happen in Raleigh. Sam put his arm around her and brushed his mouth against her hair as they walked to his car. She slipped her arm around his waist, a feeling of such longing settling in her.

He cupped his hand along her jaw, his fingers catching in her hair as he brushed an infinitely gentle kiss against her temple.

Olivia looked at him. He held her gaze for a second, his expression taut, then he released his breath on an uneven sigh, his hand trailing down her neck as he pulled away.

He started the car and backed out of his driveway.

Once they hit the beltline, he reached out and caught her hand, then drew it against his thigh. Olivia's heart stalled, spreading her hand against his leg, trying to communicate everything inside her by touch alone. He massaged the back of her hand with the heel of his, then laced his fingers through hers, his thumb caressing her palm. She pressed down on her emotions to keep the pain and longing she was already feeling at bay.

As they pulled into a parking space across from the terminal, Olivia's hands tightened in her lap. Once outside the truck, he offered her his hand and with the pain in her chest escalating, she took it, gently rubbing at his skin.

Once inside the terminal, Sam completed his check-in and they proceeded to the line for security.

He dropped his duffel and pulled her into his arms. "This is where we say goodbye, sweetheart."

"I don't want to say goodbye," she said softly. "I'll just say take care, Sam." Tears welled up in her eyes, and her throat tightened.

"Liv," he whispered.

"Give me your phone," she said, stepping back a bit from him.

He pulled it out of the back pocket of his jeans. She took it from his hand and accessed his contact list and added herself.

"There, now you can call me if you want to, but there's no pressure." Tears slipped down her face and he brushed them away with his thumb.

He cupped her cheek and pressed his mouth to hers. She kissed him fiercely, desperately.

"You stay out of trouble."

"That should be much easier without you around," she said with a soft smile.

"Still sassy, Team Owens?"

"Always, Lone Ranger."

He smiled and she smiled back at him as he picked up his duffel and turned away from her.

Olivia was trembling badly by the time he moved out of sight. Heading back to his truck, she drove back to his house, cleaned up a bit, grabbed her stuff and called a cab. Back at her apartment, she expected to find nothing but a terrible mess, but instead it was cleaned up, even the furniture that had been destroyed replaced.

"Kate," she said softly; she had mentioned it to Sam's mother when she had been a guest in her home while Sam was being assessed. She dropped down on her sofa and finally let herself fully and completely cry at the loss of Sam.

Four weeks after leaving Liv teary and looking lost at the airport, Sam sat in front of Lieutenant Tim Aldrich's desk.

"I've got good news and bad news," the army psychologist said.

"Oh, man, let's hear the good news."

"I'm discharging you, soldier. You're finished with therapy as far as I'm concerned."

"Really? It's earlier than I expected."

"That's due mostly to you, Captain. I credit your resilience and your willingness to open up about what happened to you fully for your early release."

"And the bad news?"

"Well, maybe it's not bad. You have to make your decision. After what you've told me about your reasons for staying in the military or discharging out, I can't say the decision is a difficult one."

"No, Dr. Aldrich. I think I've made up my mind."

"I thought so. Well, carry on. Get yourself out of here and to your next destination. Good luck."

Sam left the doctor's office and went back to his room. Over the weeks he'd been here, his clarity returned, along with his capacity to make decisions more easily. The fuzziness and the terrible Trey nightmares were all gone. He often dreamed of Liv, but they were warm or sexy dreams, far different than the terror-filled ones. The doctor had worked diligently with him and he'd held nothing back. Getting well was his top priority and he wasn't going to make a decision until he was clearer. He wanted to be sure. It didn't take him long to get dressed in his uniform and head over to his C.O.'s office. With his hand on the knob, he was at peace with his final decision.

Olivia pushed her hair back out of her face. She hated cleaning chores, but it had to be done. She'd already cleaned the bathroom and washed and dusted and even changed her bed. She'd been on a job for six days. A lot of stakeout work and her home got terribly neglected. She was just finishing up mopping the floor in the kitchen when there was a knock at the door.

She wondered who it could be. She wasn't expecting anyone. Probably someone who got the wrong apartment.

She opened the door and for a moment she couldn't breathe. Sam stood there, his duffel on his back, his hair slightly longer and his blue eyes full of anticipation.

"Sam!" She threw herself at him. Then immediately backed up before he could even get his arms around her.

"Hey! What kind of greeting is that? Are you teasing me? I've been waiting a long time to hold you."

"I'm a mess. Why didn't you tell me you were coming?" She smacked his chest. "I would have planned to at least be showered and presentable."

"You look pretty damn good to me. Still as sassy as ever." He took a step forward and pulled her tightly to him. "Even with your messy hair and sweaty body, I bet your lips are still as soft as I remember. You haven't changed. Liv, you're still as beautiful and contrary as ever."

He let her go and she stood there for a minute before bursting into tears.

At first he looked stunned, and then understanding dawned. "You're happy to see me, right? That's why you're crying?" He grabbed his duffel and snagged her around the waist, dragging them both into her apartment.

Kicking the door closed with his foot, he dropped his duffel again but picked her up and snuggled her close.

"Ah, Liv, tell me the waterworks are because you missed me?"

She smacked him again and he chuckled. "You know they are, you exasperating man."

"Well, I've been on a plane for a few hours and I could use a shower." He waggled his eyebrows, and her tears stopped and her breath hitched.

"Kiss me again, Sam," she whispered. "Just kiss me."

"Yes, ma'am."

They ran out of hot water because they were too much into each other. Sam literally was into her as far as he could go. Now sated, they were lying on her bed. He was toying with her hair. "I left the service." When she smiled at him, he said, "So I'm kinda between jobs."

She ran her hand over his thick, broad chest. His blue eyes were looking deeply into hers. "That's a nice way to put that you don't have a job."

He smiled easily and she decided that this relaxed, laid-back Sam was just as sexy as the tough, I'm-in-charge Sam. "Okay, I'm unemployed."

She gently scored his skin with her nails and he inhaled and grabbed her hand, pulling her over his chest. "I heard that you're kinda a rich guy."

He sent his hand into her hair and cupped the back of her neck, gently rubbing his thumb up and down. His touch was warm and it made her shiver. "Well, sure, but I'm not going to sit around eating bonbons."

It was her turn to smile now. "You're not? What are you going to do?"

He pulled her face down to his and nibbled on her lips, then pressed tiny kisses along her jaw. "Funny thing about that. I heard about a job opening with this P.I."

She sighed as he trailed fiery kisses down her neck. She ran her hands over his head, the silky strands of his hair tickling her palms. He felt so good. "That sounds promising."

He flipped her onto her back and settled above her, placing his elbows against the mattress on either side of her head, his hips notching right between her legs. His eyes twinkled as they gazed deeply into hers. "Yeah, it does, but I heard she's a real pain in the ass." He grinned.

She snorted and rubbed her hands flat against his broad back. "Is that so?"

His expression was sly. "It is. She doesn't take any shit, has great debating skills, is really intelligent and can handle a mean .45."

She mock-frowned. "Oh, my, she sounds like an ogre. What makes you qualified to apply?"

He looked up, scrunching up his face, and she laughed. Tickling his ribs, he jerked and gave her a quelling look. "I'm a good shot."

"Uh-huh, go on." She smoothed her hands down to his waist.

He sucked in a breath as she dragged her nails up either side of his stomach. He caught his bottom lip between his teeth and closed his eyes. When he opened them, they were an intense, deep blue. "I'm really good under pressure." He moaned softly as she did it again. He pressed his hard-on against her. "And putting other people under pressure."

The feel of him made her breath hitch. She exhaled heavily. "Check, got that. What else?"

"This is important, something I learned only recently." He pushed her thighs apart and thrust his hips forward, slipping himself just a bit inside.

She wet her lips and tried to focus on what he was saying. "I can't wait to hear."

He grinned from ear to ear. "I'm a team player."

She laughed and groaned at the same time. "Are you? Well, I have an activity that requires a team of two."

He shoved himself all the way in and whispered, "Do I need to take notes?"

Her hips rose to meet him. "Oh, no, Sam. You're a natural."

Chapter 18

Sam woke up in Olivia's arms and was quite content to lie here for the rest of his life. But he felt a bit guilty that he hadn't first gone to his family. Olivia stirred awake and her brown eyes opened. For a moment, she looked dazed, then smiled.

"Oh, good. You weren't a wonderful dream."

"Nope." The comfort he got from just that look in her eyes made his heart contract. Jeez, he had it bad. "I need to go see my family today. Want to come with me?"

"I'd love to see your mother," she said, wrapping her arms around his neck and burying her face in the hollow of his neck and shoulder.

"After that, I want to take you somewhere tropical. You up for that?"

She raised her head so fast she knocked his chin.

"Oh, sorry. Yes, I'm so ready for that. I can't remember the last time I took a vacation. But before we discuss that, there is something I wanted to talk to you about, something you mentioned last night, but I got kinda distracted by your mouth and body. You made the decision to leave the army. I hope it wasn't for me, Sam. I wouldn't want you to give up something that was important to you. I would have adjusted."

His heart turned over and over. This woman was such a treasure. "No, sweetheart. I didn't do it for you. I did it for me. I have been dissatisfied with the service for a while. Burned out even before the Cartel ambushed me. I will admit that I wanted to be with you more than six months out of the year. I'm ready for something different and new. With you, Liv. If that's something you want to pursue."

"Yes, Sam. I want a relationship with you. I wanted it before you left, but I wanted you to find your way first. To discover what it is you really wanted. Our relationship couldn't really move forward. Have you found your way?"

"Yes, straight back to you, babe."

"Oh, Sam. That makes me so happy."

"I owe you."

She looked confused. "A bra?"

"What?"

"My black silk bra. Remember? The one you destroyed."

"No, Liv, not the bra."

"The dinner, then? You said you'd take me out to dinner."

"No, Liv, not dinner."

"What, then? Owe me what?"

His throat got tight. "Saving my life, Liv. I don't know what I would have done without you. I was completely lost without your brother to help me. You kept me occupied and grounded. I feel like I would have been swallowed whole by what they did to me."

She cupped his face. "Oh, Sam. It was easy to be with you."

He snorted, "Easy. We fought like maniacs."

"I know. But that was just part of who you are. I'm sure we'll fight some more."

He nodded. "True, but the making up will be fun."

"Oh, Sam." She kissed him and held him close.

He buried his face in her hair. "I love you, Liv."

She broke away from him to look into his eyes. "Say that again, Sam."

He brushed his thumb across her cheekbone and his lips across her mouth. "I love you."

"That is really great, but you still owe me a bra and dinner."

He laughed.

He argued all the way over to his mother's about the P.I. name. Olivia wanted "Owens and Winston" and Sam argued for "Winston Owens." As they parked outside the estate, their argument ended abruptly when Sam saw a man pacing outside the gate. His eyes narrowed as he studied the man.

He was an older man, probably about his mother's age, maybe a tad older. He had dark brown hair that was mostly gray, a ruddy complexion and was quite fit.

Getting out of the truck, Sam approached the guy warily. "Who are you? What do you want?"

"You're one of her sons, aren't you?"

"I'm Sam Winston and, yes, I'm Kate's son. Why are you here?"

"I need to speak with her. It's urgent, but I can't get in. The security is so tight after all the trouble you had here about a month ago."

"What is it that you need to see her about?"

"It's private, son."

He looked at Olivia. His expression growing more suspicious, he grabbed the man's arm. "Well, let's see what my mother has to say about that."

Sam took no chances. "I need to check for weapons."

The man nodded as Sam gave him a thorough frisk.

When he was satisfied the guy wasn't carrying, he dragged the man through the gate and up past security, raising his hand when the two agents standing guard outside the door stepped forward. He opened the door and pulled the man into the foyer.

"Mom!"

After a few moments, she came hurrying into the foyer with Trey and Thad hard on her heels.

"Sam!" She ran to him and threw her arms around him. "It's so good to see you and Olivia. We're having lunch…" She broke off when she saw the man Sam had hauled inside. Her face went white with shock and she swayed. Sam went to steady her, but the man was there too quickly, catching her first.

Trey and Thad jumped forward. Sam grabbed the man and jerked him away from his mother and pushed him up against the wall, his fist clenched.

"Sam, no. Please, let him go."

She covered her mouth and just stared at the man in front of her, and Sam's heart lurched to see the look in her eyes. Not only did his mother know this man, but she knew him well.

"I need to speak with you, Kate." His expression crumpled a bit. "It's a matter of life-and-death."

"You can come into the study."

"No," Sam said, standing between the man and his mother. "There's no way we're going to stand by while some stranger talks to you alone."

"This is no stranger." His mother's voice was soft and a little broken. "This is Patrick O'Hara. I loved him before I met your father."

He approached her again, his eyes a little desolate. "Yes, and you abandoned us, Kate."

She looked up at him her face full of confusion. "Us?"

His lips tightened. "Kate, you left Carrie and me."

"Carrie?"

"Your daughter, Kate. Carrie was your daughter."

She backed up away from him, tears springing to her eyes. "What are you saying? My daughter died at birth."

"What? No, she didn't. She died after she had your granddaughter. Dear God, Kate. What did that bastard of a father do to you?"

"Not my father. My mother. She lied to me," she whispered, her face frozen in shock. Pain and agony shone in the deep blue of her eyes. "She told me that my baby was dead."

The same shock rolled through Sam and showed on his brothers' faces. He'd had a sister? A half sister? His grandmother lied to his mother about something so heartbreaking? And now he'd just discovered he had a niece.

"My greatest and most painful regret was losing my baby girl."

Olivia went to her and put her arm around her as Kate leaned heavily on her.

"Your mother came to me and told me you wanted nothing to do with us. I raised her by myself. But I lost her to a drunk driver. I raised Shelby alone after that. It was just the two of us."

His mother looked so wrecked, Sam took her hand and helped her into the living room, where she sat down on the couch. Patrick followed, looking as horrified by the situation as Kate.

"Katie, I didn't know. I thought you'd given up on us and gone to that fancy school in Europe. When I tried to find you, you were gone."

She raised her distressed eyes to his. "I would never have left her, Patrick, or you. How could she have done this to me?"

"She was probably trying to protect you," Patrick said. "But when I thought you didn't want us that was hard to take, Kate."

She took Patrick's hands and he closed his eyes at her touch. It looked as though this man and Sam's mother had a lot to talk about.

"Why did you come here, Patrick? After all these years."

"I need your help. I don't know who to turn to. Shelby has been missing for two weeks. I'm frantic and the FBI keeps giving me the runaround. They've made no progress on finding her. I thought you could help with your connections. I'm desperate, Kate. I don't know who could have taken her."

Sam's heart lurched in his chest and he swore softly

under his breath. His brothers looked at each other, thinking the same thing he was thinking.

There was complete silence in the room as his mother's face hardened. "I do," she said softly. "The Cartel."

Epilogue

Olivia woke up in a platform bed that was low to the floor. They had been traveling for so long that she'd gotten so tired she'd fallen asleep, barely waking up on the last leg of the trip. Sam must have carried her here. She looked around the quaint but beautiful cabana. Polished wood floor and walls, tastefully decorated in a modern beach theme. The gauzy curtains at the windows billowed in a soft, warm breeze.

She was completely and decadently naked against a fully nude Sam. They were lying on the bed, his leg thrown over hers, his face soft in sleep.

There had been a couple of nights when he'd had some lingering nightmares, even though he mentioned he hadn't had any really bad ones, Olivia realized that it took time to get over what Sam had endured, She'd soothed him through them. Especially after the shocking event they'd witnessed at the estate when Patrick O'Hara, Kate's first love, had dropped that bomb about Kate's first child. A child Sam and his brothers knew nothing about. The family would need some time to absorb that information and the terrible news that Shelby, Kate's granddaughter, was missing.

Kate insisted that it would be handled and that Sam and Olivia needed a break. So they had agreed to take this trip.

That soft breeze from the window wafted over their bodies in a pleasant slide.

She slipped out from under him and walked over to the doorway and peeked outside. Stunned, she looked up and down a completely empty beach. Looking behind the house, she saw nothing but jungle. No roads, no cars, mopeds, bikes, nothing but a thick green wall.

"That's right, you're all mine for seven days."

She turned to find Sam propped on his elbow admiring the view of her backside as she bent over the window frame to gaze out. His grin was so easy, so carefree, she grinned back at him. "This is a secluded island?"

He reached out his hand to her, motioning her back to bed. "Totally. No people, just water, sand and jungle."

"Wow, that's amazing. Does your family own it?" She couldn't think of one place she'd rather be than here isolated with her Lone Ranger.

"Lock, stock and barrel." He got an impatient look on his face and motioned her again. She shook her head.

Padding into the kitchen, she said, "There better be

coffee here, Sam. Or I'm going to be cranky. And what about food? Certainly we're not going to eat coconuts."

"No. No coconuts, but fresh fruit. There's plenty of coffee and a coffeemaker. We have electricity from a generator. Stocked fridge, too. We're good for the whole week."

She looked back at him. Nothing but endless sand beaches. No nightlife, no dinner out, no exploring. "What exactly are we going to do for seven days?"

He gave her a wicked grin and she laughed. "Come over here and I'll show you."

"Oh, my God, that's so…sexy. I'm glad I packed my bathing suit." She looked around the expansive room. No luggage anywhere.

"Sam, where are my suitcases?"

Another wicked grin. "You won't need clothes."

"What?"

He finally gave up trying to get her close to him. He folded his hands behind his head and the motion flexed his biceps and she got a bit distracted, so she missed what he'd said.

"What did you say?"

"Having problems focusing, Team Owens?"

She laughed softly. "I've said you're quite beautiful, Sam."

"I intend to keep you naked the whole time."

"Right. That's funny." She laughed again, but Sam's serious expression didn't change.

"I'm not joking."

"What am I supposed to wear?" she said.

"Me most of the time."

She walked to the bed and folded down onto the mattress on her knees. A hedonistic seven days of a gloriously naked Sam. She gave him a skeptical look. "You're kidding, right?"

Sam laughed. He was serious. This was how she was going to remain for seven days. Then he'd give her back her clothes. He gave her a sly look. "Wait. I do have something you can wear."

He reached under the mattress and pulled out a ring box.

Olivia gasped, her eyes widening.

He held it up. "It's…um…kinda big." He was suddenly nervous. "But I wanted to show you how much I love you."

She took the box and opened it and her breath caught again. She straddled him, which he thought probably meant she'd say yes.

"Oh, Sam, I don't need a ring."

"How did I know you would say that?"

She took the square-cut rock out of the box. "Ask me, Sam. Now."

"Hmm. You're straddling me and giving me orders. Is that the way it's going to be?"

She laughed.

"Ask me, you beautiful man."

"Will you marry me, Olivia Owens, and be my wife forever?"

She stared down at him her salty tears hit his chest.

Then she wrapped her arms around him and pressed herself against him. "A million times yes, Sam."

He leaned back and cupped her face now, both of his hands delving into her hair. "I only need you to marry me once. That's all it'll take. Just once, Olivia. I love you, babe." He took the ring and slipped it on her finger.

"I love you, too." She pushed him back and folded down on top of him and buried her wet face in his neck.

"And now we can stop arguing about a name for the P.I. business," he said smugly.

"Is that so?"

"Sure. Now we'll call it Winston and Winston."

Her laughter echoed across the beach as the waves lapped against the deserted shore.

* * * * *

ROMANTIC suspense

Available July 1, 2014

#1807 LONE WOLF STANDING
Men of Wolf Creek • by Carla Cassidy
Sheri Marcoli is searching for two things: her missing aunt and her fairy-tale prince. The damaged and fierce detective Jimmy Carmani is nothing like the man she envisions, but when the kidnapper sets his sights on her, it's Jimmy who rides to Sheri's rescue.

#1808 SECRET SERVICE RESCUE
The Adair Legacy • by Elle James
Secret service agent Daniel Henderson saves the rebellious secret heiress Shelby O'Hara from a cartel looking to pressure her grandmother to drop out of the political race. But when they're forced into hiding, sparks fly and Daniel realizes the biggest threat is to his heart.

#1809 HOT ON THE HUNT
ICE: Black Ops Defenders • by Melissa Cutler
Former black ops agents and ex-lovers Alicia and John are both on the hunt for the team member who betrayed them, but when the tables are turned, they must team up, trust each other and trust in the love they once shared.

#1810 THE MANHATTAN ENCOUNTER
House of Steele • by Addison Fox
When the commitment-phobic Liam Steele agrees to protect the shy research scientist Dr. Isabella Magnini, neither expects the explosive danger they find themselves in or the equally explosive attraction they feel for each other.

YOU CAN FIND MORE INFORMATION ON UPCOMING HARLEQUIN® TITLES, FREE EXCERPTS AND MORE AT WWW.HARLEQUIN.COM.

HRSCNM0614

REQUEST YOUR FREE BOOKS!
2 FREE NOVELS PLUS 2 FREE GIFTS!

◆ HARLEQUIN®

ROMANTIC suspense

Sparked by danger, fueled by passion

YES! Please send me 2 FREE Harlequin® Romantic Suspense novels and my 2 FREE gifts (gifts are worth about $10). After receiving them, if I don't wish to receive any more books, I can return the shipping statement marked "cancel." If I don't cancel, I will receive 4 brand-new novels every month and be billed just $4.74 per book in the U.S. or $5.24 per book in Canada. That's a savings of at least 14% off the cover price! It's quite a bargain! Shipping and handling is just 50¢ per book in the U.S. and 75¢ per book in Canada.* I understand that accepting the 2 free books and gifts places me under no obligation to buy anything. I can always return a shipment and cancel at any time. Even if I never buy another book, the two free books and gifts are mine to keep forever.

240/340 HDN F45N

Name	(PLEASE PRINT)	
Address		Apt. #
City	State/Prov.	Zip/Postal Code

Signature (if under 18, a parent or guardian must sign)

Mail to the **Harlequin® Reader Service:**

IN U.S.A.: P.O. Box 1867, Buffalo, NY 14240-1867
IN CANADA: P.O. Box 609, Fort Erie, Ontario L2A 5X3

Want to try two free books from another line?
Call 1-800-873-8635 or visit www.ReaderService.com.

* Terms and prices subject to change without notice. Prices do not include applicable taxes. Sales tax applicable in N.Y. Canadian residents will be charged applicable taxes. Offer not valid in Quebec. This offer is limited to one order per household. Not valid for current subscribers to Harlequin Romantic Suspense books. All orders subject to credit approval. Credit or debit balances in a customer's account(s) may be offset by any other outstanding balance owed by or to the customer. Please allow 4 to 6 weeks for delivery. Offer available while quantities last.

Your Privacy—The Harlequin® Reader Service is committed to protecting your privacy. Our Privacy Policy is available online at www.ReaderService.com or upon request from the Harlequin Reader Service.

We make a portion of our mailing list available to reputable third parties that offer products we believe may interest you. If you prefer that we not exchange your name with third parties, or if you wish to clarify or modify your communication preferences, please visit us at www.ReaderService.com/consumerschoice or write to us at Harlequin Reader Service Preference Service, P.O. Box 9062, Buffalo, NY 14269. Include your complete name and address.

HRS

SPECIAL EXCERPT FROM

HARLEQUIN®

ROMANTIC suspense

Sheri Marcoli is searching for two things: her missing aunt
and her fairy-tale prince. The damaged and fierce detective
Jimmy Carmani is nothing like the man she envisions,
but when the kidnapper sets his sights on her, it's
Jimmy who rides to Sheri's rescue.

Read on for a sneak peek of

LONE WOLF STANDING

by *New York Times* bestselling author
Carla Cassidy,
available July 2014 from
Harlequin® Romantic Suspense.

That's better than being poisoned, right?"

He was aware of the weight of her intense gaze on him
as he pulled out of the animal clinic parking lot. "I'm no
veterinarian, but I would think that definitely it's better to be
tranquilized than poisoned." He shot a glance in her direction.

She frowned. "That man in the woods broke Highway's leg.
I don't know how he managed to do it, but I know in my gut
he probably broke the leg and then somehow injected him
with something. Highway would never take anything to eat
from anyone but me, no matter how tasty the food might
look or smell. Jed and I trained him too well."

They drove for a few minutes in silence. "Sorry about the
pizza plans," she finally said.

He flashed her a quick smile. "Nothing to apologize for.

I'm guessing you didn't plan for a man to attack your dog an then chase you in the woods tonight. I think I can forgive yo for not meeting up with me for a slice of pizza."

"Thank God you came to find me." She wrapped he slender arms around her shoulders, as if chilled despite th warmth of the night. "If you hadn't shown up when you did, think he would have caught me. I will tell you this, he seeme to know the woods as well as I did, so it has to be somebod local."

"We'll figure it out." He seemed to be saying that a lo lately. "Maybe in the daylight tomorrow we'll find a piec of his clothing snagged on a tree branch, or something h dropped while he was chasing you."

"I hope you all find something." Her voice was slight husky with undisguised fear. "I felt his malevolence, Jimmy. smelled his sweat."

"You're safe now, Sheri, and we're going to keep it that wa Highway is going to be fine and we're going to get to th bottom of this."

"So…so, what happens now?" she asked.

"Since we didn't get our friendly meeting for pizza, we' going to do something else I've heard that other friends do, he replied.

"And what's that?" she asked.

He flashed her a bright smile as he pulled in front of he cottage. "We're going to have a slumber party."

**Don't miss
LONE WOLF STANDING
by Carla Cassidy, available July 2014 from
Harlequin® Romantic Suspense.**

HARLEQUIN®

ROMANTIC suspense

HOT ON THE HUNT
by Melissa Cutler

ICE: Black Ops Defenders

**Lust and danger collide in the Caribbean in this
ICE: Black Ops Defenders title!**

Burned black-op ICE agent Alicia Troy spent years
plotting the perfect revenge on the man who left her for
dead...until her plan is foiled by her ex-teammate and
lover, who taught her the meaning of betrayal. She can
trust John Witter...so why can't she stop wanting him?

Look for *HOT ON THE HUNT* from the
ICE: Black Ops Defenders miniseries by Melissa Cutler
in July 2014. Available wherever books and
ebooks are sold.

**Also from the *ICE: Black Ops Defenders* miniseries
by Melissa Cutler**

*SECRET AGENT SECRETARY
TEMPTED INTO DANGER*

Available wherever ebooks are sold.

Heart-racing romance, high-stakes suspense!

www.Harlequin.com

HRS278

HARLEQUIN®

A *Romance* FOR EVERY MOOD™

Love the Harlequin book you just read?

Your opinion matters.

Review this book on your favorite book site, review site, blog or your own social media properties and share your opinion with other readers!